For One Night Only

A Killer Thriller

First published in 2019 in Great Britain.

Copyright©Foronenightonlywendyreakes2019

ISBN:

ISBN: 9781694234827
Imprint: Independently published

Wendyreakes.com

.

1981

FROM WHERE HE WAS HIDING in the bushes at the side of the road, Drake Fisher could see the entrance to Seaview: a small gated community upon a narrow headland on Lynton Bay. He didn't live there, nor was he born there, but somewhere around there, on the banks of the river Lyn, he'd been conceived.

He had to admit he thought about his conception a lot, ever since he was bestowed his damn stupid name, Drake, after a dumb duck. In post-war Britain, he was just five-years-old when his idiotic parents took it upon themselves to share that particular moment of intimacy, and now, in his adult years, whenever he chanced upon a river bank somewhere, a picture always popped into his head of his mother and father 'doing it'. So vivid was the image in his mind, that whenever it popped in there, he was forced to bang the side of his head three times on the left and twice on the right. He didn't know why it was three on one and two on the other. It was just how it was, no explanation necessary.

Now, with his Walkman's headphones covering his ears, he listened to Phil Collins playing on the radio, singing *In the Air Tonight*. Lying belly down on the grass verge, hidden from sight, as he waited for a certain car to come past, he thought about his parents and the time they'd recounted the story of his conception, along with the momentous occasion they made him 'out of tadpoles and eggs'.

Drake had been sitting at the Formica kitchen table. He wasn't allowed to get down until he'd finished his broccoli, so said his parents who had their backs to him as they performed the same washing-up ritual they performed every night. He recalled his mother wearing a flowery pinafore over a new dress, a lime green short-sleeved crimplene shift, where the zip down the back was slightly puckered. That's how she'd got it on sale, she told father, 'because the zip wasn't quite right.' Holding a tea towel and a wet dish in one hand, his father, Mannie, moved his free hand from around her waist, up to the neckline where he took hold of the little pulley piece and tugged the zipper down. As his mother screeched and whipped Mannie with a wet sponge, five-year-old Drake noticed red welts on her bare skin below the horizontal strap of her off-white bra.

"Ooh, Mannie Fisher," mother said. "Our little Drake is watching you get all flirty." She laughed, and his father chuckled with a deep sounding ho-ho-ho, like he was Santa Claus, except it was more of a dirty haw-haw-haw, not sounding like Santa Claus at all.

Drake's intense dislike for green vegetables did nothing to temper his bad mood. He was a tired five-year-old so he should have been treated with a lot more caution than they'd given him credit for. *He* should have been the subject of their attention, not hanky-panky as his mother often called it. He watched them with a scowl on his face as father's hand slid underneath the tie of mother's apron and down to her backside, squeezing it with one large hairy hand, making the flesh bulge through the gaps of his fingers. That was when Drake banged his dinner knife down on the table with one loud crash.

Mother swung around giggling, just as Mannie's hand came up and squeezed her left breast, as meaty as the cheek on her arse. "Haven't you finished that dinner yet, my little Drake," she'd said, brushing off Mannie's indelicate advances with a look that said, 'don't go doing that in front of the baby'.

"I don't wan' it," Drake yelled as he picked up his fork and threw it so hard across the table that it fell on the floor at his mother's feet.

"Bad boy, Drake. Bad boy." She kneeled down and picked it up, just before Mannie stepped forward and placed his hands on her, gyrating his hips against her bent body. Mother squealed and got up as Mannie began kissing her neck with that haw-haw-haw moan of his.

"Drake," his father yelled after he'd removed his lips from mother's red neck. "You stay there and don't get down until you finish that broccoli. You hear me, boy?"

"Mannie…" mother chided with a twinkle in her eye.

"Come on," he said, leading her by the hand, taking her to the lean-to, just off the kitchen at the side of the house. That old lean-to held all the stuff they couldn't cram into the small terraced dwelling; clothes rack, floor sweeper, ironing board, and lots of old dirty boots.

Within seconds, six-year-old Drake heard that familiar bang-bang-banging he heard most days and nights, bang-bang-bang and moan-moan-moan. Day and night, every day, every night. As the noise became faster, Drake chewed his broccoli, mixing it with saliva until it was pulp in his mouth. The taste was revolting, but he had no intention of swallowing. He hated vegetables, especially the green ones.

The noise stopped and they came back in. Father's face looked flushed, as mother took the chair opposite Drake. And as father carried on drying those dishes, mother told Drake the story of how he got his name. 'Father had gotten all amorous,' she said, 'down by the river near Clovelly Waterfall.' That's where you were made, little Drakey," she said, "Just when father's little tadpole swam up to mother's eggs, we heard a duck quacking." She laughed, remembering the event. "That's when we decided to call you Drake."

"Quack, quack, quack," his parents chanted together, intent on making him laugh. "Quack-quack-quack."

When they both leaned down in front of him, quacking their stupid quacks, Drake pulled in his stomach and opened his mouth to let that broccoli and saliva pulp spray all over their stupid faces.

As they coughed and spluttered, Drake clutched a dinner knife under the table. If they kept up their bang, bang, banging and their quack, quack quacking, he'd shove that knife into mother's neck until she dropped down dead. And then afterwards he'd do it to father. That'll show 'em. Instead, as his rage was unleashed, he slapped himself on the face, three times on the left and twice on the right.

Now he could hear a vehicle coming along the road. The lights got brighter as the car got closer, and as the fabulous Mr C sang *In the Air Tonight*, Drake's mind was soothed and stimulated all at the same time. When the Cortina turned into Seaview, he got up from where he was hiding and rushed through the gates before they closed, singing the lyrics softly. "There's something in the air tonight..."

Chapter One

At No.6

WHEN RHIANNA LOXLEY LEFT HOME and moved in with her uncle at Seaview, little did she know she'd be fighting for her life that night in 1981.

She had barely unpacked when the whole matter occurred and if anyone in the future happened to ask her about it, she could honestly say she had simply been in the wrong place at the wrong time and that perhaps it was all meant to be. That was Rhianna all over. People called her Miss Positive.

The night before, on Friday, she'd driven along the road through the valley of rocks, with her map of Devon spread out on the seat next to her. It was the peskiest thing. Why couldn't the map people invent something more user-friendly? she pondered as the dark of night prevented her from reading the thing.

She was listening to Phil Collins singing *In the air tonight* on the radio when she remembered she had her lights on full beam. She was made to regret that when she looked up and realised she was blinding the driver of the car in front. She quickly dimmed them and decided to overtake, so that she could wave her apologies. In response, as she passed, the man driving had offered her a rude gesture and an expression that made her feel she was a nuisance on the road. Before she went by, she noticed an old lady in the back looking as miserable as can be. As a self-confessed writer, Rhianna wondered why she looked so sad and that maybe it was the fault of the driver who was clearly rude and aggressive and certainly not a person anyone would want to know. Still, she ought to give people the benefit of the doubt and not be so quick to judge. With that in mind, she offered a cheery wave and went on by.

Now she was back giving a sideways glance to the massive and un-foldable map on the seat next to her.

Her car was a white Cortina. Mother had bought it for her twenty-first birthday, two years ago. It enabled her to get about a lot easier, now that she was a fully-fledged reporter for the Devonshire Post. They'd offered her a permanent contract only last week, and mother had arranged for her to stay with her uncle who lived in Devon. He apparently lived on a rather nice place near the sea, so she was excited to see it and to meet him for the very first time.

Actually, that wasn't entirely accurate. Apparently, he had attended her Christening when they were all on speaking terms. Father had fallen out with uncle Rolf, and they still hadn't mended those particular wounds. When Uncle Rolf had agreed for Rhianna to live with him on a temporary basis until she got on her feet, she had been very grateful. She could hardly afford the rents around Taunton until she got her first month's pay.

"There it is," she announced to herself when she saw the gates of Seaview looming. She quickly slowed down and switched on her indicator to turn right. It had a light shining up at it and Rhianna likened it to heaven's pearly gates. She stopped and grabbed a piece of paper from the glove compartment. It was a letter from Uncle Rolf stating the numbers for the security panel. *Don't worry*, he'd written, *the gates will open automatically, so you don't have to get out of the car.*

She had to stretch her arm to reach the panel and then she tapped in *95873*. The gates opened immediately, albeit slowly. A car was behind her and was now waiting in the road to follow her into Seaview. The driver dimmed his headlights and Rhianna saw that it was the man with the old lady in the back. Just her luck. She hoped he wasn't following her to give her a piece of his mind.

The gates were fully open now, so she drove in. The road in front was a figure eight, so uncle had said in his letter. She should look for No.6 in the top right-hand corner of *the eight*, next to the rather large house at the top. She looked in her mirror and saw the car behind her pull into one of the houses not far from the gate, and just before she decided to forget the horrible man, she saw another car come behind him, to park in the first house on the left. Seaview was a busy place, Rhianna thought.

Then, quite by chance, before she looked away, she saw a small dark figure dart through the gate before it closed up. She looked again, but then she decided her eyes were playing tricks on her and that she should simply drive on and find uncle's house.

UNCLE ROLF HELPED HER with her luggage, which wasn't very much, just a rucksack and a couple of bags with essential supplies.

"Well, Rhianna," he said, "Your photographs don't do you justice. What a pretty young lady you are."

Rhianna thanked him but decided he was just being kind, especially since she was wearing her glasses and her long dark hair was tied back into a messy ponytail. When she had her hair down, she looked more her age and a lot tidier.

He was shorter than her, but she was 5'10 so that wasn't hard to imagine. She got her height from her father's side and seemed to tower over everyone she met. It was an embarrassment at school, especially when wearing platform shoes in the early seventies. Hers had lifted her up another two inches, so it had been an unfortunate item of fashion.

Uncle Rolf was grey. He had a moustache which was also grey and a speckled grey unshaven chin. He wore a cardigan over a shirt and tie, just like her father did when he was at home until he went out and then put on a jacket. Rhianna had often tried to update his fashion, for him to at least wear a nice cashmere vest occasionally, but he still hadn't worn that red one she'd bought him for Christmas.

"Come on through and have a cuppa tea," uncle Rolf said. She followed him into the lounge, which was a strange looking room. The house was modern, but the furniture looked like it had been bought in the fifties, complete with antimacassars over the backs of the chairs.

He brought in a tray laden with tea things and placed it on the coffee table sporting a Formica top and four splayed legs. In the centre was an ashtray with a pipe resting on its side and a green marble table lighter.

"I'll pour," she said.

"I've got a casserole in the oven. We'll have that when you've unpacked."

"Lovely." She picked up the stainless steel teapot. "This is a lovely place," she said as she poured.

He nodded and accepted the cup and saucer. He put in his own quantity of milk, followed by one sugar. "I take it you know the story."

"Vaguely."

He stirred his tea with a silver spoon. "Me and your aunty Barbra bought it when it was built two years ago, but she never got to live here. She died the day we moved in. All the stress of moving, the doctor said." He stared longingly at a black and white photo displayed on the mantelpiece. It was a picture of uncle and Barbra on their wedding day. Rhianna felt sorry for the man who had clearly loved his wife dearly.

"That's very sad."

He perked up. "Tomorrow, I'll show you around. The beach will be a bit windy and the sea too rough, but we might be able to manage the steps if it's not raining."

"I can't believe we're so close to the sea."

"Well, you've lived in London all your life, so I can imagine Seaview being a bit strange."

They both sipped their tea. "Hmm, lovely," she said.

"You're starting your new job on Monday then."

"Yes, I'm terribly excited."

"So why down here? You could have got a nice job in London, couldn't you?"

"Yes, but I wanted to get out of the city. It's all such a cliché don't you think?"

"I suppose." He looked like he didn't know what she was talking about.

"I just think there may be some meaty stories to cover in the country. Things that people in the big cities don't get to see."

He chuckled. "Oh, I don't know if you'll find much going on here. Especially not in Seaview.

"Well, I may have to go beyond the gates."

They both laughed, enjoying each other's company.

Then the doorbell rang.

Uncle Rolf got up to answer it. He came back into the lounge followed by a man he introduced as Clive from No.2. "Pleased to meet you, young lady," he said as they shook hands.

The two men stood up in the centre of the room while Rhianna finished her cup of tea. She bit into a Custard Cream.

"What can I do for you, Clive?" Uncle Rolf asked.

"I was wondering if you fancied coming down the pub for a game of darts, but I can see you've got company."

"My niece is going to be staying with me for a while. She's got a nice job in Taunton."

"Ah, I see." He looked at Rhianna. "You'll have to come over and meet my wife Marigold. Shame you weren't here last summer. We had a bit of a bash for our anniversary."

"Well, she didn't have her job, then, Clive."

"No, of course not." He looked down and shuffled his feet as if he had been told off.

"You can go and play darts, uncle Rolf. I don't mind."

"No, I can't leave you on your first night. Your mother would never forgive me."

"Won't you be coming on the golf weekend, then?" Clive asked.

"No, I won't leave my niece."

"Oh, Uncle Rolf," Rhianna said. "Don't put aside your plans for me."

"It's tomorrow, dear. I would have to leave very early, so it wouldn't be fair on you."

"I'll be fine. I'll probably sleep until midday."

"No, I don't think so. And it's a trip."

"How long?" Rhianna asked

"Just for one night," said Clive.

Poor Clive thought Rhianna. It seemed like the two men were friends and now his buddy was letting him down.

She stood up and grabbed the tray. She needed to prove to her uncle that she was self-reliant. Before she left the room, she said. "Go on, uncle. It's only one night."

Chapter Two

At No.1

SHE REMEMBERED THE SEVENTIES and the eighties well. But there was one night in 1981 Kimberley Cutter remembered better than the rest. How could she forget?

The night before, she recalled getting home later than usual, after joining her colleagues in the wine bar across the road. They'd all gathered in Barneys, as they did most Friday nights, but that particular night she had offered to buy a round for the three men made redundant that week. Two of them had taken her up on the offer, but one was missing.

The moment she drove into Seaview, as the gates closed, in her rearview mirror she could have sworn she saw a small figure darting in from the road, going quickly behind the bushes near the eight-foot wall.

Okay, so that last glass of wine had got to her. She realised that. Especially when she wound down the window to look back at the gate. When she noticed nothing untoward, she deemed herself lucky to have gotten home safely after four glasses of Hock. Those days, she was often mindful about how many she had before driving home, especially since they'd brought in the drink driving restrictions. What a shock that had been for all the dedicated socialisers. Frankly, Kimberly Cutter thought it was a tactical move by the government to spoil everyone's fun. Bloody Tories! And Bloody Maggie! What a disappointment she was.

Sometimes, Kimberly wished she'd never moved to Seaview. She didn't mind the area, it was scenic, and the house she rented wasn't too bad, quite sizable for the amount of rent she paid, but the neighbours...well, sometimes she didn't get them *at all*.

She lived at No.1, just inside the security gate, surrounded by newly planted trees and shrubs with herbaceous bushes divided by empty flower beds. No.1 was fortunate to have an older tree in the front garden if you could call it a garden; more like a patch of grass that needed cutting each week, which a pain since she didn't possess a lawnmower and had to rely on the old guy over the road at No.8. When he got fed up with her overgrown front plot, he often came over and cut it all back without even asking her. Still, that suited Kimberly, especially if she didn't have to talk to him.

Comprised of eight houses, the small estate was set out like a figure eight which was annoying for Kim, because the road, like a car race track, was classed as a one-way system. It was preposterous for her at No.1, since she was located next to the gate, where *the eight* joined the main road leading to the real world. If Kim was going to follow the highway law, then by rights she should pull out of her little drive sloping down from the garage, turn left, and go up through the houses, around the top circle and back down the second circle to the gate and the main road. As it was, and since the whole system was ridiculous, she simply reversed and went the wrong way for twelve metres before driving out. Not normally classified as a lawbreaker, Kim liked to think of it as her one defiant act, to do what she wanted to do and to hell with everyone. That gave her a small amount of satisfaction, small as it was.

The house inside was furnished. *Furnished* in the already-furnished sense in a rental property. The all-through lounge at eighteen feet long displayed two camel coloured two-seater sofas in front of a modern electric fire set into the wall. The floors in all the rooms were covered in teak herringbone with two beige shag-pile rugs in the sitting and dining areas. An MFI table and four chairs were at the far end next to the patio doors, and a sideboard stretched along one wall, displaying a rather chic oversized brandy glass where Kim kept her keys.

When she initially viewed the property, Kim thought the decor was elegant as can be, especially the basket weave swing chair suspended from the ceiling. At the rear of the property was a view of the sea over a sheer cliff face dropping to rocks and tumultuous waves. She spent many an evening sitting out on the patio watching the sky turn pink. It was her favourite place to be, as long as she was alone.

Now, as she stepped inside the front door and turned on the lights in the porch, she was startled when the doorbell rang. Still with her coat on, she backtracked and swung it open.

It was Marigold from next door. "I saw you drive up," she said, putting one foot inside. She pulled her cardigan tighter around her as her breath in the cold evening air made it look like she was smoking. She sidestepped in and Kimberly sighed. Marigold was in and she'd be staying until Kimberly chucked her out. Bloody neighbours!

As she closed the door, Marigold marched inside the lounge as if she'd been invited. The neighbours in Seaview all did that. They were permanent intruders. Annoying, desperate and needy, the lot of them. "You're late home," Marigold said.

Kim frowned with a creased brow. Only that morning she'd checked out the lines on her face. She was just thirty-six, but already they were beginning to show. She often wondered why there wasn't a proper remedy for wrinkles. *Still*, they haven't cured cancer yet, so she guessed that would come first. "You've been watching and waiting for me to come home? Isn't that rather strange behaviour?" she asked Marigold. Did the woman have no shame!?

Marigold ignored her. The woman wasn't ashamed or embarrassed. She simply accepted Kimberly's normal grumpy disposition as if she was a good friend who did things like that, accepting everyone for their faults! More fool her.

"I was going to have an early night." Even when she said it, she knew Marigold wouldn't take it as a hint. She was too stupid to see hints, even when they were staring her in the face. No, you can't argue with stupid, Kimberly pondered. Least of all someone who was named after a pair of rubber gloves.

"An early night!" she hooted. "It's Friday. Who goes to bed early on a Friday?"

"Erm, people who work for a living."

She hooted again and sat down. "Well, one day you'll get married and then you can give that up."

Kimberly snarled behind her back, as she took off her coat and hung it on the hook next to the telephone table. "I wouldn't want to give it up."

Marigold laughed. "Don't be silly."

Kim went into the kitchen. She opened the fridge door and pulled out a half bottle of white wine.

A voice travelled through the door opening. "Shall I get myself a Cinzano?"

Kimberly ignored her. That bottle she'd bought at Christmas was almost gone, drunk by Marigold over the course of the past fortnight. She went back into the dining area where Marigold's skinny arse in tight crimplene slacks poked out from the sideboard. She grabbed the bottle by the neck and set it on top then, after pouring a double, she used the soda syphon to top it up. Marigold preferred lemonade, but Kim didn't buy it in. Marigold had commented on it once. "No lemonade?"

"No."

"Oh. Shall I pop next door and get some?"

"If you like."

When Marigold came back, she found all the lights were off and the doors locked tight. She never did that again. Now she stayed put and took soda.

She watched Marigold pick up a Co-Op carrier bag, filled with a few bags of nibbles. She raised her pencil drawn eyebrows and said "I've got cheese and crackers too. We can have a cosy night in."

Kimberly closed her eyes and counted to ten. She'd had enough! "Weren't you listening when I said I wanted an early night?"

"Oh, I know what you're like. You say one thing and mean another." Carrying her drink in one hand and the carrier bag in the other, she went into the kitchen. Marigold had finally taken charge.

KIMBERLEY LIVED ALONE. She'd never married and possessed no kids. In fact, she had no baggage whatsoever, so said her disapproving mother often enough. It was true, Kim had nothing a prospective suitor would feel threatened by, except perhaps a job. She was a career girl. Had been since she left school when she turned her back on so-called domestic bliss. She just felt that her life wasn't supposed to turn out that way.

Kim's blonde hair and blue eyes did nothing to dispel the illusion of her just being a pretty girl with no brains. Her boyish frame was an attraction to men who liked that sort of thing, so admirers were not in short supply. She'd once fallen for her boss at the other place she used to work. He'd pursued her relentlessly, despite being engaged to another girl, but when she finally reciprocated the attraction, he ran a mile. Good job too. That could have messed up her career for good.

Now, she worked for Philips at their manufacturing plant in Taunton. She was a supervisor, in charge of packaging and distribution. She had thirty-five men under her, -just where she liked to keep them- until this week when three were laid off. One of them was that weirdo, Drake Fisher.

Chapter Three

At No.7

PHIL COLLINS WAS PLAYING ON THE RADIO. *In the Air Tonight.* One of Eddie's favourite songs. "You all right back there, mum?" he called, looking in his rear view mirror.

His mother didn't reply since she was deaf as a post. He turned up the volume. She'd enjoy a bit of Mr C, he reckoned.

He was smiling to himself as he drove along the road towards home, through the Valley of Rocks to Seaview. Eddie and Sandra had moved there when the houses were first built two years before. He liked the idea of being safely tucked away behind an impenetrable gate, but the part that appealed to him most was the rear and side aspects, dropping away to the sea.

The small beach, on the right of the headland below the forty-five-metre cliff face, was accessed via man-made stone steps cutting down through the rock. The beach was white sand mixed with pebbles, which got covered entirely when the tide was in. When it was out, the residents of Seaview were able to enjoy the beach during the summer months to do a spot of jogging or even a nice swim. In the winter, and usually alone, Eddie would dive into the freezing Atlantic and do a couple of miles before coming back out again to pace up the cliff steps to get warm. Then, when he was at the back door of their house, he would strip off his wetsuit and don a robe waiting for him over the back of a chair. He'd dry his feet after putting them under the garden tap to get the sand off. He didn't like dragging sand onto Sandra's clean floor.

While he drove, he thought about his swim that morning. Something strange had happened, when normally, nothing strange ever happened in Seaview.

He'd been on his final lap of the bay, between the two jutting cliffs that protected the beach from easterly and westerly winds. His body had tingled from the effect of the stabbing saltwater and he began to flag. He took a rest, stopping just for a moment to get his breath back. Treading water, he looked up to the top of the cliff, where he thought he saw his wife, Sandra, staring out to sea, dressed in nothing but a yellow floral nightie. After a small wave lapped over his face, he opened his eyes once more and looked again. Sandra had gone. *Odd.* The incident was even more peculiar fifteen minutes later when he went back into the bedroom dressed in his robe and found her tucked up in bed still fast asleep.

So convinced that it had been her watching him from the cliff top, he felt compelled to pull back the covers to see her nightie. Lo and behold, she was wearing the pink one, making him feel a fool for suspecting her in the first place. In the end, as he showered and dressed, he thought he must have been seeing things, or at the very least, saw someone else standing there in a nightdress similar to Sandra's yellow floral.

His thoughts were brought back to the present when a car came up behind him with its full beam shining in his eyes. He cursed as the Cortina overtook him and speeded up as if the Highway law didn't apply to them. '*Pigs*,' he cursed again as he turned up the volume on the radio to calm him dow.

Phil Collins belted out *There's something in the air tonight…* but Eddie had lost all desire to sing along. He thought about the phone call he'd had with Sandra after he'd picked up mother from the care home. "I'll be home in an hour," he'd said. "Have tea ready. Our mother will be ready for something by then. They told me she never had her lunch."

"Of course, I'll have it ready. I always do. Every weekend when you bring her home."

"What?" he'd said slowly with a low commanding voice that would scare the shit out of his ungrateful wife. He'd make her regret that little outburst when he got home. She wouldn't say anything against his old mum again. He'd make sure of it.

"I didn't mean to sound…"

"We'll talk about it when I get home."

"Eddie…"

"What?"

"I didn't mean…How is mum? Is she well?"

"You'll see for yourself in an hour, won't you?"

"Yes. Of course. I'll have her room ready.

"You'd better." Then he hung up.

THE CALL ENDED and Sandra put the phone back on the hook. She stood trembling, wondering about his mood. Wondering if...

"Are you okay, Sand'?"

She turned and saw Marigold peering out of her front window. She was looking out for the girl who lived at No.1. Marigold was good friends with Kimberly, but Sandra couldn't stand her. Too high and mighty for her taste. She worked all the time -odd in itself- and she was single, which made Sandra nervous. Probably, because Sandra had wished she was single many times in the past and she didn't like the girl at No.1 rubbing her face in it. Of course, she kept all that sort of thing to herself. She couldn't afford for it to get back to Eddie. She'd pay for it big time if it did. "Yeah, I'm fine."

Sandra busied herself in the kitchen, anticipating her husband of five years coming home with his goddamn miserable mother. The kitchen was a modern open plan room, with a dining table and six chairs down one end just inside the patio doors that led to the garden and a side angle view of the sea. Sandra loved that house, despite Eddie living in it.

Thinking of her husband, she went to the fridge and pulled out a fresh round lettuce. She'd do some salad with the lasagne she'd prepared earlier. Sandra was into cooking big time. Ever since pasta arrived on the British shores, she'd raved at the diversity of the stuff, especially since she'd cut a lot of potatoes out of her diet. Of course, she couldn't cut them out completely since Eddie favoured a nice buttery mash, but she often made a cottage pie to satisfy that particular whim of his. His other favourite was garlic bread. She often joked about how continental they'd become, but when Eddie ate that garlic, his breath always reeked of it.

She glanced once again at Marigold who was still hovering next to the window. Why couldn't she go to her own house to stalk the girl at No.1? But Sandra wouldn't say anything. She didn't have many friends, so the ones she did have, she kept on their good side.

She threw a comment across the room. "She not back yet, then?"

Marigold looked at her watch. "No, she's late tonight."

"You know Eddie and his mother will be home soon," she hinted, as she sliced some tomatoes to go with the mixed salad.

Marigold dropped the curtain and walked towards the centre counter of the kitchen. The island was the height of elegance as far as Sandra was concerned. Not many of the eight had one of those. She was proud of it and she was sure Marigold was jealous she didn't have one.

"The mother again?"

"Hmm, every bloody weekend."

"Why don't you tell him to leave her at the care home next weekend to give you a rest."

Sandra almost spat. "Are you joking?" she said. "He'd never do that."

"You've got to put your foot down, Sand'. We can't let these men walk all over us. Not in this modern age. The war's over, remember," she added, condescendingly.

Sandra didn't say anything back, but she did think the comment was uncalled for. She was a war child, so the comment was insensitive, especially since she still remembered the sound of the bombs coming from London.

She went to the fridge and took out a bowl of sliced cucumber from last night. The lime green glass bowl was covered in that new cling film wrap. Whenever she used it, she always thought of Katie Boyle holding a glass of milk over her head. Tight as a drum!

"Shall we have another Cinzano?" Marigold asked.

Sandra's nerves were getting the better of her. "Well... Eddie will want his dinner ready." There, she'd said it. Hopefully Marigold would get the hint.

"Do you want me to give you a hand?"

"What?" Sandra splashed water over the lettuce, and it sprayed over her dress.

Then, just behind her, Marigold made her jump when she took a hold of her arm. "What's that bruise?"

She looked. It was actually two bruises, fused to one big one, "Nothing. I just banged it on the handle of the bathroom door."

"Opposed to you banging your head on the bathroom cabinet?"

"What?"

"That's what they say, don't they? Abused women, I mean."

Sandra laughed. "Abused! Don't be ridiculous." She laughed again. It was forced, but Marigold didn't know that. No one knew that Sandra used to be an actress. A well paid one too. She'd given it up when she married Eddie since he'd claimed, 'no wife of his would ever have to work'. He took pride in the statement, and

Sandra, -fool that she was- thought his beliefs were sweet. Now, not so much.

"You think I haven't noticed how you are around him?" Marigold said.

"What do you mean?" Sandra had her back to her when her eyes went from side to side, wary of where Marigold was going with her statement.

"You're always scuttering around him like you're scared of him."

"No, I'm not."

Marigold walked away. "Whatever!" She went back to the window where car lights were shining into the room. "She's back," she said, announcing the arrival of the woman at No.1.

Just as Marigold opened the front door, she bumped into Eddie coming inside with his mother. Sandra thought, she's just got rid of one nuisance and another two turn up. When would she ever get some peace?

SANDRA PUT ON HER SMILING FACE; her 'welcome home' face; her 'so-glad-to-see-you' face. Eddie's mother was eighty six. Sandra often wondered why the old bat had hung on for so long. Sandra was positive she did it just to annoy her. The woman had never suffered an illness in her life except for painful bunions on both feet and the odd swelling of the ankles when she retained water. Apart from that, much to the annoyance of Sandra, everything worked well for someone so aged.

"How was the journey, Gladys?" Sandra raised her voice since the old girl was practically deaf. Why couldn't she wear that hearing aid she'd been given by the NHS six months ago. It would make their life a lot easier. Instead, they had to raise their voices to communicate with a woman who didn't give two hoots about what they were saying to her. Sandra wouldn't have minded so much if she was interesting, but as she'd got older, she had nothing to say for herself at all. She was just hard work.

"She was all right," Eddie replied on her behalf, "Weren't you, mum?"

Doris nodded with a glum expression on her wrinkled face. For all Sandra knew, the old lady didn't enjoy coming to their house, any more than Sandra enjoyed having her there.

"I've made lasagne for tea." She smiled at her husband, hoping she'd get a smile in return. She didn't.

She turned her back on him as she thought about that morning when she'd gone to the cliff. Last night had been particularly hard, so she must have been in some sort of trance when she left the house in her nightie and went along *the eight* to the path leading to the cliff. She'd stood there, watching him swimming in the cold sea, thinking about the night before when he'd given her a blow to the head. She'd passed out and woken up with dried blood inside her ear.

She was surprised when he stopped swimming and looked up. At the time, she was wishing he'd get eaten by sharks, despite there being no predators in those waters.

As soon as he spotted her, she gasped and stepped back, turning and running back to their house.

Fifteen minutes later, she heard him walk into the bedroom. She held her breath when he pulled the covers from her motionless body. With her eyes closed tight and her breath caught in her lungs, she thanked God she'd thought to change her nightie. She just hoped he wouldn't see the yellow one inside the Ali Baba basket in the bathroom.

Now, as Sandra grabbed a thick cloth, she turned off the oven and took out the lasagne, baked to perfection. He should be happy with it, she thought. Please let him be happy with it.

"What was that Marigold doing here?" Eddie asked as she put three warm plates on the table. She went back for the food, taking each item one at a time. Once, she'd made the mistake of trying to carry two together and dropped one. Eddie had made her pay for that. She didn't do that again.

She sat down and began serving up the pasta. She'd used that dried packet stuff, boiling it before layering it neatly with mince and cheese sauce. She had perfected the recipe two years ago after she'd discovered the strange foreign staple at the local co-op. They'd gone to Italy once when they were younger, and Eddie had always enjoyed it. "Can't you try making it?" he'd said at the time. Sandra had hooted and replied, "I wouldn't know where to start." Now they had cooking programmes on the television, where she picked up a lot of new ideas.

"Marigold was just waiting for the woman at No.1 to get back," she said, spooning some salad on her plate and serving Gladys too. Eddie helped himself.

"Why couldn't she wait in her own house?"

"She can get a better view from here."

Sandra thought it made sense, until Eddie said, "Next time, tell her to take a hike. We don't live here for her benefit."

"She wasn't in my way. I still made dinner…"

He banged his knife on the table. It was a sign to tell Sandra to shut up and stop arguing. "Are you trying to start something?"

Sandra looked at Gladys, whose eyes were lowered as her fork pronged her pasta.

"No, I was just saying…"

"Well don't."

Sandra remained quiet. How she hated him.

How many times had she wished him dead, each night hoping he'd crash his car on the way home? She would pretend to be a grieving widow until she cashed the insurance policy. The papers sat in the top drawer, taunting her every day when he came home safe and sound. When the man from the Pru visited each fortnight, he always asked if they wanted to up the payments for bigger dividends. Eddie always said yes to *her* life insurance policy, but not to his own. It made Sandra feel eternally suspicious of him. Still, he'd never get away with killing her. The insurance wouldn't pay out when the coroner discovered the bruises on her body.

"Did you pack a bag for me?" he asked before he shoved a big fork full of pasta into his ugly mouth.

"Of course. And I put in that tie I got you for Christmas last year."

"Will I need a tie?"

That stumped her. "I can ask Mrs Lang."

"Stop calling her that."

"I can't call her Eva anymore, can I?"

"You shouldn't have taken that cleaning job. It undermines us."

"You said you were fed up of me scrounging from you every time I wanted something." She looked him right in the eye, daring him to deny it. "I didn't have much choice, did I?"

"I already give you an adequate allowance."

Through his eyes, she could see his temper rising, but now she was on a roll. He made her sick. She preferred being confrontational. Better than being meek and mild, like a bloody doormat. But her bravado only matched her moods and most of the time her mood was fearful and cautious and in downright survival mode. But she wasn't a fool, her bravado was only short lived.

She took a swift glance at Gladys. The old lady had fleetingly raised her eyes. Eddie hadn't noticed but Sandra had. She was enjoying Sandra's humiliation, she could tell. The old hag was as bad as her violent son. They were both cut from the same cloth and Sandra hated them both.

"What time are we supposed to be leaving?"

The minibus will stop at the gate at 8.30. Roger said you can take your own clubs, as there are only four going now, so there will be plenty of room."

Eddie chewed the pasta. "Only four?"

She nodded, pretending to enjoy her food. "Mr Butler from next door won't be joining you. I think Roger felt he was too old, and of course, there's no man at No.1. She's single, remember?"

"Tart!"

"Just because she's single?"

He shook his head. "It's indecent if you ask me."

And Sandra thought, *no one's asking you, you pig!*

"Well, if the bus is coming at 8.30, I'll still have time for a swim before we leave."

"I suppose so." *And maybe you'll drown before you get a chance to go on your golfing weekend with 'the boys',* she thought.

"By the way," Eddie said. "I thought I saw you this morning, up on the cliff." He was staring right at her.

"Me?" she chuckled. "No chance of that in this weather."

He responded with a slow nod of the head. He wasn't sure about her story. He somehow knew she was lying.

Now she'd have to be on her guard again until he forgot what he saw.

Chapter Four

At No.5

EVA CALLED FROM THE BEDROOM. "Darling, I've packed for you."

"What?"

She went onto the landing to find him in the office. "Unclog your ears, Roger the Dodger." She went up behind him and flicked his ear lobe. Then she bent down and kissed him.

He didn't take his eyes from his work, but he did manage to bring up his hand and pat her on the bottom.

"What are you doing?"

"Just checking the itinerary."

"Again! You must have it memorised by now."

He looked up and smiled. "Almost."

She sat herself down on the chair next to his desk. The room had been designed for him. A bedroom turned into an office. The height of sophistication. "How many are going now?"

"Four of us from here, my brother and Harry."

"Harry's going?"

"Yes. Why not?"

"I thought you'd fallen out with him."

"We're okay now. Worked it out."

"But he accused you of having an affair with his wife." Eva looked down and realised a button was undone on her silk blouse. She did it up.

"A misunderstanding, sweetheart. It happens to the best of us."

"Well, I'm not happy about it. It was my husband he accused. Perhaps he should be apologising to me too."

"I'm sure he will when he sees you."

"Is he coming here in the morning?"

"Actually, darling. I forgot to mention it, but he's coming to spend the night."

"What?" She shook her head. "You forgot to mention it?"

"Sorry," Roger said again. "It's easier for him since the bus will be leaving early in the morning."

"I'm not sure I'm happy about that, darling."

"Well, he asked, and I could hardly say no."

"I suppose not." She thought about the clean sheets in the airing cupboard. "I'll make the bed up in the spare room then."

"Okay. Thanks."

EVA LANG SHOOK THE SHEET from its folds over the single divan bed, while pondering Roger's best man, Harry, and the dinner party they'd had in the summer. They were always having people over. Roger liked to show off his home: an exclusive property within an exclusive community, boasting an exclusive panoramic view of the Atlantic from the exclusive sweeping terrace. Exclusivity was what Roger was all about, since his high paid job at Philips Electronics, afforded him to be.

The dinner party had comprised of just seven guests. One was Kimberly from No.1 since she worked at the same place as Roger. The evening had gone well until Harry drank one glass of Blue Nun too many. Jade, his beautiful exotic wife, had taken the brunt of his drunk talk when from across the table, he openly accused her of having an affair.

Sipping a Dubonnet, Jade had sat in silence, shaking her head in quiet disbelief. It was a terribly awkward moment.

"Come on, Harry, old mate," Roger had said. "Tone it down."

"Tone it down?" Harry spat. "You're the one who needs to do that, mate."

"Harry!" Jade admonished. "Please, Stop it."

"You stop it," he said back. "I mean, really, honey, stop." He leaned back in his chair staring at his wife with her dark tanned skin and her bosom bulging over the low cut dress. Her long black hair was draped over one shoulder, making her look exotic and erotic, all in one go.

Eva didn't like her much. She was always batting her false eyelashes and moving her body seductively. Eva often noticed Roger staring, admiringly. He did it openly while offering a comment now and then, like 'I see you didn't bother dressing up for us tonight'. When in fact she was dolled up to the nines. Eva had seen him do that before, in the past. It was a 'thing' of his; openly admiring a woman while trying to prove he had nothing to hide. Nothing but his lust.

That night at dinner, Harry had scraped his chair over the stone flag patio and stormed into the house. The guests around the table had gone silent, probably enjoying every damn minute.

Eva had followed him into the house, while obstinately, Jade remained where she was. Harry stayed with her. Eva found him in the kitchen pouring the last glass from a bowl of punch. He discarded the fruit. "Are you all right?"

He shrugged and closed his eyes as he leaned on the counter top.

Their kitchen was the best in *the eight*. Actually, their entire house was the best of the eight. The other seven houses paled in comparison since theirs was the original builder's home. The guy had inherited the property from his late mother. Once an old fashioned bungalow, it had a view to die for, so he went on to capitalise on his good fortune, believing that property was the way forward, to invest in for the future. The entire headland was also his, so he developed it into a gated community built on a figure eight -his lucky number. His mother's old bungalow became No.5, and it was the best of the bunch after he trebled the square footage and put in all mod cons. Finally, when the eight properties were complete, the guy went bankrupt and the estate taken from him in a heartbeat. He died a year later, some said of a broken heart.

Harry looked up and stared at Eva for longer than necessary. "Why do you put up with him?"

"You don't know him."

"I know enough. He's at it with my wife."

"That's not true." She went up next to him and stroked his arm. "You've just had a few too many. That all. You're imagining things."

He looked at her hand on his arm and then at her. Their eyes locked and for a moment there, Eva felt a desire she hadn't felt for years. Could it be that she found Harry attractive? How was it possible after knowing him for so long? What on earth was she thinking? She felt her cheeks burn. She went to walk away, but Harry turned suddenly and pulled her into his arms. His harsh lips found hers as she moulded her body against his. She felt as if he was about to break her, which made her feel feminine and terribly sexy.

They pulled apart and he apologised. She felt her neck burning and she knew it must have been glowing red by now. It was one of her reveals. Whenever she was embarrassed or guilty of something, her neck turned crimson. That's why she'd tried to keep on the straight and narrow all her life. Otherwise, her neck would have given her away instantly.

Roger's voice could be heard behind them. Eva spun about and covered her neck with a conveniently placed tea-towel. "Are we okay in here?" he asked. Harry coughed while Roger patted him on the back. "Are we good, old friend?"

"Yeah. We're good. No problem," Harry said before he left the room and went back out to join his wife."

Eva wondered if he had seen them. "Don't clean this up," Roger said. "Ask Sandra to come in and help in the morning."

"I would have to pay her extra."

"That's okay by me. Nothing is too good for my lovely wife."

That was five months ago and now Harry was coming to stay the night.

As she made up his bed in the spare room, smoothing the sheet with slow hands, Eva Lang wondered if she should wear a turtle neck sweater when he arrived.

THE DOORBELL RANG at eight-thirty. Eva went slowly into the hall to answer it. She knew it was him, and her pulse had already quickened. Her heart missed a beat when she saw him standing in the frame of the door. He seemed unfazed by seeing her. *Maybe* the potential passion between them had been short-lived.

"Roger's in the lounge."

She watched him go through as she closed the door. She needed a moment to pull herself together. She went into the downstairs bathroom and leaned on the sink, staring at her face in the mirror at her face. She was thirty-five, but she didn't look a day over thirty. Many said so. It was that particular compliment she'd come to rely on when thinking about Harry those past few months. Her eyes were green, her hair dark, short to the neck. Her figure was slim, athletic looking and she dressed down, never wanting to follow the damn awful fashions of the era. *No*, she wore slacks and a tunic top by day, with muted colours, and at night, a plain shift dress just above the knee. Her style was conservative, sensible and easy to wear. She didn't believe in flaunting her body. That was for the desperate ones. Not the ones who'd already snagged a husband for life.

She'd met Roger at a nightclub when she was just a girl, a young virgin, out celebrating her seventeenth birthday with her other virgin friends. Roger was with a group of boys, he was six years older than her, but he was by far the most handsome boy in the room. He was medium height with hair that fell over his forehead, which he combed every hour on the hour. Their eyes met across the room and when he asked her to dance, Eva almost swooned. He took her breath away and after he'd courted her for two years when she was nineteen, she agreed to get engaged. They married when she was twenty years old and he was twenty-six. Everyone said it was a match made in heaven.

In those days, Roger was an apprentice at Philips Manufacturing plant in Taunton. He was there when they started up, launching the Philips audio cassettes upon the world. In the early days, he was promoted monthly, rising to great heights in his career as a workforce manager. Now he was Managing Director, involved in the battle of the video cassette innovation, along with VHS and Sony.

His job was high pressure, but he never took out his troubles on Eva. No, he'd been a good husband. The only low point of their marriage had been Eva's inability to conceive. In the early days, they'd longed for children. Now it was a faded memory since Roger never wanted to talk about it anymore.

Eva washed her hands and dried them on the soft pink towels of the downstairs toilet. She adjusted the collar of her white roll neck sweater, took a deep breath and left the safety of the small bathroom to face the two men in her life whom she claimed to love.

"EVA, DARLING, ANY CHIANTI?" Roger called as she entered the kitchen.

She looked straight at Harry, but he acted as if she wasn't even there. She was sure he'd regretted that summer kiss. Whilst she had been dreaming of him, kissing him, walking along a beach with him, making love with him, he in comparison had completely blocked her out. She was sure of it. What an old fool she'd been.

"In the back-up cupboard in the garage."

"I'll get it," said Harry. She watched him leave the kitchen to go through the back porch.

"He won't find it," she said as she followed him.

He was looking in the wrong place. "It's in here." She opened an old kitchen cupboard, an antique, once belonging to the developer's mother's kitchen. She pulled out a wicker covered bottle and when she handed it to him, their fingers touched. His was deliberate. She looked up at him. He was staring down at her with a serious expression on his face. "I've been thinking about you," he said simply.

Eva almost gasped, so sure that he couldn't have meant it. "Why?" she asked, almost losing her voice.

"Since the dinner party in the summer. Since we kissed."

"Oh."

His hand went to her shoulder. She looked at it, resting there, as she'd so often dreamed of him touching her. She looked towards the door leading back to the house. "I should go."

"Tell me you feel the same," he whispered.

She paused as she wondered if she should tell him the truth. She shook her head. "No, I'm married."

"So am I. Our marriages are shams."

"Not mine."

"Yes, yours too."

THEY WERE SITTING IN THE LOUNGE. The fire was on and the lights were turned low. Jim Reeves was crooning in the background as Roger rested his arm around Eva's shoulders. Her legs were tucked under her and her feet were bare. Harry sat opposite them on the easy chair. The glass coffee table in the centre was laden with bottles of wine and bowls of nuts and crisps. She'd put out some stuffed green olives, but no one had touched them.

They were all holding a bulbous brandy glass, swirling Hennessy at the bottom.

"Look, old boy," Roger said, "I want you to know that nothing has happened between Jade and me.

Harry rested his arm on the chair and nodded. "Think nothing more of it, Roger," said Harry.

"Just the drink talking, huh?" Roger chuckled.

Harry pouted. "Something like that."

Eva was grateful for the brandy that warmed her and calmed her and increased her desire for the man sitting opposite her husband. The feeling was strangely sweet, making the whole scenario exciting by its obvious danger.

"Anyway, it's all forgotten now, eh?" Roger patted Eva's thigh. She smiled, not meaning it one little bit.

"How's work?" Harry asked.

"There's a lot of pressure right now. The 'video wars' we call it." Roger pursed his lips. "We think VHS will take the crown there."

"I heard that soon every home in the country will have a video cassette player."

"Yes, it's possible, if the price comes down."

"Jade loves ours. She can actually record Coronation Street while she goes to Slimmer's World on a Wednesday night."

"I don't see the sense in it," Eva said. "Who goes out on a Wednesday night. I certainly wouldn't. At least not until *the street's* finished."

"If it was left to you, Eva darling, no one would ever want to buy a video recorder. You'd put us out of business," Roger laughed.

"I suppose I'm old fashioned."

"Not in all things," Roger said. A pause as they sipped their drink. "Actually, we had a bit of upset at work this week."

"Oh?" said Eva, "You haven't mentioned anything."

"It was all a bit strange. A bit spooky actually."

"What was it?"

"We had a strange chap working for us on the manufacturing side of things. He's worked there for ten years."

Eva and Harry remained silent, waiting for Roger to finish the story.

"He's always been a bit odd. Not very well liked, if you know what I mean. Anti-social, if you like." Roger lit a small cigar. He offered one to Harry, but Harry declined. Eva leaned over and slid the green marble ashtray across the table. Roger placed it on the arm of the sofa. He tapped it with the tip of his cigar before he carried on with his story.

"Anyway, we had to lay some people off, what with the video wars going on. It was ordered from above. Nothing to do with me at all. But you know what people are like, they always want to shoot the messenger." He gulped and drew on the cigar as the smoke wafted upwards.

Eva liked the smell, but not the odour it left in the morning.

"It was quite uncomfortable. I called him into my office and offered a handshake, but he was quite nasty about it all. I told him it wasn't my call and that if it was up to me, I would keep him on until he retired, but he wouldn't have any of it. He became quite irate…sinister almost. Made me feel quite queer." Absentmindedly, Roger rubbed Eva's hand. "He made some terrible threats."

"What sort of threats?" Eva sat up and looked her husband in the eye. *Why hadn't he mentioned it before?*

"Oh, just silly, random stuff. Watched too many cowboy films if you ask me."

"Tell me," implored Eva.

"He threatened to kill me, which is wholly ridiculous," he said nervously. "I can't take the matter seriously."

Eva was unnerved by the story, but she wasn't about to ruin the evening. Not while Harry was there. She'd talk to Roger about it when he got back from his golf weekend. Then she would propose that they call the police to report the despicable man for making such vile threats. Honestly, she couldn't understand why Roger hadn't done that already. She decided to change the subject. "So, what are you boys going to get up to on your golfing weekend?" Eva asked. She looked at Harry when she asked that, wondering what *he* -not Roger- would be doing tomorrow night.

"Just dinner and then a drunken evening in the clubhouse, no doubt," Roger replied with a chuckle.

"When will you be back?"

"Sunday afternoon. It's just one night."

"I understand all your neighbours are coming," said Harry.

"Most of them. The old boy from number eight won't be joining us. He's seventy-nine, so I didn't invite him."

"Won't that be a little awkward, Roger?" Eva asked. "He'll see you all leave in the bus."

"Can't be helped."

"What about the ladies?" asked Harry. "You have any plans?"

"Well, I've asked the neighbours over for cocktails on Saturday evening."

"That's nice."

Eva shrugged. "Well, as Harry said, it's just for one night."

Chapter Five

At No.2

THEY MOVED INTO NO.2 when the Seaview estate was brand new. Their house was an elegant two storey dwelling with three bedrooms, but the one thing that sold it to Marigold when they'd viewed it, was the kitchen. A kitchen to die for! It was open plan, like Sandra's, but it was bigger, and better decorated, in Marigold's opinion. Cream coloured cabinets lined the walls at one end with a breakfast island in the middle and a neat glass-fronted wine fridge underneath. Marigold and Clive thought it was so sophisticated when they'd viewed it. She was particularly enamoured by the double stove in the middle, placed underneath a mock chimney with a tall mantle over it housing her little china pigs.

The view from the kitchen was wonderful, so said everyone who visited. They had a much better view of the sea than Sandra's and Eddie's, but not half as good as No. 5, the cream of the crop, taking prime position at the top of *the eight*. That one dominated the view, taking a corner piece of land too, just beyond their garden.

Marigold and Clive's house also had a bigger terrace than Sandra's. The garden at the front was Clive's pride and joy, packed with shrubs and flowers of all sorts. He also had a shed at the back, close to the edge. That's where he went to get away from it all when the kids were around.

Marigold grabbed a bottle of wine from the fridge and gave the glass door a wipe with a tea towel where she'd noticed a little finger mark. Probably made by Zara, their part-time cleaner. Zara was Portuguese, but she spoke quite good English since she'd been living in the UK for fifteen years. She was a small woman, about fifty, with long black hair she kept tied up in a knot at the back of her head. She had been good with the kids before they'd left home, but Marigold still kept her around to take the load off when it came to keeping the house clean.

"Hey kiddo."

Marigold turned about to see Clive come into the room. She smiled. "Hey, yourself." They kissed on the lips, just a peck which they did at least twenty times a day.

"What have you been up to? Seen Sandra today?"

She knew what he was thinking. "To see if she had more bruises, you mean."

Clive shook his head. He leaned on the centre island as Marigold went to the fridge and pulled out a couple of steaks.

"I'll go over and see her after tea before that husband of hers gets home."

Marigold and Clive always had an early meal. They didn't eat lunch, so it worked for them. Before bed, they often munched on snacks: cheese and biscuits, something like that.

"Does that mean I won't see you for the rest of the evening?"

"Well, I might pop over and see Kim. Take a bag of nibbles and some wine." She suddenly remembered something. "Do you think I should take some lemonade?"

"A bit presumptuous. Especially after what happened before."

"You mean when I popped home and by the time I got back, she was in bed." Marigold remembered that evening well. she wondered if Kim had felt ill or something. She certainly wouldn't have gone to bed knowing Marigold was coming back with lemonade.

"If you're going to be at Kim's all night, I might go down the pub for a game of darts," Clive said.

"Shouldn't you be getting an early night, love? You've got to be up with the lark in the morning."

"Honestly, I wish I hadn't agreed to it. I don't even like golf that much."

"Oh, that's silly. You'll enjoy it when you get there."

"I don't get on with Roger very well, you know that. And to be stuck with Eddie for a weekend after finding out what he does to that poor wife of his, just makes the whole thing abhorrent. I'd much prefer to stay home with you."

It was true, Clive and Roger didn't get on that well. In the summer last year, they'd thrown a bit of a bash for their anniversary. Naturally, they'd invited all the neighbours and they'd had a few family members. The kids didn't come, they were still teenagers, so a party at home wasn't their thing. Clive had been a bit put out about it, but Marigold had said, 'They're spreading their wings. Seaview has nothing to offer when you consider their own social life at Bristol Uni.'

The party was in full swing. Everyone who said they were coming arrived in time for the food, the toasts and the anniversary cake made by Mrs Butler at No.8. She was a self-confessed cake decorator who'd trained herself in the art. They were fine words, but when the monstrosity turned up that morning, Marigold had almost dropped it, so taken aback by its ugliness. There was nothing to be done. She had to use it, but she had to confess to a bit of satisfaction when she made a little card which she'd placed in front of it on the buffet table. *Made by Mrs Butler.*

Over the course of the evening, Marigold offered a glance that way, enjoying the look of disgust coming from the faces of their guests when they saw the cake, especially when they discovered it wasn't her creation.

Over the course of the evening, Clive had gone to their shed at the bottom of the terrace. The shed was turned back to front, allowing the entrance to overlook the sea. Clive often enjoyed an evening on his own sitting in the doorway of his shed, looking out over the bay. He always said it was his little bit of heaven.

That evening, it was dark when he stepped inside and turned on the light. Roger Lang was in there with a dark skinned lady in a state of undress, doing what he could only describe as the act of an animal. 'A four legged animal,' he said when he recounted the tale the next day.

Marigold had been horrified and vowed she would tell Eva about the unfortunate incident at the earliest opportunity. Clive had persuaded her otherwise, saying they shouldn't make waves in their peaceful community. "Just forget it,' he'd said to Marigold, but she never had, of course, and even to that day she always claimed it was her responsibility to do the right thing, to inform Eva about her unlawful, cheating husband.

"What time is the bus leaving?"

"About 8.30. You should get up at 7.00 to give yourself some time."

"I'll never beat you in that department," Clive said, sipping his wine.

It was true Marigold was an early riser. Five am every day without fail, except for that morning after their anniversary party. *Then* she'd woken late at six. Messed her up all day, that did.

The phone was ringing. "I'll get it," Marigold called. She went into the hall where the phone sat on a glass half-moon table. They'd recently bought a modern cream coloured telephone, which matched the cream walls in the hall. Marigold made sure it was thoroughly cleaned each week. She couldn't begin to imagine the germs hiding in that mouthpiece.

She picked up the receiver and politely announced the number. Telephone etiquette, she called it.

"Marigold, this is Elsie Butler. Could you send your Clive over to have a look around the gate?"

"What on earth for, dear?"

"I heard some noises out there. Mr Butler is in bed with a nasty cold, so I thought your Clive could come and inspect things."

"Of course. What sort of noise?"

"I'm not really sure."

"I'll send him along then. Stay inside the house until he knocks."

"Alright. Goodbye.

"Goodbye, Mrs Butler." Marigold hung up the phone. She called Clive's name as she went back into the kitchen. She'd pull the steaks out from under the grill until he got back. "Can you pop along to the gate? Mrs Butler thinks she heard some noises."

He didn't answer. At her door, he removed his slippers and put on his shoes. "Back in a minute," he called.

Marigold looked at her watch. Another hour and Kimberly would be home. She quite fancied a nice evening in with her good friend Kim.

Clive returned twenty minutes later, and she pushed the steaks back under the grill.

Clive pouted as he washed his hands.

"You couldn't find anything then?"

"The cat had knocked over a flower pot. I found it smashed on the path. Told her to leave it till the morning and I'll go over and clean it up."

"Was she all right?"

He nodded and dried his hands on a small towel hanging on the hook at the back of the door. "Mr Butler's laid up."

"Yes, she told me on the phone." Marigold leaned her back against the cupboard. Everything was ready apart from the steaks. "Five minutes and dinner will be ready."

"He's getting on a bit now."

"I wonder what she'll do if he goes?"

"Well, she won't stay here. Probably go to her sisters in the north."

"Then we'll have new people move in." Marigold didn't know if she should be happy about the prospect of new neighbours or not.

"She'll get a good price for that place."

"How much do you reckon? It's only small, her house."

"She'll still get about twelve thousand for it. Nice little place like that."

"Right next to the gate too. You know, if we downsized and bought that, I'd be directly opposite Kimberly's house."

"Keep an eye out for her, you mean?"

"Yes, I do. An attractive young girl like that with no man to protect her. Shame!"

They sat down and tucked into their steaks. "After tea, I'll go over and see Sandra. May as well keep an eye out for her too. Just until Kim gets back from work."

Later, after tea, Marigold left via the back, where double French doors were always left unlocked. It was hardly a security risk. No one ever intruded on their gated community, so it was safe to be lax. Whenever Marigold talked to outsiders about their estate, she always spoke with reverence, since Seaview was completely exclusive and private. "We don't have to worry about things other people on the west coast worry about. We've never had one burglary in the two years we've been there. 'And not many people could say that,' she often added.

Chapter Six

INSIDE THE HIGH WALLS, Drake Fisher crouched behind the bushes, keeping out of sight of the heavy traffic that seemed to be entering Seaview. He watched the first white Cortina go up along the eight, then another car, and then the one he'd been looking out for all night long, Kimberley's. He was glad when the headlights were turned off so that he could hide in the darkness. If anyone had seen him come in, his plan would have been over before it had begun.

He kept his eye on Kim. The others held no interest for him. Not yet.

He recalled the time Kimberly told him he was to go up to Lang's office. He thought he was in for a promotion since she'd given him a nice kind smile. More fool him. She was like all the rest. A dirty, scheming scumbag. And a woman to boot. Drake didn't mind what gender his victims were. 'People' in general were his enemy and he would kill anyone for just being 'them'.

He watched Kimberley get out of her car. Just as she was going inside her house, a woman dressed in slacks ran across the road, pulling her cardigan around her while her breath looked as if she was smoking. Just as Kimberly shut the door, the woman rang the bell. Even from that distance behind the bushes, he could tell by Kimberly's face she wasn't happy to see the woman. But she let her in anyway. That was people all over. They did things they shouldn't do. Not like him. Everything Drake did was precise and right. He'd made good choices.

He'd kept his nose clean all that time, apart from that one unfortunate occasion when he was twenty five when he met Jane. She was the love of his life, even though she was reluctant to reciprocate his affection. She was shy, Drake realised, so he'd taken the matter in hand and got her over her shyness. She was a mess when he buried her out on the moors, but he made up for it by giving her a posy of pansies in her hands, crossed at her bloodied abdomen as if she had been interred properly. It was the least he could do for the love of his life.

Now, as the temperature dropped, he realised he needed to find a place to get warm before someone saw his breath rising from the bushes.

The house nearest him was No.8. Earlier, when he was outside the gate on the other side of the road, he'd seen the old lady come out. A cat had made a flower pot crash to the floor and made a ruckus doing it. She'd gone back inside and then a man came sprinting towards her house as if he was the cavalry. He had a look around and eventually saw the broken pot. Drake had watched him as he walked to the back door and entered the house. Then two minutes later he left.

Now, as Drake darted past the broken pot on the path, he noticed it had been filled with pansies. Ahead of him, at the side of the house, near the back garden, he saw a greenhouse. He slipped inside as he thought about Jane and her little posy of pansies, then under the cover of darkness, he hit himself on the face three times on the left and twice on the right.

Chapter Seven

At No.1

KIMBERLEY HAD HAD ENOUGH OF MARIGOLD. She
needed to get her out of her house before she screamed. The woman
had made herself comfortable in the lounge in front of the electric
fire. She'd kicked off her shoes and even had the audacity to bring
along a pair of slippers. She put them on her feet with a sigh. "That's
better," she said.

"You brought slippers?"

"Well, you know what we're like when we get started. I end
up staying half the night." She laughed as if it was a shared joke.

"What about Clive? Doesn't he want your company?"
Please say yes, Kimberly pleaded silently.

"Oh, no. Our Clive's all right. Besides, he's gone down the
pub to play darts."

"Well, that means he'll be back when the pub closes around
eleven, so you won't want to stay here beyond that."

"I don't mind."

"I'm keen on having an early night." She couldn't be any
clearer than that.

"I tell you what, I'll disappear around about twelve and let
you get some peace and quiet."

"That's good of you," Kim said, sarcastically.

"My pleasure."

Kimberly Cutter had long ago learned to tolerate people
like Marigold. She was a *person cliché* as she liked to call them,
having met several people like her over her lifetime.

Kimberly had been raised by an alcoholic father. He was a
good man, a hard worker, but at night, when he came home, he hit
the bottle hard and the family suffered for it. She couldn't help
loving him for the man he was by day, but by night, her childish
optimism was often shattered by the dreaded drink.

He was a whiskey man. One bottle a night. But at weekends
he doubled that and was often found passed out on the sofa, drunk
beyond all drunkenness. There was no word for it. It was his infinity,

his bottomless pit, his own private hell. No one knew the cause of his self-destruction -he would say there wasn't one- but it was something Kim had always tried to get to the bottom of, hoping that one day, even while she was still young, she would find the answer and make him well again.

She'd suffered at his hands many times, but his biggest and most supreme weapon was his words. He destroyed her with them, her two brothers too, not to mention their mother. He had a gift for dragging people down to his own darkest depths. He would lift them one minute and destroy them the next. He was unpredictable when he was drunk, but unlike her brothers, Kim learned how to use that treatment to her advantage.

Later in life, someone told her that children of alcoholics were highly skilled in recognising body language and micro-expressions; the look on a face; the light in an eye; a sleight of hand, all from imperfect strangers. She had developed the gift very early on, the result of her living with a verbally and physically aggressive abuser, she was told. It was the mind's natural defence system, a way of protecting oneself, premeditating the abuser's actions, defending herself from verbal and physical torture.

She'd harnessed the skill when she turned eighteen.

It was her first boyfriend. He was a cad and a cheater, but she thought she was in love. She knew his movements, his cheating ways, his lies, just by his body language and the excuses he made, the look in his eyes when he lied to her, and at the end of two years, she finally caught him out.

She was standing at the bus stop and a girl stood next to her. They'd caught a glance at each other, and Kimberley saw a look in her eyes that she called 'curious'. She saw the girl again at a nightclub when she was talking to her cheating boyfriend, and then Kim knew. Just by that single expression at the bus stop, Kim realised she was the girl whom he had cheated her with. It had befuddled her, as she wondered how she could possibly know someone just by looking at them. It never made sense, until she realised, she was inherently skilled at non-verbal communication and micro-expressions.

She'd dumped the boy!

Now, as Kimberley was about to lose her rag with Marigold, the telephone rang. She went into the hall to answer it, closing the door behind her, leaving her intruder on her own, where she deserved to be. "Hello?"

"It's me."

"What is it?"

"I'd like to see you."

"So does everyone else." She took a quick glance towards the door to the lounge. She hoped Marigold didn't have her ear up to it.

"Hmm?"

"Nothing. Just being sarcastic."

"I thought I'd come over tonight."

"After what happened last time?"

Kimberley had been seeing Tyrone on and off for over a year. He once worked at Philips as an office manager, but he left after an unfortunate incident on the shop floor.

He'd pursued Kim relentlessly, but she refused to go out with him, stating quite categorically, that she would never have relations with a colleague. It had been a difficult decision since he was extremely good-looking. One day he was walking along the factory floor when he was almost knocked down by a forklift truck. He told her the tale after the event, saying he'd had a narrow escape, but it was pretty hard to imagine. He claimed it wasn't an accident. That he had, just a week before in the distribution depot, almost been crushed by a crate falling from twenty feet up. It had missed him by inches. Another time, he was in his own office, when a brick came hurtling through the window. He was covered in glass, and after it had taken him a few minutes to get back on his feet, when he looked outside, there was no one there.

He said the incidents were extremely odd and that he couldn't think of one person who would want to harm him. After an investigation, it was discovered that the one driving the forklift truck was none other than Drake Fisher. Of course, Fisher said he didn't see him and that maybe Ty should stay in his office rather than risk his life on the shop floor. The Unions agreed.

A week later Ty resigned after realising that putting his life in danger for the sake of a job, wasn't worth it. But the real reason, she'd discovered, was that he was in love with her and if he didn't work at Philips, she would agree to go out with him.

Actually, Kim went the other way. She'd suddenly lost respect for a man who would abandon his position in life just because of some silly little accidents. Eventually, he caught her at a low point, and she agreed to go to the pictures with him. *The Blues Brothers* was amazing, and it put her on a high. So much so, that night she'd slept with Ty, which was the start of something quite new.

"What happened last time?" Ty was now saying on the phone.

"One of the neighbours saw you leave."

"So what?"

"I told you before," she whispered. "These are small minded people who live small lives. You have no idea." She looked once again at the closed door and hoped Marigold wasn't listening.

"I'll make sure no one sees me, and I'll be out early."

"Well…I've got one of them here. She's hard to get rid of, but I guess I could get her out by midnight. How does that sound?"

"Sounds great to me. Can't wait to see you, baby."

Kimberly hung up the phone. *God*, she thought, the guy always sounded so damn desperate.

THE EVENING WENT SLOWLY. Marigold kept the conversation going while Kimberly tuned out and stared into the fire. That was until Marigold said something a lot more interesting than anything she'd said so far.

"I don't know whether I should say anything," Marigold said.

"What about?"

"What happened at our anniversary party last summer."

"Which was?"

Marigold was suddenly coy. "No, forget I said anything."

"I'll get you another drink." Kimberly brought her a glass of port. Marigold accepted it and sniffed it. "It's port," Kim said.

"Ah, I wondered why it was in such a small glass." She took a sip and nodded her approval. "This stuff usually sends me to sleep."

Thank God, thought Kimberly vowing to get in another bottle. "What were you saying about your 'do'?"

"You were there, weren't you?"

"Yes."

"You were with a rather handsome young man."

"Tyrone."

"That's right. Very friendly." Marigold was staring right at her, trying to read her thoughts. Kim looked away.

"He stayed over. Nothing going on. He's just a friend."

"Of course."

"So, what was it that happened?"

"It's a bit delicate and I'm the last person to gossip." She made it look like she was struggling to voice the words that would surely shock Kimberly to the core. "Clive went down to the shed to get another tin of *Party Seven*. He stores them down there in a little fridge he rigged up." She laughed. "We went through four of them that night. That's twenty-eight pints. What a hoot."

Kimberly wished she'd get on with it.

"Anyway, he opened the door and there were a couple on all fours, doing it."

Kimberly's eyes widened. "You're joking? Who was it?"

"That the awkward part. You'll have to promise me to keep it to yourself."

"Of course."

"It was Roger from No.5."

"With Eva?"

Marigold shook her head. "I'm afraid not," she rushed, "Not that I think Eva would ever be found in a position like that."

Kim chuckled. "You mean in that predicament? Not position!" She raised her eyebrows suggestively.

Marigold caught on after a few seconds had passed. "Ooh," she hooted. "That's definitely what I meant."

Kimberly leaned forward. She was all ears. "Tell me, then. Who was with Roger in that awkward predicament?"

"I don't know her name. She had dark skin…oriental looking…a foreigner, anyway."

"I remember her. Jade! Her husband's name was Harry. He was talking to Ty most of the night."

"Yes, friends of the family apparently."

"Well, what do you know? Poor old Eva." Kim couldn't help enjoying the gossip. Now she could watch them and read their thoughts. A great source of pleasure.

"Speaking of which, are you going to her cocktail party tomorrow night?"

"I'm not sure. I'm not into 'all girls' parties."

"Go on. It'll be a laugh. All the men will be away on their golfing weekend. Tine to let our hair down a bit."

"At a six o'clock cocktail party?"

"Well, we could keep it going. I'd be happy to have everyone round my house."

Kimberly's eyes darted to the clock. "It's quarter-to-midnight."

"I should get off then." She placed her empty glass on the side table.

Kimberly was thanking her lucky stars. *Good timing*, Ty would be there soon.

HE ARRIVED AT TWELVE-TEN. She kept the lights off and let him in. He grabbed her and kissed her, deliciously. "Where did you leave your car?"

"Outside the gates, just along the road a bit."

"Good. You remembered the code, then."

"I'm an office boy, I always remember numbers."

They went through to the kitchen and she poured him a glass of port. If she knew Ty, they'd be in bed inside of ten minutes.

"Something strange just happened."

"What?"

"The gates opened and as I walked near to the light, I heard someone gasp."

"What do you mean, gasp?"

"You know, like…" He made a gasping noise. "As if someone recognised me."

"Damn! Probably one of the neighbours. A weird lot."

"I'm not sure. I couldn't see anyone. I thought I saw the bushes move next to the house on the other side."

"That's No.8. Old couple. My neighbour told me that her husband had to go over there tonight, but it was just a cat or something."

"Cats don't gasp, do they?" He walked towards her with a smile on his lips and a look in his eyes that made her realise it wouldn't be long before he took her up the stairs.

"Only when they see someone who shouldn't be there. Like a good looking guy visiting a single girl at midnight."

He laughed. "Let them gossip. Who cares? I need you in my life all the time, Kimberly Cutter," he whispered huskily. "No more excuses. I don't work at Phillips any more. You won't compromise your position."

"It's lucky you left when you did. We had a few redundancies this week, one of them from your department."

"Good timing for me then."

"Yes, but you missed out on a potential redundancy payment."

He leaned into her and kissed her neck. "No problem. Money means nothing to me."

His comment almost put Kimberly off. Who doesn't care about money? Still, she was anxious to get him into bed now, so any doubts she had about his moral code would have to be put at bay. For tonight at least.

Chapter Eight

At No.7

FRIDAY NIGHT WAS POSSIBLY THE WORST and the best night Sandra had ever experienced. It started when Mrs Butler popped round. They had just finished dinner and Eddie was settling his mother, Gladys, into a comfortable chair in the lounge. From there to the kitchen, sliding glass doors divided the rooms, so Sandra could see them watching the television. BBC2 was showing live coverage of the inauguration of Ronald Reagan as the fortieth President of the United States. Sandra wondered what were those Americans doing voting for an actor? Seemed odd to her.

Sandra had her hands deep in soap suds when Mrs Butler tapped on the patio doors. She often slipped through the back gardens to borrow something, or to bring Sandra a home-baked treat or two.

"Only me," she said.

Sandra quickly put her finger to her lips to hush her. "Eddie's in there with his mother," she said with a whisper.

Mrs Butler whispered back. "Ooh, sorry. I don't want to disturb you so late."

"You're alright Mrs B. It's only seven o'clock. I'm making coffee if you fancy one."

"I'd better not. George is in bed."

"Still not well?"

"Yes, poor thing."

"Have you had the doctor out?"

"He came this morning. He said it was just a bit of influenza, but George's chest sounded terrible."

"Did he give him anything?"

"Penicillin, but I'm not a fan. I've still got some M+B693 from before the war. I've given him a dose of that."

"Good idea."

"I had a bit of a fright earlier on," she said.

Sandra looked up from the coffee pot she was filling. Mrs Butler was a frail looking lady, but she was mentally strong, even after surviving two wars. Rumour had it, they lost a son in WW2, but they didn't talk about it and Sandra felt it was wrong to ask. She always wore a nylon overall over her house clothes. Sandra couldn't remember her ever wearing slacks.

"What happened?"

"I thought I heard something outside. Clive from No. 2 came over to have a look, but it was just our cat. He'd knocked over a plant pot. Little Minx. I've only just put those pansies in."

"Bit early for pansies isn't it, Mrs B?"

"I know they won't last long, but I like to see a bit of colour outside in the winter. George grows them in his greenhouse. A lovely purple colour."

"Hm. Lovely."

"I'll bring you a couple of plugs over if you fancy it."

"Not if they won't last long."

"You'll get a week out of them," she said. "Anyway, I heard another noise just half an hour ago, so I thought I'd pop over and tell you to make sure your doors are locked."

"I don't think you have to worry on that score, Mrs B. We're safe as houses in Seaview."

"I don't like being so near the gate. The light used to shine in our bedroom at night, so we had to move into the back bedroom. Me and George often say we wish we'd taken that one up in the far corner, No. 4."

"Well, at least you've got the big wall on one side. We're open to the elements here. Gets quite blowy in the winter."

"We still get the wind though. Have you met them up at No.4? He's in a wheelchair, you know."

"I've seen them out and about and we've said hello once or twice, but I don't know much about them. They keep to themselves a lot."

"Yes, strange for Seaview, don't you think?"

"We all like our privacy once in a while."

"No.3 is still empty."

"I've heard there's a family moving in next week. Two young children, apparently."

"That'll be nice having some youngsters. I'd enjoy seeing them ride their bikes along *the eight*."

Sandra nodded as she placed two chocolate cupcakes on a plate.

"Is your Eddie going on that golfing trip?" Mrs Butler asked.

"Yes. He's looking forward to it. I suppose George won't be going, what with him being laid up."

"He wasn't even invited."

"That can't be right. Roger invited all the men."

"Not George."

Sandra picked up the tray. "Let me just take this through." She went through the sliding doors to the sitting room. Ronald Reagan was holding up his hand, pledging! His wife Nancy was at his side. Her hair was lovely and puffy, but she always looked like her head was too big for her body. "Here's your tea."

Then Eddie snapped. "Shush. And tell her from next door to sling her hook."

Sandra was mortified. Her face must have been as red as the cushions on the sofa. "She'll hear you."

"I don't sodding care."

Sandra hurried to close up the doors. Back in the kitchen, she mouthed 'sorry' to Mrs Butler.

"Don't worry, dear. I expect he's had a hard day."

Sandra shrugged. She was so embarrassed. She leaned on the counter to get her breath. Suddenly Mrs Butler came up beside her and placed her hand over hers. "Don't worry," she repeated. "You just look after yourself."

Sandra looked at the old lady's wise eyes and she knew then that Mrs Butler *knew*.

WHEN SHE LEFT, the whole evening dissolved into plain misery.

Eddie came straight out and closed the doors behind him, leaving Gladys alone in the front room. "How many times have I got to tell you to keep that old bag out of here."

Sandra went on alert. She was an expert at it since it was a well-practised ritual. "She was just warning us to lock the doors because she'd heard a noise." She backed up and turned away from him, pretending to wipe the draining board. She kept her head down, praying he'd forget the whole thing and leave her alone. Instead, she felt his fingers squeeze her arm. He swung her about and she almost lost her footing. Her legs were twisted so she was unsteady on her feet. One of her slippers came off.

Suddenly, she felt a surge of defiance. She knew it would spell trouble, but there were times when she just didn't care. She stared into his eyes and snarled at him. He looked aghast that she should demonstrate such venom when she was usually so easily manipulated.

Words weren't spoken. It was as if time had stood still. There was an invisible wall between them, but she knew if he wanted to, he would get past that. And he did.

He looked sternly into her eyes, threatening her with his steady unwavering gaze. Then he placed his hand on her throat. He held it there, the tips of his fingers tightening and his eyes glistening with carnal joy. He was going to strangle her. She felt such relief.

He loosened his grip. "You do this every damn time, don't you? Winding me up when I've worked my socks off all day! Who do you think you are, eh?"

She didn't speak. There was no point. She'd said it all before. Nothing ever made a difference, and nothing mattered anymore. She would gladly die right now so that she never had to look at his ugly face again.

Instead, he dropped his hand and shoved her. Her twisted feet gave way so that she was forced to slide down the cabinet beneath the sink. She kept bleach in there. She should grab it and throw it all over his face so that it burnt him like acid, and he would wither and die. What joy.

But she just sat there for a moment contemplating her life, allowing tears to stream down her face. She lifted the skirt of her pinafore and wiped her eyes, pressing the cloth hard to hide in the perfect darkness and solitude. Then she pulled it away and she was faced with the glaring strip-light overhead. Back to the real world, where Eddie reigned.

SHE COULD HEAR THE TELEVISION in the front room. Canned laughter filled the house and she imagined him in there with his mother laughing at the antics of Morecambe & Wise.

Sandra turned off the lights in the kitchen and went slowly up the stairs. She felt such fatigue brought on by raw emotion, and she could barely get to the top. She went into Gladys' room. The bed was already made. She turned down the blankets and with a slow hand, smoothing the corner of the flannelette sheet. She closed the curtains and turned on a small table lamp at the side of the bed. Gladys would read for a while. She often had trouble sleeping.

She went into their bedroom. They had single beds with a small table separating them. It was her one small mercy. Eddie never wanted her that way. Hadn't for years. She just had to abide his snoring in the bed next to hers, every night, until he got up and went for his swim.

That swim.

She'd thought about 'his swim' for the whole two years they'd lived in Seaview. He assumed she was asleep when he was gone, but she wasn't. Each morning she would lie awake thinking about him in the Atlantic, thrashing about, until a large wave went crashing over him and took him under. The current wouldn't allow him to surface and only when he was half-drowned -just so he was aware of the moment he died, a wave would throw his body against the cliff, time and time again, until all that was left of him was a bloody mashed pulp. When he was still on the verge of passing, a shark would come at him and he would open his eyes for one last time, seeing the jaws and teeth snap down upon his torso, breaking him in two. Even then, she still thought about his death when he travelled to hell itself. No heaven for him, Sandra thought, enjoying her daydream immensely.

Now, she got into bed and turned out the light. Soon he would come upstairs and if she was awake, he'd make her pay for upsetting him so much. And in the bedroom next door, Gladys would hear her sobbing and Sandra hated the thought of that most of all.

Chapter Nine

At No.5

"I'M GOING UP," Roger said, Eva was taken aback since she thought he would be awake for ages yet.

Harry looked equally surprised when Roger picked up his glass and finished his drink. He watched Eva still sitting on the couch with her legs tucked under her. She leaned her head back idly on the cushions and Roger bent down and kissed her on the forehead. "Goodnight. No need for you to rush."

"Night, Roger," Harry said while still watching Eva.

"Don't forget to set your clock. We've got an early start." Then Roger left, closing the door behind him.

A mood fell over the room as the two looked at each other across their half empty glasses. The tension was obvious. Eva had been thinking about Harry all night and she was sure he'd done the same. They were alone now. No wife and no husband to stop them doing what they wanted to do. The music played softly, Simon & Garfunkel, *The sound of silence.* The words soothed her mind while stimulating the notion of a long lost romance. Perfect.

She watched as he got up and came towards her. He sat down where Roger had sat. The seat must still have been warm. Eva leaned forward, placing her head in her hands, contemplating the mistake she was about to make. Would she regret it in the morning? Could she help it? She felt his hand on her shoulder. She looked up and his face was right next to hers as he stroked her hair. He leaned in as she closed her eyes and he kissed her, tenderly, as a lover would.

"We should stop," she croaked when they pulled away.

She had her hand flat on his chest. Pushing him from her, but not hard. She hoped he would make the decision himself, that he would see sense and retire. His eyes were glassy, his lips together, about to yield. She looked at the small dark hairs sprouting from his neck above his sweater. She thought of her own neck and for once it wasn't burning red.

She moved away from him and stood up. She went to the door and opened it slightly, looking up the stairs, wanting to hear something to give her a reason to stop.

She closed it again and she felt him behind her. It was going to happen. They were going to make love, and there was nothing she could do to stop it.

At No.6

JUST BEFORE MIDNIGHT, Rhianna switched off her bedside light and opened the curtains. She had a good view of the other seven houses, most of whom had their lights turned off. It was quiet out there on *the eight,* as uncle called it. Cars were parked in driveways or inside the garage for the night, and just a few exterior lights were turned on above the entrances.

Next door at No.5, the bedroom light went on. She watched a man go to the window and draw the curtains closed. Downstairs, the dimmed lights in the front room were still on. She could see two figures moving around inside, close together as if they were skating on ice.

Rhianna looked directly into the window of the house opposite, No.3. Uncle Rolf had told her it was empty, but there was a new family moving in next week. There were no curtains up, but she still couldn't see much of the interior since it was dark inside. Next to that, house No.4 also had their lights off. A man in a wheelchair lived there, uncle said. She would pop around tomorrow and see if they had a story to tell. Maybe it would be published. She could always send it to one of those magazines that print tragic life stories. *Woman's Own* or something.

Her eye caught movement out on the road. She shuffled her knees on the bed to get a better view while her elbows leaned on the window sill. She saw a woman hugging a cardigan around herself, while her breath looked like she was smoking. Still wearing her slippers, she'd just left the house at No.1. The woman inside the house had waved her off and then closed the door quite forcefully as if she was glad to see the back of her. The lady staggered along *the eight.* She must have had a drink or two. She walked to the side of

No.2 and opened the wooden gate to go around the back. That must have been Clive's wife, Marigold.

Speaking of which, the front gate was now opening. A car was waiting to enter with its lights dimmed. The lone driver went straight to No.2 and parked the car on the sloping driveway. When he got out, she saw it was Clive, coming home from his darts match. Lucky his wifey got home first, Rhianna thought, chuckling to herself.

Wait! The gates were opening again. A man! He'd used the security keypad to open them, but he was on foot. Where was his car? He came through the gates before they had opened fully and then he went directly to house No.1. But then he hesitated as if he'd heard something. He tapped the door. A woman answered and he slipped inside like a thief in the night. A secret rendezvous! Seemed like Seaview wasn't so quiet after all.

Rhianna decided to open the window slightly so that she could get a bit of air in the room. When she did, she heard a muffled scream. She gasped as the noise made her skin crawl. She closed the window again. It must have been the couple next door. Uncle had told her about how the man, Eddie, abused his poor wife. Uncle said if Rhianna heard anything untoward, she should ignore it. 'Nothing anyone can do,' uncle Rolf had said.

Chapter Ten

THE TURN OF EVENTS ON FRIDAY NIGHT began after that cat tipped over the flower pot. Then after that man from No.2 had gone, Drake had slipped into the greenhouse where the cat followed him as if they were best friends. Maybe he'd keep him, Drake thought, stroking his back to his tail.

He'd been hiding out in the greenhouse with the cat, when, feeling a little warmer, he decided to have another scout around. He went down the side path of No.8 to see if there was anything going on, but everything was quiet, which was a shame because he was in the mood for a bit of excitement.

He knew the lay of the land in Seaview very well. He'd taken a part-time job there last summer, just so he could keep an eye on Kimberley Cutter. He'd taken some odd jobs, cash in hand, from all the residents except Kim, and Roger Lang at No.5. They would have recognised him, so he kept his distance. If he ever noticed them go past, he would pull his cap down over his face.

He knew the old people well. Mr and Mrs Butler had used him to do a few things around the place. Once he had to clean out the gutters. Up his ladders, he had a good view of what was going on in Seaview and he pretty much knew all the residents now.

He was disturbed from his thoughts when the old lady, Mrs Butler, came out of the side door of her house to go into the back garden. Caught unaware, in the shadows, Drake stood still, pinned up against the eight-foot wall, hoping she wouldn't look too hard. If she did, he'd have to quieten her, but that didn't faze him. He watched as she went across the back garden to the house next door. When she came back half an hour later, muttering something under her breath, Drake went back into the bushes near the gate so that he had a better view of *the eight*.

At a quarter to midnight, Kim's front door had opened. He was surprised to see her. He had always admired her, but that week she was the one who sent him to Lang's office where he got his cards and now he didn't know how he felt about her at all.

He watched that woman Marigold, still in her slippers, come out of Kim's house to rush next door to her own place at No.2.

It was a cold night. Even from where he was hiding, he could still see the breath coming from her mouth as if she was smoking.

Drake had to step back into the shadows when a car stopped at the gates. The driver dimmed his lights as he worked the keypad and then the gates opened, and he drove in. It was the man who had gone over to the Butler's house earlier that evening. As he parked his car on the drive, and as if there wasn't enough going on, lo and behold the gates opened once more, and a man walked in.

When the light caught his face, Drake recognised him immediately. It was Tyrone from the office, the one who had relentlessly pursued Kim, who was much too good for the likes of him. He was so surprised to see him, Drake had accidentally gasped out loud and Tyrone turned about. 'Who's there?' he said suspiciously.

Drake wanted to jump out of the bushes and put a knife deep into his neck, but there was still too many people wandering about, and he was sure he'd get caught. Then he wouldn't be able to carry out his plan. *No*, better to leave Tyrone alone for now. Still, he couldn't help remembering the 'accidents' Tyrone had had at work. When Drake hurled the brick through his office window, he left Tyrone wondering who had done it. Another time in the depot, the crate Drake had pushed off the shelf above his head was a bit of a surprise too, and when he'd almost ploughed him down with the forklift truck, Drake's satisfaction was complete, only made better when he heard that Tyrone had resigned and left the company. That was a good moment in Drake's life.

As Drake watched avidly, Tyrone went to Kim's front door and tapped on it. The tap was like two crashing symbols in his ears, and by the time Kim had let him in, Drake had no choice but to slap himself on the cheek three times on the left and twice on the right.

He'd gotten so wound up, that when Mrs Butler came out to put out her empty milk bottles, he grabbed her and forced her back inside.

That's when she'd screamed. He loosened his grip and she crumbled to the floor in a fainting heap. He hoped no one heard her scream. Daft old biddy. What was her problem?

End of Part One

Part two

Chapter Eleven

At No.7

IT WAS BARELY DAWN when Sandra was roused from her sleep. She wasn't a habitual early riser, but after everything that happened last night, she could barely sleep a wink. In her own bed, faced away from him, she heard him get up, shuffling his bare feet into his slippers. She knew his habits. He would go downstairs, strip off his pyjamas in the kitchen and pull on his wet suit. He was always naked underneath and whenever she thought about that, she cringed at the notion of his dangly bits beneath that rubber suit. She often wished he got it caught in the zip, to put him out of action of a while. That would serve him right after what he did last night.

Sandra's eyes were swollen. Not from him lashing out at her, but from the constant stream of tears that had soaked her pillow. She felt exhausted, mentally and physically and she was sore, *down there,* after he'd left his mark on her.

Last night, she thought she would just go to sleep while he stayed downstairs watching television with his mother. The incident in the kitchen after Mrs Butler left, had shaken her, but it wasn't anything she hadn't experienced before. Not that it made the things he did any easier. It was just that now, after five years of being married to him, she accepted his abuse as a regular part of her life.

The first time he laid his hands on her had been a shock. They were on their honeymoon, of all things. They'd taken a caravan in Porthcawl. He paid for it out of a bonus he'd been awarded at work, and all week he didn't stop reminding her that he had to work long and hard to earn that bonus and he was spending it all on her. She didn't see his reasoning at the time. She was his wife, so surely, he should pay for everything anyway.

It was raining that evening in the caravan in Porthcawl. She was sitting inside doing a spot of crochet when the subject of her work came up. She'd given up her job as an actress. She only did *extra* work at the BBC studios in Bristol, but it was a living.

"Have you handed in your notice yet?" he asked.

She shook her head. "There's no need. I only work when they want me to. I'm not obligated in any way."

"But you should tell them so that they don't keep contacting you."

"I'll see what I'm doing at the time," she said, "I could always do a bit of work occasionally."

"But you're married now."

She dropped a stitch off her hook and had to work back to pick it up again. *Annoying thing.* When she finally retrieved the strand of baby blue wool and looked up, there was Eddie standing over her, bent down, with his arm resting on the back of the seat behind her shoulder. She didn't know what to make of it when his face got closer to hers and she thought for a second that he was going to kiss her.

But he didn't kiss her. He headbutted her.

She was dazed by the blow, and her nose had bled profusely, but then he placed his fingers over her face and squeezed. "Eddieee," she cried dropping her crochet hook to grab his wrists. She didn't know what she'd done or why he was acting that way, why he was hurting her.

"No more acting," he said simply as he let her go. She grabbed some tissues and held them to her nose. "I'll go down the pub for a while," he said as if nothing had happened. Then he grabbed his coat and left.

Sandra was stunned more than anything else. Her face hurt and she knew her eyes would turn black from the force of the blow.

When she looked down at her baby blue crochet and saw it splattered red, she stood up, got her balance and then dropped it in the peddle bin at the side of the sink.

That was the very first time he assaulted her. It wasn't the last.

Now, she heard the back door close and she knew he'd left for his swim.

She got out of bed and put her dressing gown on. She needed a cup of tea to soothe her stomach.

Going downstairs, her shoulders sagged beneath the weight of her burden. She knew she'd reached her tolerance level. It was time to end it.

She switched on the kettle as she thought about last night. She'd woken up with him on top of her, her legs spread apart as he fumbled to get himself inside her. It was made worse by the fact that she hadn't woken straight away, that she had been in such a deep sleep, he had gotten that far.

Only an hour before, she had been thinking about how he never had sex with her any more, glad of it too, and there he was forcing himself inside her as if she was an object to defile. He wasn't even looking at her. She could have been anyone or anything. He was using her. She'd sobbed when he finished and got off. She heard him take a long sniff to get the catarrh out of his nose and he repulsed her more than anything she could describe.

Sandra now looked up at the sun coming up across the bay. He was in the sea right at that moment, feeling free, swimming the surf with carefree abandon.

Without knowing where the time went, she suddenly found herself outside. She was in a trance and she couldn't rouse herself out of it. She walked to the end of the garden, going along the path, past the vegetables and herbs. At the end, where the garden dropped away to the 30ft cliff, next to a stack of rhubarb, she stood like a haunting statue looking out to the sea. She was going to jump. She wanted it to end. She could stand it no more.

Then she felt a hand on her arm.

She swung about in the quiet of the morning as the wind lashed her body.

The hand belonged to Gladys, Eddie's mother.

SHE WAS RIGHT NEXT TO HER, wearing a thick flowered nightdress with sleeves down to her wrists, secured by elastic. The bottom whipped about her frail legs, and her small bony feet were tucked inside fluffy slippers.

On her head, she wore a hairnet with some bobby pins securing a couple of curls at her brow. Cotton wool was tucked under the net each side of her ears, keeping two curlers from hurting her head while she'd slept. Then she said. "It's not you that deserves to die. It's him."

Sandra shook her head. She was conscious that time had passed, and that Eddie could be on his way back. Without saying another word, Gladys guided her by the hand along the garden to the house. The exterior light was turned on and Eddie's robe was draped over the patio chair. "Get that," Gladys said, pointing to an overly large stone. It was one of the rocks Eddie had used to build up the rockery.

Gladys turned off the exterior light.

At the side of the house, next to the tap jutting from the wall was a panel of fencing he'd used to disguise the bin and garden tools. Gladys guided Sandra behind the fence as if she had the whole thing worked out.

The two women stood inside the nook. Sandra was trembling from the adrenalin coursing through her body. When they heard footsteps coming around the rear through the side gate, they both quickly hushed.

He was back.

From the shadows, with no light to guide him apart from the breaking of the dawn, the two women watched as Eddie unzipped his wetsuit and peeled it off. He pulled on his robe, white in the darkness, wrapping it around himself and pulling the tie belt tight across his hips. He went to the tap and turned it on, balancing himself against the wall while he washed each foot in turn.

Gladys nudged Sandra, and Sandra knew what she had to do.

She stepped out from behind the panel as the splattering tap water drowned out the noise of her footsteps. At his side, as he bent over, washing his feet, she lifted that rock above her head and brought it down on Eddie's skull with a strength she didn't know she possessed. His crown cracked like an egg, spurting red everywhere.

As Gladys stepped out of the shadows, the two women looked down, watching the flow of water from the tap washing away the blood. "Just like his father," Gladys said.

Chapter Twelve

At No.5

UP WITH THE LARK, Eva Lang went about her daily routine. The first thing she'd do is make a pot of tea and take one up to Roger. Who could get anything done without a cuppa first? she thought. He was still snoring when she went in. She smiled to herself. He won't like being woken so early, but better he started stirring if he was to be in time for the golfing trip. "Roger," she whispered as she rocked him awake. "Cup of tea here."

He grunted and she placed the drink on the bedside table.

On the chair in the corner, balanced atop the two wooden arms, his small overnight bag was open, awaiting toiletries and last minute essentials. His suit, wrapped in dry cleaner's plastic, hung above it for the dinner they'd be having in the night. On the floor at the side of the case, was his golfing shoes alongside a *best* pair of smart loafers she'd bought him for the anniversary party at Marigold and Clive's house last summer. She decided to take them down and give them a polish.

Back in the kitchen, she poured her own cup and bit into a Rich Tea biscuit. The sky outside the south-facing window was beginning to change colour with the dawn. She always loved that time of the morning, watching the day awaken, listening to the early bird.

She wondered if she should take up a cuppa for Harry. It was only five, so maybe it was a bit too early for him.

Harry!

Suddenly she stopped what she was doing and looked out across the bay. Her eyes became transfixed on a flock of birds, against a backdrop of grey clouds. How odd that she had gone about her business for the past half hour without thinking about what had happened the night before. It was as if she'd tried to block it out, by doing things that were normal to her.

Oh, God. She had betrayed her husband, with the man that stood up for him at their wedding. His best friend, Harry.

Last night they'd made love. It was wonderful at first, but the longer it went on, the more her head had cleared, and she began to think about Roger coming downstairs to catch them at it. On the sofa, Harry lay on top of her, thrusting, while her once passionate disposition gave way to harsh reality. She'd heard stories about 'danger' sex and she'd read a few risqué novels in her day, but that did nothing to spur her on. In fact, she went the other way, turning her cold.

Before he finished, she'd pushed him off. She felt bad, especially when she saw his flushed face and those eyes of his, looking strangely confused.

She sat up and tidied her clothes, wiping his saliva from her mouth with her sleeve. *Yes*, that was reality. The passion had long gone at that point. Only the wet remained.

They didn't speak, only talking with their eyes, before Eva rushed from the room and up the stairs.

When she came out of the bathroom, she bumped into him on the landing. He didn't speak. What was there to say? The best thing she could do at that point was to forget the whole thing. After he closed the door to the spare room, she went into hers and leaned against the door watching Roger snoring away under the blankets of their double bed.

Now she was riddled with guilt. She had betrayed her husband. How could she ever forgive herself?

At No. 6

WHEN RHIANNA AWOKE at six-thirty, she had to quickly orientate herself. Where on earth was she, in that strange room in that strange house in that strange place called Seaview?

She looked out the window. The day was cold, but the sky was clear of any potential downpour. She wished she could see the sea, but uncle Rolf had that privilege from the window of the back bedroom. She quickly pulled on a pair of high-waisted jeans, a t.shirt and an old blue jumper her mother had knitted for her. Rhianna had made a hole in each sleeve for her thumb to poke through. Her mother had been horrified and never forgave her for ruining a good jumper. 'Maybe I'll start a new fashion,' Rhianna had said, but her mother had scoffed. 'As if! Who in their right mind would want to deliberately look tatty?'

With the smell of bacon wafting upwards, she walked down the stairs and into the kitchen. Uncle Rolf was already up and he had a fry-up on the go.

"There she is," he said. "How did you sleep?"

"Fine!" She looked out of the window and saw the view for the first time in daylight. It was splendid. "Wow. That's a great view to wake up to."

"I never get tired of looking at it."

"I'm not surprised. Mum would love it here."

"I invited her down for my wife's funeral, but your dad wouldn't allow her to come."

Rhianna was shocked. "I find that hard to believe," she said, pulling out a chair and sitting down.

He whisked up some eggs in a lime green Tupperware bowl. The kitchen was warm and cosy while the rest of the house remained quite cold at that time of the day. She guessed he kept the heating off in the other rooms until they were to be used.

"What did you fall out about?" she asked, pouring herself a cup of tea from the pot. The old wooden table had been covered in adhesive shelf liner, now peeling at the edges. The tea service was the old willow pattern she remembered her gran having in her house. She wondered if it was the same set. Maybe he'd inherited it when gran died. The matching sugar bowl had a chip in the lid.

"Didn't your mother tell you why there was rift?"

"No. She always said what happened in the past should stay in the past."

"We fell out over a dog."

"A dog?" The smell of melted butter wafted around the room. The heat from the pan steamed up the window above the stove. Now she realised how cold it must be outside.

"This was before you were born. We were all going to get together for a family reunion," he said as he kept stirring the eggs in the pan. "Your parents were coming down to stay with us and they wanted to bring the dog." He threw a quick glance her way. "My wife Barbra didn't like pets...so she wrote and asked them not to bring it. They took umbrage and in the end, they didn't even come for the reunion. Your mum and Barbra never spoke again, and your dad blamed me."

"That all sounds silly to me. Why hold grudges? Shouldn't 'time heal'?" she crooked her fingers in the air.

He chuckled as he spooned the creamy eggs onto two plates. "Well, that's family for you."

He sat down next to her and sprinkled pepper all over his eggs. She remembered her mother doing exactly the same thing.

Rhianna was ravenous. The breakfast looked and tasted delicious, the bacon so crispy that she could pick it up with her fingers. Rhianna felt like she hadn't eaten for days and wolfed it down within minutes. Triangles of toast were propped upright in a silver rack, the butter was a soft block in a butter dish with a chipped lid, and marmalade half-filled a matching bowl with a silver spoon protruding from it. The bowl of the spoon was in the shape of a leaf. She kept on feasting as if she'd been starved for days.

He poured another cup of tea from the pot. "Glad to see you've got a good appetite."

"The breakfast is delicious. Thank you." Rhianna wondered if she would be getting a fry-up every morning. "So, what's your plan? What time are you leaving for the golfing trip?"

He wiped his mouth with a napkin. "Honestly. I'm not sure I should go."

"Why? Not because of me. I would feel really bad about that." She looked straight at him. "You wouldn't want me to feel bad, would you?"

He chuckled. "Well, alright, I'll go for the day, but I'll come back tonight. I won't leave you alone all night."

"There you are then. A compromise. Go enjoy yourself."

"I do enjoy a round of golf."

Her chair scraped along the floor. "You get yourself sorted out and I'll do these." She picked up the dirty plates and took them to the sink. Then, as she looked out across the bay, observing the morning light and the waves breaking on the rocks, she thought she saw a man swimming in the sea.

At No. 7

SANDRA WAS LEANING on the table with her hands over her head, wanting more than anything to block out the recent memories running through her mind. "Oh God, *oh god*. What have I done?"

Gladys was sitting across from her, drinking a cup of tea. She was staring at nothing. "He's gone now," she said as if she'd just finished a book. "It's over."

Sandra looked up and shook her head. She could hardly comprehend the actions of her mother-in-law. They were wholly unexpected. "I had no idea," she said. "I thought you were both close."

"No, that went south many years ago. He was a troublesome child and he became a bully, just like his father before him."

"But you've hardly said a word over the past couple of years." Sandra was bewildered. "I thought you hated me."

"I just hated coming here. I have friends where I live. He took me away from that every weekend. I couldn't say anything. He would have declared me insane. I would have lost all my rights."

"How?"

"He had power of attorney over my finance and my care. He could have had me locked up before you could say, *gone in the head*."

"So, you just tolerated it…coming here, I mean."

"Every damn weekend."

"I wish I'd known. I could have helped you."

"You couldn't even help yourself. How could you have helped me?"

Sandra knew that was true. "Yes, I was useless…I am useless."

"No, not anymore."

"Because he's dead, you mean?"

She nodded. "Take it from someone who knows. You'll get your mojo back in time."

"In prison!"

"You're not going to prison. If it comes to it, I'll say I did it. That'll get you off the hook."

Sandra couldn't believe what she was hearing. Gladys, the woman who had hardly breathed a word to her, now offering to save her. "Why would you do that?"

"Because once someone saved me. Now it's my turn. To save you."

They jumped when they heard a knock on the door. "Oh god."

"Don't panic," Gladys said. "No one knows. Remember that."

Sandra took a deep breath and went from the kitchen to the hallway. She reminded herself she was an actress and a good one. She needed to pull it out of the bag right now before she opened that front door. Through the glass, she saw a figure waiting.

ROGER LANG STOOD THERE waiting for her to speak. He was looking at her, curious about her appearance, perhaps seeing the tiredness in her eyes…the exhaustion. "Hi, Sandra. Is Eddie here?"

The colour must have dropped from her face. She couldn't speak. Actress or not. The curtain was up but now she'd lost every functioning part of her body. She was going to collapse on the world stage, a snivelling wreck. Behind her, a hand gently moved her aside.

"He hasn't come back from his swim yet," Gladys said.

"I see. Well, that's kind of awkward. The bus is leaving in five minutes."

"Oh," Sandra piped up, finally finding her voice. "I think he said he wasn't going to go after all. "

Roger frowned. "Really?" He nodded several times while he stared at his feet.

Oh, God. He didn't believe her.

He looked up. "But he didn't say anything. I've got his room booked. If he wasn't planning on coming, he could have let me know."

He was pissed. At Eddie. "I'm sorry."

Roger pouted. "Honestly. Nothing surprises me about Eddie anymore."

Then he turned and went along the path to the road

Sandra stepped forward and looked out across *the eight*. The minibus was waiting outside No.5. Soon they would be gone and then she would be left to deal with her problem accordingly.

Chapter Thirteen

At No. 5

ROGER CAME BACK INSIDE. "That prick Eddie isn't coming now," he said.

Eva was packing his newly polished shoes into his small suitcase. "Why not?"

He shrugged. "Changed his mind, apparently."

"That's a bit naughty. He could have told you before now."

"He wasn't there. I talked to Sandra. He's still out swimming in the bay according to his mother."

"Really? Bit dangerous this time of the day. The tide will be up."

"I don't care. I hope the bastard drowns."

"You don't mean that. Come on," she said, as she put the latches down on his suitcase and picked it up. "Wow. That's heavy. They should make cases with wheels. Now, that would be a good invention.

He took it from her. "I'll take it out to the bus. Give Harry a shout for me. We're leaving in three minutes."

Eva almost faltered. She didn't want to give Harry a shout. She'd have to say his name out loud and she didn't want to do that. She certainly couldn't go into his room. How would that look?

Earlier, before he came downstairs, she had gotten herself into a right state, thinking about what had happened last night. Strange how she kept going back and forth with her emotions as if she was indecisive. But never in her life had she been that.

She had begun life as a nurse. Her father was a doctor in Bristol Royal Infirmary, and her mother, a sister, so it was natural for their only daughter to follow in their footsteps.

Before she met Roger, she met the biggest and greatest love of her life when he was admitted to the infirmary with a broken leg. His name was Cary, just like the movie star, and he had a movie star's looks too. He'd been in a motorcycle accident. "You should see the other guy," he said when she watched him having his leg cast. Complications resulted in him spending six weeks in traction and Eva hardly left his side. When they fell in love, one day a woman showed up claiming to be his wife. Cary said he didn't love her anymore, but still, everything fell apart. He left the hospital with his wife and she never saw him again. She married Roger on the rebound, but she never got over Cary. Even now she still thought about him when she had a quiet moment to herself.

The situation with Harry had given her food for thought, comparing it with her love affair with Cary. She had always said she'd never be unfaithful, let alone with a married man, but now she could never claim that again.

She heard Harry come down the stairs.

They stood side by side next to the front door. She put her hand on the latch, but he stopped her. They looked at each other as if they were the only two people in the world. "Can I phone you later from the hotel?" he whispered.

She felt her neck turn red. "I don't…"

"Just to speak to you for a minute."

"Alright."

Time stood still as they stared deeply into each other's eyes. The moment was special until they were forced out of their spell by the sound of a key turning in the lock.

It was Roger. He hadn't noticed their discomfort at being discovered so close together. He spoke directly to Harry, "There's someone to see you out here."

Harry looked confused when Roger stepped aside and saw his wife, Jade

Eva felt her neck turn red as Harry went through the door and kissed Jade on the cheek. "What are you doing here?" he asked as if he was pleased to see her. That made Eva feel as jealous as any adolescent.

"Thought I'd come and wave you off," Jade said, slipping her arm through his. He turned to glance back at Eva, but she didn't return his gaze. The arrival of Jade was a game changer.

Roger said, "Well we'd better be leaving. Everyone's waiting."

Then he turned to Jade and said "Why don't you stay here with Eva? All the girls are getting together this evening for cocktails."

Eva closed her eyes and cursed Roger. Honestly, she could murder him. She willed Jade to decline. How dare Roger make such an arrangement without discussing it with her first. As if the matter of Harry wasn't complicated enough, she'd now have his wife to deal with.

"I wouldn't want to impose," said Jade. "Eva may have plans that don't include me."

"You don't mind, do you, darling?" said Roger.

"No, I don't mind at all," Eva said.

RHIANNA STOOD OUTSIDE the house watching the men load their luggage and golf clubs. Uncle Rolf seemed hesitant, not happy at all about leaving his niece. He came back over to speak to her. "I wish I could tell them I've changed my mind," he said.

"No…" She was about to persuade him to go and not worry about her.

"But Eddie at No.7 isn't going now so the numbers are down. I'd feel awkward pulling out of the trip as well."

"Good. I want you to go and enjoy yourself."

"I've asked Eva to keep an eye on you. She lives next door at No.5, so just pop around if you need anything."

"I'll be fine."

"Don't go down to the beach until after eleven. And be careful with those steps. They can be slippery."

"Okay."

"The tide will be back in at five, so make sure you're not down there after that. You'll be trapped with no way out."

"Got it." She chuckled. "Go on, off you go. Don't worry about me." Rhianna was touched by his concern, but she was a big girl now. She'd manage just fine.

He left her then and got on the bus.

MARIGOLD WAS WAITING FOR CLIVE to load his bags. She had her arms crossed over her body, wondering where Sandra and Eddie were. She glanced over to their house and saw all the curtains at the front were closed. *Strange!* She decided to go over and give them a knock. Maybe they hadn't realised the time.

Then Clive was at her side. "I'm just going to pop over to Sandra's."

"Don't bother. Eddie's not coming."

"Oh! Why not?"

Clive shrugged. "Roger told me he'd changed his mind and he was still swimming in the bay."

"That's odd," Marigold said.

"What is?"

She looked at her watch. A gift from Clive for their anniversary last year. "The tide is in. Bit dangerous to be out there."

"Roger said he hopes he drowns."

"That's not very nice."

"He feels let down."

"Still no reason to wish a man dead." Just at the right moment, she looked across the road to No.7. The curtain moved as Sandra peeped out, then she ducked back in when she saw Marigold looking. *Strange!*

"By the way, will you look in on Mrs Butler later?" Clive said. "I went over and cleaned up that broken flower pot, but I couldn't get an answer when I knocked. They might still be in bed."

"Okay, I will."

"I'll get aboard then," said Clive.

They kissed. "Have fun and stay safe," she said, stroking his arm.

"I will. And you too."

She waved to him before she strolled over the road, towards Sandra's house.

WITH JADE AT HER SIDE, Eva watched as Roger arranged the men's cases and clubs. Harry was already on the bus, sitting on the back seat, facing forward, deep in thought.

She avoided looking at him. She didn't want their eyes to meet. Not with Jade at her side.

She looked over to Rolf's niece, standing outside No.6, waiting patiently for the bus to leave. Rolf had asked Eva to keep an eye on her while he was away. She was young but she looked nice, pleasant. Eva would ask her to the cocktail party later.

She looked further down *the eight*, near the gate, hoping that Mr and Mrs Butler wouldn't come out and see the bus leave. Eva was embarrassed, that Roger hadn't invited Mr B when he'd invited everyone else. She hoped they wouldn't be offended.

She looked to the empty house at No.3. Pity the new family hadn't moved in yet. It would have been a great opportunity to get to know them. *That's odd*, Eva thought. She thought she saw someone move about inside. But then she decided it must have been her eyes playing tricks on her.

Now, Roger was about to kiss her goodbye. Out of earshot, she whispered to him. "I wish you hadn't asked Jade to stay. I felt really awkward."

"Don't be daft. She won't be any bother. She'll probably go home after the party."

"You could have asked me first, Roger."

"Wasn't time." He kissed her on the cheek. "Right then, we're off. I'll try and phone you later."

"No need," she said. "Don't worry about things here. You go and enjoy yourself."

"Okay. I'll see you tomorrow afternoon, then."

"Yes, alright."

Just as he was about to board the bus, without thinking she tugged his arm. He turned around. "I'll miss you, Roger," she said.

He chuckled sympathetically. "Don't worry, baby. It's just for one night."

She nodded and let him go.

The doors closed.

Eva took one more glance at Harry in the back. He was looking right at her. She blushed and averted her gaze to her husband.

The driver pulled away as the women watched and waved. When they got down to the bottom of *the eight*, the gates opened, and the bus drove through.

Just before the gates closed, Eva had an awful sense of foreboding.

Chapter Fourteen

THEY WERE GONE.

Drake couldn't believe his bad luck. His reason for being there, doing what he was doing, was all about Roger Lang, but now, the devious pig had left on some sort of stupid golfing trip. Watching them, it was clear that Lang had arranged the whole thing, which made Drake even more resentful since he hadn't been asked along. He used to be a trusted employee, and that week he'd been let go. Surely, it would have been a good opportunity for Roger Lang to make it up to him. They could have had a 'do' for him, given him a gold watch, allowed him to make a speech. He could have used that platform to release his rage, to talk about the injustice of it all. Instead, he was left there at Seaview to deal with everything on his own. Just like the time his mother left.

If anyone should ask him years later what that incident was, this is how he would tell it:

I was just a teenager when father left. We still lived in that small house in town with the lean-to just off the kitchen. Father still bonked mother every day and night, but by then, after years of living with their unhindered sex play, I hardly noticed it anymore. I'd been smart with the drill holes I made in the walls. I used the smallest of father's drill bits and disguised it next to a picture, or something else less noticeable. The best one was the peephole in the bedroom wall just above the dresser between a vase of artificial silk roses. Sometimes mother rearranged the flowers when she dusted, so occasionally, I had to pop in there and part them so that I could get a good view. Each night, from the wall opposite their bed, I could see father's arse going up and down, up and down, grunting and grunting all night long with mother's legs spread wide apart and moaning her moaning, all night long. I sometimes resented that particular hole above the dresser, since it made me feel disgusted, making me slap myself around the face when they were finished. Once, I put a sticky plaster over that peephole, just so I could get away from it, but it always called me back and told me to unpeel it. I hated that plaster, and in the end, I pinched a whole box from the chemist down the road, so that I could replenish it each day.

The day father left was like a dream, which was what I always thought it was…a dream.

I'd gone into the kitchen one morning and found father with his toolbox out.

"What are you doing, then?" I asked. In those days I used to have a sulky adolescent voice that was deep and croaky. I had hairs sprouting from my chin and over my top lip, but I cared nothing about learning to shave. My hair was always lank and greasy, but it served to hide most of my face and the acne covering my skin. My eyes were blue, but they were dull, with my lids always looking like they were half-closed. Girls never gave me the time of day and I always put it down to how I looked. My reckoning was that I couldn't help it much since it was the face I'd been born with after I was conceived on that river bank. In fact, I always put it down to the fault of my parents who should have known better than to name their son after a dumb duck.

In the kitchen, father had chuckled when I asked him what he was doing. He had a screw between his teeth. "Getting ready for tonight," he said with a wink. "Here, give us a hand."

He made me hold a big frameless mirror, which he was screwing to the wall next to the table. "Why are you putting a mirror up here then?" I asked. It seemed strange to me. The mirror was too low to look in, and why would we want to see ourselves when we were eating our tea?

As I held up the mirror, he took the screw from his mouth and bored it into the wall. "It's a surprise for your mother," he said, winking again.

"Why?"

"God, you're a big oaf, boy. Listen, you're almost a man now and you should be thinking manly things. You'll want to do this sort of mucky stuff I should imagine...when you're older that is," he laughed when he looked at my face. I almost knew what he was suggesting, but I didn't want to admit I knew. It didn't seem right, somehow.

"Christ, you're clueless," father said.

I felt put down by that comment, but he always did know how to crush my mood.

"See this," he said holding up a silver screw. "I'll be doing this to your mother later, after tea, and she can see herself getting well and truly screwed. You know what I mean?" He laughed that stupid laugh of his and then that red appeared before my eyes like it often did when I thought about my father. Suddenly, I felt like I should be slapping my face, three times on the left and twice on the right.

The blood from my father's neck had sprayed everywhere because of that drill I put in it. It was his own fault. He shouldn't have left it plugged in with a child around. Funny how most of the blood went over that mirror he'd been hanging. All I had to do was clean up around it, so, fortunately, it wasn't a big job.

It was handy that we weren't far from the lean-to, because inside was a door leading to an old cellar we never used because the steps were dangerous. Still, it didn't matter about the steps because I didn't need to go down there myself. I didn't even have to fetch the torch. His body just rolled and bumped down those steps into the darkness below. I heard a bit of splash when he landed at the bottom, so maybe the cellar had a lot of water in it. The mirror had smashed on its way down, which was exactly where that mirror should be.

When mother got back, carrying her co-op bags down the hall from the front door into the kitchen, I watched her face when she saw me standing there with my clothes stained red. She looked to the surrounding area and picked up splashes of blood that had so far evaded the cleaning sponge, but I guessed I could leave that to her now that she was home. She was the one who did the cleaning. Not the men!

I held up the key to the cellar. "See this," I said. "No one gets to keep this key except me. Do you hear me, mother? This is my key. I'm the man of the house now."

"Oh, Drake," she said with a horrified whisper. "What have you done?"

I never got to answer that question because the next day I realised it had all been a dream. I was sure it was a dream…pretty sure!

So, that was how Drake Fisher would tell the story of the day his father left. But the day his mother left, was quite a different story altogether.

Chapter Fifteen

At No. 1

KIM WATCHED THE BUS leave Seaview loaded with husbands. So, the men were gone, she thought, and that included Tyrone.

He'd stayed until four am.

After making love, *twice*, they'd fallen asleep. Ty wasn't like the others she'd slept with. He understood the stigma attached to single women sleeping around. It was 1981, but still, people frowned upon the idea of an unmarried woman, allowing a man to arrive or leave their house during the early hours. Last night, Ty had arrived around about twelve, and when she awoke around four, she saw him pulling on his trousers at the side of the bed.

"What time is it?" she croaked.

He turned his head to look at her, naked, with the sheet covering only her lower half. Her breasts were unleashed, and her tousled hair fell upon them, enticingly. She knew she looked desirable and she knew that he'd find it hard to leave.

But leave he must, she thought, covering herself up.

"Why do you always push me away?" he said.

"Hmm? What?"

"I always feel like when you're openly affectionate, you then close down and shut me out."

"That's an awful lot of clichés you've thrown at me," she said laughing, hoping to deflect his comments with humour.

He shook his head and buttoned up his shirt.

"What's wrong. We had a good time last night, didn't we?"

"Yeah."

"So, what is it."

He sighed and glanced over his shoulder. "I just told you." He stood up and grabbed his shoes. Now he was sitting on the chair across the room tying his laces.

Through the curtains, just nets really, a faint glow of light filtered into the room, illuminating his face. Soon it would be dawn and when she looked out of the window, she would see the sea in all its beautiful glory. The view from No.1 was the best thing about that house. It didn't match the views the other houses had, but it came close and it was good enough for her.

The house she grew up in, with her alcoholic father, was a three-bed semi on a council housing estate. They were built after the war when more public housing was needed, especially in the south of England. By the time she left home when she was eighteen, the estate was a place where everyone knew everyone, and she hated it for that. *Everyone* knew about her father, especially the kids who rode their bikes along the road or kicked balls into makeshift goals. They taunted Kim and her brothers, calling their dad an alkie. Fist fights were common in those days and Kim's brothers were often kicked and beaten. Their father never did anything about it, telling them to fight their own battles, regardless of the fact it was because of him they fought in the first place.

Ty was pulling on his shoes. "Will you ring me?" she asked seductively.

He shrugged and grinned. "Maybe."

She leaned back against the pillows. "Would you like me to make you a coffee for the road?"

"No, stay in bed."

"You can remember the number of the gate."

"Yes."

He came around the bed and kissed her. It was a warm kiss, a satisfying kiss, one that made her want him all over again.

He pulled away and tugged the blanket up over the sheet. The eiderdown had been left on the floor.

"See ya," he said, and he was gone.

Now, as Kim watched the bus go through the gates, she thought about Ty and how he'd made love to her last night.

At No. 7

SANDRA WATCHED THE BUS leave before she leaned against the wall at the side of the window with a deep, rueful sigh. They were gone. Thank god. That was one less matter to deal with. Roger seemed to have believed her story about Eddie no longer wanting to go with them on their golfing trip. He'd said, 'nothing surprises me with Eddie anymore'. She knew exactly what he was referring to.

For a short time, Eddie and Roger had been pals.

It was the opening of Seaview when two families moved in on the same day. The timing of the other neighbour's arrival had been staggered, agreed by the developers that the weight of eight removal vans arriving at the same time, would put too much pressure on the new road. Only two new residents were given access and that first day, it was Sandra and Eddie, and Roger and Eva Lang.

Given that they were the first, they'd naturally introduced themselves. Roger had invited them over for drinks and sandwiches at teatime.

It was a fine summers day when Eddie and Sandra knocked on the door of No.5. When they got no reply, they went tentatively inside. They worked their way around boxes and eventually found the couple and their two children out on the terrace. The view from the back of the house was spectacular since No.5 was on the tip of the headland and took in a panoramic view of the Atlantic.

Eva greeted them with open arms, which seemed a bit over the top for Sandra. The two men shook hands and the kids, teenagers, simply nodded, before taking off to their room with plates laden with open sandwiches. The sandwiches seemed odd to Sandra. Who didn't put two pieces of bread on a sandwich? It made the concept of the word 'sandwich' meaningless somehow. But she didn't say anything. Eva said they were Danish. *Fancy!*

They sat down under a yellow garden parasol and talked about their moving-in experiences.

"The gate will take some getting used to," Eva said, and Sandra agreed.

"The ground rent is a bit much, don't you think?" Eddie said while Roger agreed.

"I love being so close to the sea," Sandra said.

"I hope the other neighbours are acceptable," Eva said to Sandra. "I wouldn't want *young* children living here making a noise, would you?"

Sandra shrugged at that one. *Children* was a sore subject. Sandra thought Eva seemed okay, but Roger was a bit big for his boots. He told them he worked at Phillips Electronics. Higher management!

"And I was a nurse before we got married," Eva said. "At Bristol's Royal Infirmary."

"That's exciting."

Sandra meant it, but Eddie chimed in with a remark that made Sandra's cheeks turn red. "Just because you were an actress," he snapped in her direction, "doesn't mean other professions are less exciting. At least Eva saved lives."

Sandra was indignant since she hadn't meant anything by the remark, but now Eddie made it look like she had. She didn't know what the Lang's thought about it, but her embarrassment was made worse after Eva said, "An actress? Wow. What parts have you played?"

Eddie chuckled condescendingly while shaking his head. "She was just an extra. You wouldn't even notice her if you saw it on the TV."

"I was on Coronation Street once," Sandra regretted saying that. She looked as if she was trying to justify her career.

"As an extra," Eddie said, snidely. "Stop making it out to be more than it was."

"I wasn't…" Then Sandra clammed up. She knew if she carried on objecting, she'd pay for it later.

The mood of the rendezvous had changed suddenly. The Lang's appeared uncomfortable by Eddie's attitude toward his wife and Sandra just wanted to leave to go back to the house she was moving into. She was over visiting people who were watching her being verbally abused by her husband.

Up above, while the windows were opened, music blasted from the teenager's rooms. It was annoying, but it didn't seem to faze Roger and Eva. Roger poured himself another glass of wine. He didn't offer any more to Sandra and Eddie.

A week later, Roger invited Eddie to his club for a round of golf, perhaps to offer him a second chance at being friends. Eddie won the game and let everyone know it, which put an end to any kinship the two men might have had.

Now, this morning when Roger said that nothing surprised him about Eddie any more, Sandra knew what he was referring to. It stemmed from that time six months ago when Roger had knocked on the door in the middle of the night. Eddie had been particularly cruel that evening and when she fought back, they'd made a lot of noise and she remembered being past caring what the neighbours thought. When the doorbell rang, just as Eddie had pushed her halfway down the stairs and she was lying at the bottom, sobbing, she looked towards the front door. Through the opaque glass, she saw Roger standing outside. She rose to her feet and opened the door. Roger saw the state she was in, dishevelled and bruised. He looked up the stairs to see Eddie at the top in his pyjama bottoms. "What the hell, man," Roger yelled. Eddie looked embarrassed at being caught beating his wife. Roger looked at Sandra and said, 'Come on, you're coming back with me." After putting a coat around her shoulders, docile and worn out, she let him guide her away.

The following day, when she went back home, Eddie was in the kitchen demanding breakfast as if nothing had happened at all.

WELL, THEY'VE GONE, Sandra thought, watching the gates close behind the bus. Now she can be left alone to deal with the matter of her dead husband.

Gladys was in the kitchen making a pot of tea. Sandra felt like she couldn't drink another cup.

"The bus has gone," she said.

"Good," Gladys offered. 'That's one problem out of the way."

Sandra went to the window and looked out. It was daylight now. She'd been dreading that most of all, dealing with the issue in the cold light of day. The vision of Eddie's crushed skull kept repeating through her mind like Groundhog Day, as she lived the horror of it over and over again.

That morning, in the early hours, they'd devised a plan to explain Eddie's unfortunate death, but first they had to get rid of the body.

Gladys had taken charge. Outside on the terrace, while it was still cold and dark, she'd instructed Sandra to remove her clothes. Sandra was appalled. Gladys simply explained that she couldn't afford to go carrying any traces of blood into the house. That made sense, so Sandra, concealing her modesty with her hands, stripped off and left her nightie on the floor of the patio. "Wash your feet under the tap," said Gladys. "Then go inside and fetch something to put on. A robe, or something."

Sandra did as she was instructed, leaving Gladys fixing the hosepipe to the outside tap.

Sandra ran inside leaving wet footprints over the kitchen floor. She went straight upstairs and took her bathrobe from behind the bathroom door. She wanted to shower, but she couldn't leave Gladys down there alone. As her mother-in-law had instructed, she went to the airing cupboard to find a specific sheet. 'One of those fitted ones with the elastic around,' she'd said.

Sandra's mind had drifted to her bed. It was unmade, untouched since he'd raped her only a few hours before. She went into the bedroom and pulled the blankets off. She saw the stain in the middle, the final remnants of her marriage, she thought bitterly. With one easy tug, she pulled that pink flannelette sheet from the bed and rolled it into a ball. Then she headed back downstairs.

Outside, she was appalled when she saw Gladys hosing down Eddie's naked body. "What are you doing?" she whispered loudly.

"Got to get rid of any traces of the terrace. Can't afford forensic to pick anything up like that."

"Forensics?"

"I watch all the detective series, Kojak, Streets of San Francisco. Cannon…"

Sandra's mouth was agape, discussing television was so inappropriate. She wondered if Gladys was completely sane. Then she decided *no*, she couldn't be, because she certainly wasn't right then.

Sandra handed the sheet to Gladys. Eddie's body was face down. "Take the two corners," she said as if they were about to make a bed. She put the elastic parts around his head and told Sandra to do the same with his feet. His lower body was at an angle, so she tucked the elastic around his knees and his feet. Ironically the sheet covered him into a nice little package as if he was a big sack of potatoes. "Now we have to turn him," Gladys said.

"What? Why?" Sandra was losing it. It was one thing killing Eddie, but quite another to touch him. And how was Gladys dealing with it all? He was her son. Shouldn't she be distraught like any mother would be?

"We need him to be on the sheet," she said simply. "Make it like a body bag."

Then somewhere on the estate, a light came on.

"We should hurry up."

Sandra nodded and did as Gladys asked. With the help of the elastic sheet, they turned his body over so that it was now under him. His face startled them both. Gladys obviously wasn't *that* resilient. She quickly covered it over, his cracked skull now hidden from sight.

"You need every bit of strength you've got now, dear," Gladys said.

Gladys had called her *dear*. Hearing such an affectionate term, made Sandra's knees almost give away beneath her. But with renewed strength, as if a kind word had spurred her on, Sandra took hold of that sheet and with Eddie's body tucked inside, the two women dragged it up the garden towards the cliff.

They came to a stop at the edge. The tide was in. It was crashing again the rocks, spraying almost half way up. Gladys and Sandra looked at each other and Sandra nodded. It was time to be rid of Eddie once and for all. They took a firm hold of the sheet and spilt his body over the side, leaving Sandra with the pink elastic, so-called body bag, as his corpse careened down the sheer cliff and into the sea.

They both stopped and looked. They could no longer see him. He was gone, to be taken by a current after the turbulent waves had smashed his body against the rocks, cracking his skull in the process. He'd been out swimming, they would tell the police. He never came back.

Then a breeze came up over the cliff face as if Eddie's soul had come back to blow the hair from her eyes, Sandra had a notion. She looked at Gladys and said. "If he was out swimming, why would he be naked, while his wetsuit is here at the house?"

She thought Gladys would have an answer to that, but Eddie's bemused mother just looked over the cliff, realising too late that she must have missed that episode of Kojak.

Chapter Sixteen

At No. 7

"SANDRA?" MARIGOLD CALLED through the letterbox. "Are you there? Are you okay, Sandra?"

Marigold couldn't understand why Sandra wasn't coming to the door. And why were all the curtains closed? She suddenly had an awful thought. What if something had happened to her? What if Eddie had done something bad? Marigold knew she wouldn't be able to let it lie. If Eddie had done something to her friend, she intended to find out about it before she called the police.

She decided to go around the back. She opened the gate at the side of the house, went down the path and stepped onto the terrace. She startled the two women inside when she knocked violently on the patio's doors. They were sitting at the kitchen table drinking tea. Even through the window, Sandra looked white as a sheet. She got up and slid open the door and Marigold stepped inside, out of the cold.

She held her hand against her chest. "Thank God. I thought something had happened to you."

Sandra's voice was shaky. "What do you mean?"

"The bus has just left and then I couldn't get an answer." Marigold frowned as she suddenly remembered Sandra's face peeking through the curtains while the men were loading the bus. "Why didn't you answer the front door?"

"I didn't hear the bell."

Marigold was sure there was something afoot. She'd yelled through the letterbox. How could Sandra not have heard her? And since when were Sandra and Gladys pals? She couldn't remember a time the two women had sat together so intimately as if they were suddenly best friends. "What's wrong?" she said, looking for an answer from either woman. "Where's Eddie?"

"He's…he's still out swimming."

"What?" Marigold was stunned. "How could he be out swimming? The tide's in and it's rough as hell out there."

Sandra simply shrugged, which made Marigold even more suspicious. Then as if a curtain had gone up on stage, Sandra became a different person. "Oh, don't worry about Eddie," she said. "He's a strong swimmer. I'm sure he'll be back soon."

Marigold admitted she wasn't the brightest bulb in the basket, but she knew that Sandra was lying. The woman was acting! It was obvious…maybe not to a stranger who didn't know her as a quiet person, who never made many optimistic statements, but Marigold was no stranger to Sandra's habits. She was a timid character, not overly chatty or sociable, so right then, the image didn't fit at all.

"Sit down and have a cup of tea," Gladys said.

"I'll get the biscuit barrel," Sandra offered.

Marigold sat down and recalled that time when Sandra had come to her house at No.2. It was just after the anniversary party, which Sandra hadn't turned up for and Marigold had gotten quite peeved with her. Clearly, Sandra had gone over to make some lame apology.

"I'm sorry about the party," Sandra had said as she sat down. She was wearing an orange flowery dress which would have looked okay five years ago, but it was the eighties now and people were ditching those loud colours. She had a cardigan on, which was odd because it was a really hot day.

"Take your sweater off," Marigold said. "You must be baking in that."

"I'm fine."

"Go on, take it off."

"I told you I'm fine."

That's when Marigold reached over the table and tugged that cardigan from Sandra's shoulders, knowing very well what she would find underneath. The bruise was huge, covering her arm and shoulder, as black and blue as a midnight sky.

Sandra pulled the sweater back around her as tears spilt from her eyes.

Marigold touched her hand. "Why do you put up with it?"

She shook her head. "I don't have much choice, do I?" she said, bitterly.

"Why don't you just leave him."

"And go where?"

"Family. They'll help, won't they?"

"Not mine. My father would send me right back to my husband. I can hear him now. 'You made your bed, our Sandra, now you have to lie in it'."

"Your sister then."

Sandra shook her head. "Never. She has a wonderful marriage. She'd scorn mine. I couldn't bear the shame."

"Friends?"

"The only 'friends' I have live in Seaview. The others have dropped by the wayside over the years."

Marigold contemplated Sandra asking if she could come and live with her and Clive, and suddenly, Marigold had lost all compassion for her friend. That wasn't a responsibility she'd like to take on at all. And she knew Clive wouldn't like it.

"Don't worry," Sandra said. "I'm not about to ask you to live here."

"Well…I…"

"I should go." She stood up and left, and that was the last time they'd talked about it in any detail.

Now, as they sat at Sandra's kitchen table, Marigold knew only too well the horrors that went on in that house and she intended to get to the bottom of what happened in there that morning…or last night!

Chapter Seventeen

At No. 5

RHIANNA KNOCKED ON THE DOOR and Eva let her in. "I'm sorry to bother you," she said, "Uncle Rolf said I could call on you if I had a problem. It seems that we're out of milk. I was just wondering if you knew what time the milkman was coming."

"He's already been. Didn't he leave you any?"

"No, but I think he took away the empties."

"That's odd."

Rhianna shuffled her feet as a notion came to her. "You know what? I think I know what's happened. Uncle Rolf knew he wasn't going to be here this weekend, so he probably cancelled the milk."

"But he knew you'd be there, didn't he?"

"Uhm, yes, I suppose so, but maybe he forgot."

"Well, I've got some I can spare. Come in."

Rhianna stepped inside. "I can always go to the shop."

"I wouldn't. It's fivepence more in there," said Eva. "Come through."

Rhianna followed her into the kitchen. "This is a nice house."

"Thank you."

In the kitchen, sitting at the table next to the terrace doors, was a woman with dark hair, looking exotic in a sparkly coloured top over brown slacks. "Hi," Rhianna said.

Eva introduced them "This is my friend, Jade." She looked at Jade without any affection in her eyes. "Jade, this is Rolf's niece from next door."

"Rhianna," she said. She guessed Eva had forgotten her name.

"Would you like a cup of coffee?"

"Coffee? Yes, I would. Uncle Rolf doesn't keep it in."

Eva chuckled. "We're all big tea drinkers, but I like coffee. I just think it's more continental."

"We drink a lot of tea in our house too. My mother wouldn't be able to get through the day without twenty cups at least."

The two women laughed. "Sit down," Eva said.

Rhianna watched her pour black coffee from a silver pot. "I've always wanted a percolator," Rhianna said.

"It's so convenient." Eva set a mug down on the table in front of her. "Put in your own milk and sugar."

"Thanks."

"Your uncle tells me you're going to be a journalist."

"Yes, I love writing." Then Rhianna had a notion. "Hey, do you know the people next door?"

"At No.4? Yes. He's in a wheelchair. you know."

"Yes, uncle Rolf mentioned it."

"That poor wife of his. We hardly see them out and about, but they have family visit once in a while."

"I was thinking of asking him if I could do a piece on him. Do you know how he became confined to the home? Magazines and journals pay a lot for stuff like that. They call them real-life stories."

"Oh, it was a tragic accident by all accounts," Eva said.

Rhianna's ears perked up. "Really!?"

"His name is Jack. I don't know all the details. He used to drive a lorry, you know one of those tankers that transport oil…Well, he was on the M1 one day and a car almost crashed in the side of him. A woman it was…fussing over her baby while she was driving. Anyway, Jack swerved his lorry and the tanker went over the verge and headfirst into a bridge. He injured his spine on impact, and they had to cut him out. He's been in a wheelchair ever since."

"That's terrible."

"Yes. It was the woman's fault, but she got away with cuts and bruises." As an afterthought, Eva said, "I think everyone should wear seatbelts, don't you agree?"

"Yes, I do."

"And of course, his poor wife, Jo, has to nurse him. But I'm sure he must have had a good pension."

"Jack and Jo?" Rhianna said, aghast at the pairing. Eva chuckled. "I'd love to do a story on him. Do you think he'd agree?"

"Perhaps. You'd have to ask him. You can just go around. Go straight around the back. It's easier for him…rather than opening the front door."

"All right, I will." Rhianna was happy with the information. She wondered if she could get the story written up that weekend. It would be a good one to take with her on Monday when she started her new job. Maybe they'd publish it. She wondered if anyone at Seaview had a typewriter she could borrow. *Yes,* this was turning out to be quite a productive morning, she thought.

"Have you tried the steps yet?" Eva asked.

"The steps?"

"The cliff steps. They're quite a challenge. I don't go down there much."

"Uncle Rolf said I shouldn't attempt them until after eleven."

"Yes, that's a good idea. They can be treacherous."

"I thought I saw someone swimming out there this morning."

"That was probably Eddie from No.7. He always has a swim in the mornings."

"He braves the Atlantic, this time of year?"

"He wears a wet suit."

"Not this morning. He looked as if he was naked."

Eva shrugged. She clearly wasn't interested in her neighbour Eddie. Rhianna decided to change the subject to something more interesting. "So how do you two know each other?" she asked.

Then the reporter in her noticed two things:

One: so far Jade hadn't said much, only observing and listening to Eva relay her intel on the neighbourhood. And two: when she asked about their friendship, Eva had blushed. Her neck had turned red, and Rhianna had to wonder if she had an illness of some kind that caused spontaneous redness of the skin.

EVA HAD SO FAR ENJOYED the visit with Rolf's niece, but now the subject had changed, and it wasn't a topic she relished.

She put her hand up to her neck and hoped Rhianna and Jade hadn't noticed her skin turning red. She tugged at her sweater and adjusted the collar. Rhianna had just asked how she and Jade were friends, but as far as Eva was concerned, they'd never been *that*. "Well, Jade's husband is my husband's best friend," she said, putting Rhianna in the picture.

"Not right now they're not," said Jade.

"What?" Eva looked stricken. Honestly, the woman had hardly said a word the whole morning and now she was bringing up an issue that didn't need bringing up.

"They seem to have been battling a lot lately. Haven't you noticed?"

"Well, they've been friends for a long time. They wouldn't be normal if they didn't have a falling out once in a while," Eva tittered. She couldn't manage a laugh. Forced or otherwise.

Rhianna made the awkward moment worse when she asked, "Why have they had a falling out?"

Eva decided Rhianna would make a good reporter. She seemed to be sticking her nose in a lot of people's business. "We don't know."

Jade butted in. "Well, actually, we do."

"What?" Eva's neck was ablaze.

"I think they're fighting over me."

Rhianna and Eva looked at Jade as if she'd lost her mind. Rhianna's eyes had lit up, but Eva decided there was only one thing left to do. She decided to change the subject.

"You know, Rhianna, I don't know if your uncle mentioned it, but I'm having a bit of a get-together later on this evening."

Rhianna gazed at her in the most discerning way. She'd obviously noticed that Eva had changed the discussion from something quite meaty to something quite ordinary.

"It's just the girls…Since the men have decided to leave us to our own devices," she chuckled.

In exchange, Rhianna offered her a smile.

"Just Cocktails. And a few nibbles…sausage rolls, crisps…that sort of thing…You'd be very welcome. Six o'clock then?"

"Six o'clock."

Chapter Eighteen

At No. 5

WHAT A MORNING SHE WAS HAVING, Marigold thought. First, her visit to Sandra's house and now Kim at No.1 was pacing back and forth in her kitchen worried about some boyfriend of hers.

Before she went over to Kimberley's, she'd had a frank and sober discussion with Sandra about Eddie. Marigold was beginning to consider herself to be quite the sleuth after she deduced that Sandra had been spouting off a load of lies for half an hour.

Eddie still hadn't returned from his 'swim'. "Don't you think you ought to call the police?" Marigold asked.

Sandra was still in denial and had her actress hat on. Marigold was beginning to feel insulted, knowing that Sandra was making a load of excuses whilst assuming Marigold couldn't see through her little ploy.

Personally, Marigold suspected Eddie had left home and for the most part she couldn't understand why Sandra didn't come right out and admit it. It was 'good riddance to him', surely.

"Maybe the coast guard should be informed," Marigold said, pushing the issue to the very limit. Soon, Sandra would crack under the pressure and tell all.

Then, when the sun shone through a gap in the clouds, something caught Marigold's attention. Her eyes had darted to the terrace outside the window doors. "That's odd."

Sandra's eyes had followed hers. She looked alarmed. "What is?"

"Well, it hasn't rained since Thursday and yet your terrace is wet."

A silence fell between them, before Gladys piped up, "That was me. It looked like it needed a good clean."

"Really?! It's a bit early for cleaning isn't it? She looked at her watch. It was only 9.30 and she'd been there half-an-hour already.

"I don't sleep well, and I like to keep busy."

"You're not worried about the terrace freezing over…and maybe slipping on it?"

"No, I wasn't worried about that until you said it." Gladys seemed to be getting irate. Marigold was glad she was making waves. One of them had to cave any minute. Their secret was hanging in the air like a cloud full of thunder.

"It's a shame Eddie had to miss the golf trip."

Sandra kept up her side of the acting duo. "He changed his mind. He doesn't get on with Roger very well."

"Oh, I see. That's a shame since Roger was kind enough to pay for most of it."

"Eddie would have felt duty bound to him."

"None of the others felt that way. My Clive certainly didn't. It was understood that Roger was charging it back to the company. One of the perks he called it."

"I…I didn't know that."

"I think Eddie knew."

"Well, I don't know why he changed his mind. I'm just guessing."

"This is all garbage."

"What?"

"I know something has happened. I just wish you'd trust me enough to tell me."

When Sandra clammed up, saying no more on the matter, Marigold got up and walked out. She'd had enough.

WHEN SHE GOT OUTSIDE, with the intention of storming off back home, she noticed Kim's curtains were open at No.1. Marigold thought that was odd since Kim never got up before eleven on a Saturday. She called it her treat of the week.

Just as she was about to cross *the eight*, Marigold realised she'd forgotten to look in on Mr and Mrs Butler. She'd promised Clive she would.

Kim would have to wait five minutes.

She went down the path of No.8 and noticed a bit of loose fertilizer on the flagstones. She tutted. Clive had missed a bit from the flowerpot the cat had broken last night. She'd get a dustpan and brush from Mrs Butler and clean it up properly. *Men!*

She tapped the back door. No answer. She tapped again. Nothing. *Strange!*

"Yoo-hoo, Mrs B," she called. "It's Marigold from across the road at No.2."

She tapped again.

Strange! Mrs B was usually up by now. She went into the back garden and took a few paces back, to try and see up to the window. Yes, the curtains were closed up there too. She supposed they were having a lie in.

As she stood with her arms crossed, wondering what she should do, she heard voices. She stood very still and quiet at the side of a tree and listened to the voices from next door at No.7. Sandra's voice was unmistakable, and Marigold knew she was talking to Eddie's mother.

"What about the stone?" asked Sandra.

Marigold pouted and frowned. What on earth were they talking about?

"I washed it and threw it over the cliff."

"But there's a gap in the rockery. It's noticeable."

"We can fix that."

"What if the water doesn't dry up. If Marigold noticed, others will too."

"We can get some towels. Soak up the worst of it."

"Alright. But our biggest problem is the wetsuit. What will we do with it?"

"Burn it?"

"Not around here. They'd notice a bonfire. And rubber smells."

"Bury it then."

"Bury it?"

"Why not? We could go down to the beach after eleven when the tide's out."

"Alright, we'll do that then."

"We need to go and make everything look as normal as possible. You should open the curtains and make the beds."

"All right," said Sandra.

Marigold stood in the garden next door, hidden by a tree. She'd forgotten about Mrs Butler, and now she was wondering what on earth Sandra and Gladys had been talking about.

ACROSS THE ROAD at No.1, she found Kimberly pacing around the house outside on her little patch of lawn. "Kim?" Marigold called as she crossed *the eight*. "What's wrong? Are you okay?" Her friend looked extremely agitated.

"Erhm."

Marigolds put her hand on Kim's shoulder. "What is it?"

"I had a friend come around last night…"

Marigold frowned. "Yes, she laughed. That was me."

"I mean after you'd gone."

"But I didn't leave until midnight."

"Just before actually," Kim said as Marigold began counting minutes in her head. "It's just that he…I mean *she*, left quite early this morning, but she never took her car. I've just seen it parked down the road beyond the gates. He…*she* parked it there last night."

"Why didn't she drive it in?"

A pause. "She forgot the code."

"How did she get through the gates then?"

A pause. "I…I let her in. She couldn't be bothered to go move her car, so she left it there. We had a few drinks, so she didn't leave until early this morning."

"There's your answer then," Marigold said, satisfied she'd solved the mystery of Kim's friend's car. "If you both had a lot to drink, she wouldn't have wanted to drive, would she? The new drink driving restrictions are playing havoc with people's social lives."

"I suppose so…"

"What's her name, your friend?"

"Erhm…Tyra."

"I tell you what, why we don't have a nice cup of tea and you can tell me all about her."

As they walked into the No.1, Marigold thought about how Sandra had lied through her teeth and now there she was with another one who couldn't see the truth if it was staring her in the face.

What a morning, Marigold thought.

Chapter Nineteen

At No. 3

DRAKE WAS IN A BAD MOOD and in a good mood all at the same time. He realised he couldn't class himself as a patient man, but the guy he had tied up in the kitchen was seriously testing his patience. Tyrone didn't know what had hit him when he left Kimberly's house early that morning, and it was the one thing that was keeping Drake's cheerful mood up. He loved to surprise people. Not in a good way!

He often recalled the surprised look on his father's face when young Drake had put that drill through his neck. And he didn't lose that expression even when the life was sucked out of him. When he went down those cellar steps and the mirror followed him, despite his eyes being shut, Drake had called out. "Here's your mirror, you dirty bastard, take a look in that now." The irony wasn't lost on Drake's humour and he spent many days afterwards reminiscing on the whole debacle.

Mother, of course, had gone about her routine in her usual docile state. God, how he hated women. They never fought back. They never stuck up for themselves. They never objected to anything. That's what he liked about Kimberly Cutter. She was a strong woman. Not someone people could just walk all over.

Except for the guy he had tied up on the kitchen floor. *He* had tried to take over her life and Drake was positive Kim hadn't agreed to it. She had rejected Tyrone time and time again at work, so she wasn't about to welcome him into her home willingly. If she had, Drake wouldn't think kindly of her at all and he'd be forced to teach her a lesson until she complied! It didn't usually take him long to make women do that. Look at his mother. She was a good example.

After father left, she'd gone around that kitchen with her bucket and sponge and she'd cleaned everything. Then she did it again the next day. When someone knocked on the door asking about father, Drake heard her telling lie after lie about his whereabouts. He was a co-worker, someone from the plumbing firm father worked at. Mother told him that he'd run off with some tart and that he probably wouldn't be back. "It's just me and our Drake now," she'd said before she told him to send father's final wages to her.

That was the last they'd heard about father. Good riddance!

Now there he was with Tyrone, not knowing what he was going to do with him.

It began that morning when he came out of Kim's house in the early hours, and out of the dark Drake had taken a spade to the backs of his legs, making him crumble to a heap on the floor. Then Drake crashed the spade down on his head. He'd gotten the spade from the greenhouse at No.8 since they didn't need it anymore.

He was surprised and relieved all at the same time when Tyrone moaned while lying on the grass in front of Kim's house. Drake was sure he'd hit him hard enough to kill him, but it looked like his head was harder than he'd anticipated.

Drake had to admit to feeling mildly relieved. He hadn't planned getting rid of Tyrone since he had no idea Tyrone was going to be there. The spade across the skull scenario had been as much as a surprise for Drake as it had been for Tyrone. Sometimes Drake just saw red and the things he did, as a result, were almost dreamlike as if he was being forced to do it. His father maybe. *Yes,* maybe it was father who made him do the things he did.

When Tyrone passed out, Drake had dragged him by the legs all the way past No.2's front garden. He'd checked to see if anyone was looking, but it was so early, a fine mist had settled on the ground and everyone in the neighbourhood was fast asleep. Just as he'd taken a much-deserved rest from lugging the big guy about, from the darkness and through the mist, he saw a figure, a man, wearing a wet suit, going up the side path to No.7.

When he'd gone, Drake had simply carried on, not even relieved that the man never saw him. If he had, Drake pondered, he would have gone over the road and smashed his head in too. He still had the spade so that would have been easy peasy. *No*, that man was lucky he got off scot-free, and that he would live to see another day. Lucky guy!

Drake dragged Tyrone the rest of the way, across the grass of No.2 to No.3, the empty house on the left of *the eight.* He'd already been there to check the place out, with the intention of lying low until an opportunity presented itself to get that Roger Lang.

He'd taken Ty inside, and laid him out on the kitchen floor. There was no furniture in the house, but he had found some blue nylon rope in the greenhouse at No.8. Without a chair to tie him to, Drake had laid him out on the lino floor, tied his hands and his feet and taken each end of the rope to tie them to anything he could find. On one side, he'd secured the rope around the cupboard door handles and the other end he tied around the stove on the opposite side of the kitchen. Drake had to laugh when he saw Ty's body lying flat out on the floor. He almost looked like Jesus on the cross, with his arms straight out and one bloodied knee bent. Still, Jesus or not, he'd be hard pressed to get out of those cryptic knots. And even if he did, his legs were probably broken.

With one more thing left to do, Drake had taken a plastic bucket of water and lemon squeezy and gone back to the garden in front of Kim's house. There, he threw the soapy water down where some blood had spilt from Tyrone's legs after Drake had buckled his knees.

Then he went back to No.3 to wait things out.

Chapter Twenty

At No. 6

IT WAS NOON and Rhianna had finally watched the tide go out. Now she could go down to the beach.

The wind was up, lashing her hair about her face and stinging her eyes. She'd tied her hair up into a ponytail, but still, the wind managed to pull it out in strands. The sun was up over the bay, which was a blessing. It did make the whole experience a lot more pleasant.

She wore a navy blue anorak. It had a hood if the relatively good weather turned to rain. She wore ordinary white daps on her feet. She'd had them for years, after using them for PE when she was at school. They never seemed to wear out. She called them her old faithfuls. Goodness knows how many times they'd been buffed up with canvas whitener.

The top of the cliff where the steps went down was a patch of grass, now mud, covered in sand. From a giant rock, a sign protruded, warning of the dangers of the steps and the cove below. *Descend at your own peril*, it said, but Rhianna just laughed. She'd tackled worse things than that in her life. Actually, she hadn't! Honestly, she'd had quite an easy life, not like some of the kids who'd gone to the same school. She often resented her parents for allowing her to have things easy. She was never prepared for anything, even though deep down she had a great sense of adventure and a constant desire to conquer the world.

The steps were about four feet wide. They were man-made, but that was a long time ago. Now they were well worn, but that just added to their charm in Rhianna's opinion. Down one side, a natural handrail had been carved into the rock. It went diagonally down, but it wasn't straight. It simply followed the contour of the stone as if someone had hollowed it out but had difficulty in some parts. Still, it was a terrific handhold, as long as one had gloves on…which she did! Without anything to cover her hands, it would have been awkward digging her fingers into the crevices, while sand and dirt and the odd root bunged it up and threatened to bruise her knuckles. On the other side of the steps was absolutely nothing. It was almost like a floating staircase, where the sides dropped away to certain death from high up. She'd have to ask uncle Rolf why someone hadn't done something about it. Perhaps they could have added a handrail or something. It would have been less terrifying, in her opinion. Still, as her sense of adventure ruled, she was looking forward to the challenge of the climb.

The first few steps were easy since they were embedded into the top of the cliff like they were cutting down through. Rhianna took a good hold of the hollowed out crevice and began her descent. Surprisingly, she discovered the steps weren't that bad, each one better than the last, and looking less worn as they went on.

By the time she was half-way down she had a sure step and got to the bottom as if she was dancing on air. She smiled to herself as her feet touched soft sand and when she turned to look up, she saw the steps in all their glory, reaching to heaven...or Seaview at least!

She gasped when she spotted a small cave under the cliff. Wow, she thought, what an adventure! She would check out the cave after she'd had a quick run along the sand.

Just before she took off, she noticed something strange. There was a circle in the wet sand with mounds either side. Obviously, someone had dug a hole, or more likely a sand castle and the remnants were left. She bent down and picked up a small garden spade. It had a red handle and it looked quite new. She smiled and dug it into the earth, leaving it protruding from the sand next to the round patch. Then she kicked up her heels and took off to run the width of the bay in careless abandon.

SANDRA COULD HARDLY BELIEVE her bad luck. She was standing inside the cave near the steps watching a girl with a ponytail looking down at the circle in the sand. *What rotten luck*, she thought. Earlier, Gladys had said that the perfect murder was all about timing, but now Sandra realised her timing sucked.

Earlier, Sandra and Gladys had decided that the best place to bury the wetsuit was on the beach. Their reckoning was that when the tide came back in later on, it would flatten any remnants left after digging the hole. They were taking a risk, they knew that but they couldn't hide the wetsuit, nor bury it in their own back garden, not with the police sniffing around if perchance they did have a sniff around. Gladys was positive they would. If and when they discovered the body, *if* they suspected foul play, which was likely seeing as Eddie 's body wouldn't be clad in a wetsuit, then the first place they'd look was Sandra's property.

'How do you know all this? Sandra had asked Gladys just before they left the house. She'd simply replied, 'Columbo'.

At eleven o'clock, carrying the wetsuit inside a co-op bag, the two women had gone to the place where the steps, leading down to the beach, began. "I haven't been down here for a long time," said Sandra as Gladys hesitated. She leaned against the big rock where the sign protruded from it. *...descend at your own peril,* it said behind Gladys' exhausted body.

Sandra stopped when she realised Glady was way too old to manage those steps. "You stay here, or go back to the house," she said. "I'll go down."

"I can't leave you to do it on your own," she panted.

"Yes, you can. Honestly, I don't think you'll manage these steps."

Gladys nodded, and Sandra was glad she'd realised her limitations. She squeezed Sandra's arm and handed her the garden spade with the red handle. "Be careful."

"I will."

When she got down to the beach, she immediately started digging. The tide had only just started going out, so the sand was still wet, making it easier to dig. She went down about three-feet and stuffed the wetsuit deep into the hole. She had no qualms piling the sand back in and burying the remnants of Eddie's possession for eternity.

She'd asked Glady's if it wouldn't have been better to leave the wetsuit on the beach, making it look like Eddie had stripped it off himself before he dived into the freezing water. "But why would he do that?" Gladys had said, and Sandra couldn't think of a good enough answer.

Just as she threw down the spade to flatten over the hole, she happened to look up to see the stranger, the girl with the ponytail, arriving at the top of the cliff steps.

Sandra was shocked. No one ever went down the cliff in the winter. Except for Eddie!

In her panic, she rushed to the cave and hid inside the opening.

The girl arrived on the sand and then turned to see the cave. From the darkness, Sandra wondered if she had seen her, but then she figured the girl would have been more interested in watching her footing on the treacherous steps.

Sandra waited and then she saw the girl notice the hole. Her heart pumped so hard she thought it would beat right out of her chest. She watched the girl pick up the spade. *Damn*, in her haste, Sandra had forgotten about it.

Finally, the girl started to run along the beach and that's when Sandra made her escape. With the girl's retreating body in sight, Sandra took those steps up almost two at a time, not thinking at all about the danger of slipping.

BEFORE RHIANNA TURNED TO GO BACK, she looked out across the sea and the waves crashing against the tip of the headland. Wow, the place was wild, and she felt completely exhilarated. *Yes*, she was going to enjoy living at Seaview, she thought finally before she turned and ran back.

Outside the cave, she couldn't understand the footprints in the sand. They looked like they were going from the cave towards the steps. And they looked fresh. *Strange,* she thought.

She didn't notice the body on the sand, lying in the surf, naked as the day he was born.

Chapter Twenty-one

At No. 6

EVA LANG WAS GETTING READY for the cocktail party. It was four o'clock and already the daylight was fading. Despite the day starting out badly, the hours had passed relatively peacefully. In fact, if Jade hadn't been there, she'd have enjoyed it even more. The woman was a pain. She'd hung around all day waiting for Eva to entertain her, to wait on her, to cater to her every whim. Earlier, she'd made them a quick lunch of egg mayonnaise sandwiches and Jade had said, "Won't there be anything hot tonight? I'm not sure I can go a day without a proper meal."

Eva's jaw dropped. "If you want something else, you can make it yourself."

Jade looked offended. "I couldn't possibly cook in someone else's kitchen."

"Looks like you'll have to manage with a sandwich then, doesn't it?"

They sat at the table occasionally looking up at each other as they ate. Eva liked to do open sandwiches. She had seen them once when she went to someone else's house. She thought they were elegant as could be and looked forward to going home to make some herself. The appeal was in the garnish. Smoked salmon with thin slices of cucumber, egg with caviar, creamed cheese and prawns. They looked simply delightful on a plate, colourful and appetising, so the fact that Jade wasn't impressed by them, just confirmed to Eva what a low birth, low taste bitch she was.

"This is about Harry isn't it?" Jade said out of the blue.

Eva almost choked. She dug her fingernail into a gap between two teeth and gouged out a piece of bread. It gave her a moment. "What are you talking about?"

"You're being mean to me because of what Harry said at your dinner party last summer."

Eva screwed up her face. "Oh, that's ridiculous. It was the drink talking. Roger would never cheat on me. We're too close."

"Really?"

"Yes, really!" *What a bitch*! Eva thought, *bringing up that whole matter*. No wonder her husband strayed, and no wonder he suspects her of sleeping with every man she meets. That sparkly top made her look like a slut, with her long dark hair and tinted skin, and so many silver bangles on her wrist, she positively chimed. Eva often wondered if she was a Romany. What with the hoops dangling from her ears and the musky odour that seemed to follow her around. *Yes,* Eva decided, she was definitely the sort of girl who would have run away with the gypsies when she was a wayward girl.

Eva wanted to change the subject. She'd been thinking about Harry all day and she was enjoying the little quiet moments to dream about him making love to her. Last night had been the beginning. She was sure of it. She'd been a reluctant participant, but she knew she was falling for him, in the passionate sense. As for long term, she'd never leave Roger. As her old mum used to say, the grass is never greener on the other side.

Jade had spent the afternoon with her feet up on the sofa reading a magazine. The woman was downright idle. She could have hoovered or something, just to help out. Honestly, the house didn't need much cleaning. Sandra had been in a couple of days ago to have a good spruce up in readiness of the party. They'd taken her on as a daily after that unfortunate incident when Eva and Roger heard an almighty row going on at No.7. It was the middle of the night and Sandra's screams had drifted up to the top of the headland and into their bedroom window.

Eva had nudged Roger out of bed. "You'll have to go over there," she said. "It sounds like he's killing her."

Roger threw back the blankets and got out of bed. "I hate that Eddie."

"We all do. And I expect his wife hates him most of all. Honestly, I don't know why she doesn't leave him."

Half an hour later Roger brought back Sandra wrapped in a raincoat. She looked broken when Eva helped her into bed in the spare room. "Try and get some sleep," she'd said softly as Sandra stared at the wall as if her eyes had frozen over.

The following day Sandra told Eva and Roger that they'd argued over money and that it didn't happen very often. Eva had suspected that wasn't true, but she gave Sandra the benefit of the doubt. That's when she offered her the job of cleaning the house once a week. Just to give her a bit of pocket money. Sandra took her up on it and she'd cleaned for them ever since.

Now, at 4 pm, just as Eva stood in the kitchen neatly arranging bottles of spirits to make cocktails, the lights went out. "What on earth!? Oh, don't tell me," Eva cursed.

The late afternoon light still spilt through the windows, so she could still see her way around when she went to the electric box in the pantry. She pulled a few switches and then went back into the kitchen where Jade was pouring herself a sherry.

"Power cut," Eva announced.

"You get a lot around here, do you?"

"Of course. We're on the Headland. We're often at war with modern amenities." Eva picked up a plate. "It won't last long. We'll just have to wait it out." Then, she had a thought. "Of course, if you'd prefer to go home, I'd understand." *Wishful thinking*!

"No, I'll stay with you."

Great!

Frowning, Eva put the plate in the dishwasher. The breakfast dishes were still in there and it was almost full. Now she wouldn't be able to do a wash until the electricity came back on. She thought about the food she'd be making for the party. Luckily her stove was gas, but the oven was electric, so she wouldn't be able to bake the sausage rolls. *Damn!*

She had plenty of candles, but it probably wouldn't come to that. The power would be back on by then. The CEGB wouldn't dare leave them without power on a Saturday night. People would be up in arms if they couldn't watch Match of the Day, let alone get the Pool results.

For now, she'd just have to put up with it, just as she'd put up with Harry's bitch wife all day long.

At No. 4

IT WAS JUST BEFORE 4PM when Rhianna went tentatively around the back of No.6. She noticed how wheelchair ramps had replaced steps. Everything else was concreted over with just a small patch of grass down the end of the back garden. There was a wooden bench down there, facing the view of the Atlantic, and a vision popped into her head of the man in his wheelchair staring wistfully out to sea.

She knocked on the back door and waited. A light went on and she heard footsteps. A woman answered. She was medium height, with long luscious red hair gripped by a comb at the back of her head. She was beautiful and Rhianna realised she couldn't possibly be the wife of the man in the wheelchair. She couldn't be Jo.

"I was wondering if I could speak to Jack," Rhianna said.

"Who are you?" she asked gently. Her warm smile gave Rhianna the impression that she was a kind soul.

"My name is Rhianna Loxley. I'm staying with my uncle over at No.6."

"Oh, I see. Come in."

"Thankyou." Rhianna walked up the shallow concrete ramp and into the kitchen. It was a big room with plenty of space to move around, uncluttered.

"My name is Jo," the woman with the red hair said.

They shook hands. Rhianna had to ask herself why she thought the woman couldn't have been Jo. It bemused her. She'd have to think about that one.

"Follow me."

She had expected to be shown into a bedroom, where the wheelchair guy would be lying in a hospital bed with the lights turned low and a water jug at the side. Instead, a door opened to a room that had been converted to a gym.

It smelled musty. The late afternoon light was filtering through a wall of windows, the floor was wooden, the walls white, and at a weight lifting machine sat a man, his back bare to the waist, broad shoulders, muscles, tan... His hair was pulled into a short ponytail at the nape of his neck and sweat rolled off him in easy freefalling drips.

"This is Jack."

"Oh!" She was stunned to see the man Eva had described to her, the man in the wheelchair, named Jack.

He turned and smiled. His face was strong, and he was unshaven in a sexy way. Rhianna recalled her mother once saying that men always aged better than women. She wasn't wrong. Jack was drop dead gorgeous. He was around thirty-five, maybe forty, but his body was fit and he was alert, more so than she had contemplated or expected.

Jack released the bar which pulled the weights. He turned on the seat and then she noticed the chair. He pulled it toward him and swung into it using the strength in his arms. He positioned his legs onto the footrests, tugged on a white cotton shirt and then wheeled himself towards her.

At the door, he reached out his hand. "Jack," he said simply.

She pumped his hand, unable to let go. She was using it to ward off the guilt she felt for predetermining what Jack would be like. "Rhianna," she said back.

"Hey, sis," he said to Jo, "how about some lemonade?"

Rhianna turned about. "Sis?"

"You thought we were husband and wife, didn't you?" she said.

"Well, yeah. That's what I was told."

"The neighbours!" She raised her perfect eyebrows and smiled. "Let's have lemonade. It's homemade."

Rhianna held the door open for Jack to wheel himself through, but he stopped and offered his arm. "After you," he said.

"Oh…okay." She was flustered. She'd made a mess of the whole thing.

Then the lights went out.

"Power cut," said Jo.

At No. 2

IT WAS ABOUT 4 PM when Kim knocked on the door of No.2. Marigold answered straight away. She invited her in, but seemed distant, not like Marigold at all. Maybe she had a lot on her mind. She wasn't the only one. Kim needed to talk to someone…anyone.

Inside, Marigold immediately sensed Kim's distress. "What's wrong?" she asked.

"I still haven't been able to get a hold of my friend."

"Tyra?"

Kim hesitated, tilting her bottom lip as if she was saying, *well, not exactly…* "Ehm, no, it's Tyrone. He's my 'kind of' boyfriend."

"Oh, I see."

It was right to come clean. Marigold obviously didn't believe her story about a 'girlfriend' and if Kim was going to be the modern woman she wanted to be, then it was time to tell the truth. Besides, something wasn't right, and she couldn't shift a feeling of dread, that somewhere and somehow, Ty was in trouble.

"Look, Marigold, I think there's something really wrong. His car is still outside the gates at the side of the road and I can't get him on the phone."

"Well, I'm sure there's a reasonable explanation."

Kim stepped forward and stared into her face. She wouldn't look at her. She was pretending. "Oh my god, you're offended."

"No, I'm not," she answered quickly. "I realise times have changed. There's a lot of unmarried couples living together these days."

"We're not living together. I'm just using him for sex."

Marigold blushed. She looked like she didn't know what to do with herself. "Well, Kimberly, I don't really know what to say to that. I'm just not that modern, I'm afraid."

"Don't worry about it. I've always been progressive. It's held me back a lot."

That was true.

After she'd put herself through college, she acquired an engineer's degree, which was unheard of in those days. She had no social life, because, apart from working to pay rent in a two bedroom flat shared by five girls, she did a night time college course on business management, another class where women were predominantly absent.

That's what got her into Phillips. She worked her way up through the ranks and finally took the first female managerial role ever, for Phillips UK. That was how she became an entity along with being a single female resident at Seaview.

"So, have you tried calling him at home?" Marigold was saying.

"Yes, I have, hundreds of times." She walked to the window to see the headland, where she saw the waves crash over the rocks. "I'm not usually this uptight, really."

"You could have fooled me."

She spun about. "What?"

"You're always uptight. You're the most uptight person I know."

"Look, I know I haven't always been a good friend to you," Kim said. "We've had our moments, I understand that, but it's not that I never liked you. I'm just a very private person and I work a lot, so I'm always *very* tired."

"Not too tired to have night-time guests, it would seem."

"Okay, I deserved that."

She was surprised that Marigold was that observant. She always had her down as a mindless busybody who enjoyed getting into people's heads and into their homes. The very notion that she actually liked Kim was a surprise too. Kim wasn't everyone's cup of tea. She knew that only too well after a friend told her once she was always psycho-analysing everyone.

She watched Marigold remove rollers from her hair and throw them into a basket on the table. "Going somewhere?"

"Yes, the cocktail party at No.5. You are too, aren't you?"

"I'm not sure. Not until I find out if Ty is okay."

"Perhaps he couldn't start his car and he walked home, or maybe he got a lift."

Kim pouted and nodded. It was a sensible suggestion. "Maybe."

"Have you checked to see if his keys are in the car."

"No, do you think I should?"

Marigold shrugged. She either didn't know or she didn't care.

Kim wasn't used to Marigold not caring. Maybe she had something else on her mind. "Do you think I should call the police?"

"If you want to put your mind at rest, and if you really think something's wrong, then, yes, maybe it would be for the best."

"Can I use your phone?"

"Of course."

She was just in the middle of dialling 999 when the lights went out.

"Power cut," Marigold said, from the dimming daylight. She went to the wall next to the door and checked the light switches.

"Now I won't be able to report him missing," Kim said, looking at the sky outside becoming quite overcast.

"And you won't be able to get through the gate either. You'll have to wait until it comes back on."

"There must be an override to the keypad."

"Nope, we tried it before when we had a power cut. It's a modern contraption, so, it won't work without electric. Sorry!"

"That's a really stupid design fault." Kim wondered if she could fix it. She was an engineer after all. Then she decided that maybe it would be a futile exercise. The power could come back on at any moment.

Marigold shrugged again. "You've been here when we've had a blackout."

"Yes, but I can't remember ever trying the gates."

"Well, take my word for it, when the power's off, no one gets in or out."

"That's ridiculous, especially when we can't even telephone for help." She thought about that. "Wow! We're like sitting ducks. What if there was a fire or something?"

"That's what the cliff steps are for. When we bought, the developers told us that in the event of a fire, we should go down to the beach and wait for the emergency services."

Kim frowned "What about when the tide is in?"

Clearly Marigold hadn't thought about *that* eventuality. "Well anyway," she said dismissing the problem. "We haven't got a fire. It's just the power and I'm sure someone will report it. Until then, we'll just have to wait it out."

Chapter Twenty-two

At No. 4

RHIANNA WAS WELCOMED INTO THEIR HOUSE with open arms. After a glass of lemonade, Jo dug out some candles, while Jack opened a bottle of wine. The cork popped out and he poured three glasses. "Tell us about yourself, Rhianna," he said. He spoke with a deep voice. His mouth was shaped into a soft smile and his teeth were beautiful, off-white, not bright white. He wore a bangle made of leather twine on one wrist and a large gold watch on the other. He wore no ring, and his fingernails were well cared for. Not that he'd had a manicure, he was too masculine for that, but he clearly didn't do any dirty work.

"Well, I've only just arrived. Last night, actually. My Uncle Rolf offered to put me up until I settled into my new job."

"Which is?"

"I've secured a position at the Devonshire Post, as a reporter. I love to write."

"Me too."

"Really?"

Jo spoke after she'd lit the candles and she sat down. "Jack writes novels."

"No way."

"Well, it's just a hobby. I've never had the nerve to submit anything. Rejection isn't something I find easy to overcome."

"But you have overcome your disability..." She rushed..."if you don't mind me saying so. You seem very brave." Rhianna couldn't believe how blunt she was being with him. It was as if she'd known him all her life.

He stared at her. He was probably thinking how rude she was for being so blatantly honest. "I'm not brave," he said. "I just have no choice the matter."

She bowed her head. "I'm sorry. I shouldn't have mentioned it."

"Don't be sorry. You have no idea how much I resent people who avoid the subject. So much so, it's embarrassing, making it difficult for me to raise the subject in case they faint away at the notion of an invalid being so direct."

"I think I understand a bit about how you feel," Rhianna said. "I had an aunt who had MS. She was confined to a wheelchair and when I took her out, people would ignore her and talk directly to me. I found it quite shocking. It was as if she'd suddenly lost her whole identity."

"It's the 'does she take sugar in her coffee' syndrome. That's why we hardly go beyond the gates," Jo said.

"I don't understand."

"My brother and I are pretty much reclusive. We found we were intolerant of the stares and the opinions and the whole stigma attached to his disability."

"I don't really get it…but, honestly…when I spoke with your neighbour today, she said you were husband and wife, and she gave me the impression that you were a lot older than you are…and she whispered when she spoke about you as if the subject was taboo."

Jo and Jack chuckled. They seemed to appreciate Rhianna's candour. However, she had to wonder if she was pushing it a bit too far. "To be honest…I have to say, I had a picture in my head too. And when you opened the door, I couldn't believe that you were the woman she'd described to me. Is that odd?"

"No. It's normal, apparently. *Terribly* normal! More's the pity."

"How do you put up with it? I mean, you're clearly independent…young, intelligent and self-reliant…why aren't you shouting from the rooftops, complaining about how the image of you is wrong?"

"We've done that. We never gained much."

"And we never will," Jack said. "Not until attitudes change."

"Frankly, though," said Jo. "There are a lot of handicapped people who don't have a lot of drive or ambition. I'm not saying Jack is unique, but he never gave up when it happened to him and that's what matters." She was pensive when she said, "Maybe one day, people will be accepted for their disabilities, you know, not looked at, as if they had two heads. Maybe forty years from now!"

"Or maybe never," said Jack.

Rhianna didn't say anything. She didn't know what to say.

The candle was flickering. It was almost completely dark outside now, except for the moon reflecting against the dark clouds overhead. The candlelight made the room glow. "It's getting cold," Jo said. "Let's go sit in the front room. We can put the fire on."

The whole house was without carpet, and Rhianna loved the effect. Almost like it was a cosy log cabin. The furniture was seventies modern, except for an old grandfather clock in the hall surrounded by dark wooden shelves laden with books.

Jo and Rhianna carried torches as they went into the front room. Jack followed on behind. He threw a match on the fire and it flared up. "It's gas," he said smiling.

Rhianna thought it looked completely real. "I like it."

As Jo lit candles and went back for the wine, Jack swung himself onto the couch next to Rihanna. She almost backed away, but then she realised she *wanted* to be close to him. But he misconstrued her hesitation. "I should go shower," he said smiling.

She shook her head. "No hot water."

"You're right. I forgot."

They chuckled and they stared into each other's eyes. *Oh, lord*, Rhianna thought. *I've got a crush on a guy I've just met.*

At No. 7

"WE'VE HAD A POWER CUT," Sandra said to Gladys. "It's all I need." She propped her head in hands as her elbows rested on the table.

"I think you should get some rest, dear." Gladys lit some candles and put one down on the table. "While the lights are out, there's nothing else we can do."

Sandra rubbed her eyes. Maybe Gladys was right. She was very tired. "I don't think I can go up there in the dark on my own," she said. "Frightened of ghosts!" She chuckled with irony. She'd spent the last five years being beaten by her vile husband, and now she was scared of the dark. *Ironic indeed.*

"Why don't you lie down on the settee? I can watch over you. You'll be okay."

Sandra's lips trembled. To hear those kind words…Now she was about to fall apart.

She sobbed, endlessly. She couldn't stop. Her lungs pulsed and her throat constricted while tears fell in gushing waves from her blinded eyes. Her shoulders rocked and her stomach tightened as if it was twisted in an unbreakable knot. As she cried, she felt a mother's tender embrace as she was guided into the sitting room and to the sofa. She rested her head on a soft cushion while her feet were lifted up, her shoes removed, and her body covered in a blanket. She wanted to sigh if only the sobbing would stop.

Then darkness fell in the darkness, as Sandra slept.

MARIGOLD KNOCKED ON THE FRONT DOOR. She saw a light coming down the blackened hall toward the glass. Gladys ushered her inside out of the cold.

"I've come to see if you're okay," she said. "I'm making the rounds with my torch."

"That's kind of you," answered Gladys. "How long do you think it'll be out?"

"It could come on at any time. I suppose a storm is brewing. It happens in these conditions." That was true. Last year, they'd had a raging storm in winter, and they lost their power for two days. That was when the neighbours united and helped each other. All except Eddie.

"Sandra is sleeping," Gladys said.

"Oh, okay. I won't disturb her then. You're both coming to the party at No.5, aren't you?"

"I'm not sure. Sandra's not feeling too good. She may sleep through it." Gladys was still on edge. Even more so than earlier.

Marigold decided to test the water. "How's Eddie?" She was convinced Sandra's despicable husband had run off, but earlier, when she'd pondered over that, she couldn't help thinking that running off was out of character for him. Why would he leave his own personal battering ram? *No*, now that Marigold had exhausted all possibilities as to Eddie's whereabouts, apart from him drowning in the bay, she couldn't help wondering if something more sinister was going on.

Gladys took her time answering. "Actually, he never came back from his swim."

Marigold suddenly went cold as chills ran up her spine. "What?"

They were still standing in the hall. Gladys was leaning on the door frame, looking all done in.

Marigold went into care mode and chided herself for thinking bad thoughts. She took Gladys' arm and guided her into the kitchens. She sat her down at the table where a candle burned and flickered in the centre. The sitting room doors were open, and Marigold looked inside. She saw a sleeping Sandra, lying on the couch with a checked blanket over her. The gas fire was on low, casting shadows over the walls and the ceiling. Marigold turned off her torch and closed the doors. She sat down at the table with Gladys, reaching out to touch her hand. "What's happened?"

Gladys bit her lip. "He never came back from his swim," she said.

"Oh my god."

She nodded. "Sandra went down to the beach when the tide was out, but she couldn't find him." Gladys' face was drawn. Her wrinkled skin was tired and opaque looking, and her shoulders were slumped as if she were a hunchback.

"Did you call the police?"

"Yes."

"What did they say?"

She looked toward the patio doors where their reflection in the glass blocked any images of the weather outside. "They said they would call the coast guard and start a search."

Something didn't seem right to Marigold. "But they came to the house, didn't they, to ask questions?"

"Oh, yes," Gladys rushed. "Yes, they came earlier."

"That's strange. I didn't notice a panda."

"Erhm. It was plain clothes. And a plain car. You wouldn't have noticed that."

"They couldn't have been here long. I think I would have seen a strange car inside the gates."

Gladys sighed as if she wanted to end the conversation.

Marigold wondered why on earth she had just spieled all that bull. She looked towards the door to the sitting room where Sandra slept. "You know, I'm wondering…"

"What are you 'wondering'?" Gladys tilted her head and stared directly at her. Her skin was ashen in the candlelight as it cast shadows over her creased face. By that one look, she had offered a challenge to Marigold.

Marigold decided to take it. "I was just wondering when you were going to stop lying and tell me what the hell has been going on here?"

At No. 5

EVA COULDN'T BELIEVE WHAT ROTTEN LUCK she was having. For the power to go off just before she was expecting people over was just about the sum of it.

She had arranged candles all over the living room. There could be nine coming to the party, so they would probably congregate in there. Shame it wasn't nicer weather. They could have gone outside on the terrace. Still, she'd have to make the most of it now. Especially since it looked like a storm was brewing.

Jade had placed two candles in the downstairs cloakroom and one in the hall next to the telephone, which was currently dead as a dodo. She couldn't even telephone people to let them know the party was still going ahead, or if they were coming at all.

She hadn't seen Mrs Butler all day. She'd gone over earlier and knocked on their door, but there was no answer. She supposed they'd been picked up by their daughter. At least Eva didn't have to have the conversation about why Roger hadn't invited Mr B on the golf trip. Just in case, she'd popped a note through the letterbox telling them that they were welcome to come over at 6 pm for cocktails with the rest of the neighbours. As for the non-invitation to golf, she'd just have to bluff her way through that.

Marigold was definitely coming and Kim too.

She'd invited Sandra and her mother, but she'd kept Eddie off *that* invitation. He couldn't be bothered to inform Roger that he wasn't going on the trip, so she couldn't be bothered asking him over for drinks. *A tooth for a tooth!*

She'd invited Jo (and Jack) from next door, but Eva doubted they'd come. She couldn't remember one social occasion they'd turned up for. Talk about keeping oneself to oneself. Jo and Jack must have invented the concept.

The new girl Rhianna would come. She'd said so earlier when she visited. That left Eva and Jade.

Assessing the house once more, she checked she had enough plates and glasses, enough food, laid out on the table in the kitchen, clean towels in the loo, enough candles, and that the fire was lit. Yes, everything looked in order and the place looked quite homely.

There wasn't much else she could do now but wait.

End of Part Two

Part Three

Chapter Twenty-three

DRAKE FISHER THREW WATER over Tyrone's face. The cold blast didn't waken him fully, but it was enough for him to recognise Drake so that the fear of god was instilled in him. *What joy!*

The day had turned out to be quite eventful.

After watching the bus depart Seaview, he'd hung around inside the empty house at No.3. From the darkened room, he'd watched the residents come and go like rats caught in a cage. It made him chuckle. If only they knew who was watching them.

After the milkman had turned up, removing the empties and leaving new, he noticed that No.5 had taken six bottles of fresh orange juice and four pints of milk. *Curious*, seeing as Roger Lang wasn't there for the weekend. He also noticed a woman turn up just as the bus was leaving. He wondered who she was, dressed up like a tart with that sparkly top on.

After the milkman had driven his van back through the gates, and after the postman had delivered the mail, and after the newspaper boy had delivered the papers, Drake decided that he couldn't have people coming and going all day long. Later, that afternoon, when things had quietened down, he'd go to the gates and cut the cable to the keypad. That will prevent anyone else coming in…and leaving.

Earlier, just before midday, he saw the woman from No.7 walk along *the eight,* carrying a co-op carrier bag. An old lady was with her. They were going toward the steps that led down to the beach.

He'd already checked out the steps before anyone got up that morning. He wanted to see if the people of Seaview had another exit, but when he looked down at those well-worn steps with the water at the bottom, he became quite giddy as he remembered his father and the cellar steps that had led him to purgatory. When he finally stopped the giddiness by leaning on the big stone with a sign that said *Descend At Your Peril*, he immediately slapped himself on the face, three times on the right and twice on the left. That had sorted him out, clearing his head of all intrusive thoughts and dreams. After all, he needed a clear head if he was going to do what he wanted to do when darkness came.

Drake thought it was odd when he saw the old lady on her own, go back along *the eight* and enter No.7. Why did the woman with the carrier bag go down to the beach alone? he wondered.

Twenty minutes later, from where he observed, he saw a girl wearing an anorak come out of No.6 and walk towards the steps. She went down, out of sight. He decided to keep an eye on them, so he fixed his gaze on the top of those steps and waited for one of them to emerge. Eight minutes later, the other woman came back up. She had the carrier bag screwed up in her hand, and it was empty.

Funny lot thought Drake.

In the afternoon, around about 4 pm, he decided he needed to get the ball rolling.

No one was around when he went down to the gate and cut the wire.

When that was done, he took some ladders from the Butler's garden and put them up against the nine-foot wall. He was happy that he could walk around freely at No.8. *They* wouldn't be catching him doing *anything* anymore.

He climbed the ladder and looked over the wall. With no one about, except for a car parked on the verge at the side of the road, he pulled up the ladders and put them down on the other side. After he climbed down, he went straight to the electrical box. He took out the lock, found the right wires and cut them with a pair of secateurs from the Butler's greenhouse. He knew he'd taken out the power when the lights on the gate went out. Tonight, when it was dark, he could work more freely, he thought, as he went back over the wall the way he came.

Now, while Tyrone was laid out on the kitchen floor, moaning from the pain, Drake leaned down and spoke close to his ear. "Where are your car keys?" Drake asked in that menacing way his father used to do when it put the fear of god into him. "They're not in your pocket, so where are they?"

Tyrone's eyes flickered from side to side before coming to rest on Drake's face. His eyes bulged in recognition as the one who had almost run him down with the forklift truck at Phillips Electronics factory floor. Drake smiled. "Yes, it's me. I'm back."

Chapter twenty-four

At No. 7

"I HEARD YOU EARLIER," Marigold said to Gladys. They were still sitting at the table while Sandra slept on the sofa.

"What do you mean?" Gladys asked.

Marigold could tell that her resolve was crumbling. Soon she would cave and tell all. Marigold was sure of it. "You and Sandra were talking in the garden. I was next door and heard everything you said."

Gladys' eyes widened as she recalled what they'd discussed.

"You were talking about a stone, about how you'd tossed it over the cliff," Marigold whispered. "Sandra remarked that there was now a hole in the rockery."

Gladys gulped and lowered her eyes.

"Then you talked about a wet suit. You talked about burying it on the beach."

As Gladys rubbed her tired eyes, a voice came out of the darkness and startled Marigold. "Tell her, mum," Sandra said. "Tell her everything."

Marigold turned to look at Sandra, standing there with a blanket around her. She was white as a sheet, with dark patches under her eyes. "Sit down, Sandra," Marigold pulled out a chair. Before she spoke, Marigold put her arm around her shoulders and hugged her. "Whatever has happened, I understand. I wouldn't blame you for anything."

She bowed her head.

Gladys began. "There was an accident…"

"No, mum," Sandra said softly. "Tell her the truth."

A pause crept between the three women, the 'truth' hanging in the air like a suspense novel. The candle on the table burned and flickered, illuminating their faces with foreboding. Around them, darkness reigned as if they were three witches sitting around a midnight campfire while casting spells and throwing potions into a cauldron. Then, before Sandra spoke, a draught came from somewhere and snuffed out the candle. One of them screamed before Gladys picked up a match and relit it.

Sandra took a deep breath. "I killed him," she said simply.

Marigold gasped. It was one thing to suspect the truth, but quite another to hear it coming from Sandra's lips.

"Last night…he raped me. He hurt me badly and somewhere in my mind something snapped. I was going to throw myself over the cliff, but mum stopped me."

Marigold looked at Gladys' gloomy face. Somehow, the death of Eddie had brought the two women together and it felt good. It felt right.

"When he came back from his swim. I hit him over the head with a rock. He died instantly."

Marigold covered her mouth with her hand. She couldn't speak.

"We got rid of all traces of blood and then we threw his body over the cliff to the sea."

With her hand still covering her open mouth, Marigold shook her head.

"We thought we could make it look like he'd been thrown against the rocks by the waves, but then we realised we'd killed him *after* he'd removed his wet suit. When his body is recovered, we won't be able to explain that." Sandra sighed at her own incompetence. "I buried his wetsuit in the sand, but I'm afraid it was a mistake we can't rectify. The police will know I killed him."

"Did you call the police. Like Gladys said you did?"

Gladys shook her head. "We were too afraid, and then, when we decided it would be for the best, the power went off and we couldn't use the phone."

A silence came between them then. The three were in cahoots, all wondering what the hell they were going to do.

At No. 3

RHIANNA LOOKED AT THE CLOCK. It was five-thirty.

Jack sat next to her with his empty wheelchair at the side, as if it was waiting for him. He looked normal as he sat staring at the fire, but while he moved his arms and his hands and his upper body, his legs remained still, lifeless, as if they were made of stone. In the darkness with just the flickering flames of the fire lighting he room, he looked more handsome than he had an hour ago, when Rhianna, just like that, had fallen head over heels in love. Love at first sight! She couldn't fathom it, but it had happened. She had been struck with the ability to see into a stranger's soul, his mind, his eternal desires and ambitions. It was a miracle, not something you could plan. It could only happen when you never expected it. To premeditate it was impossible. But the love…well, it was there, as clear as a blue sky on a summer's day.

She didn't know what to do. She could hardly come out and say it, to tell him that she was smitten. He wouldn't believe her, much less his sister. She would tell him to stay well clear of a woman who gave her heart so freely.

"Thanks for telling me about your accident," she said trying to stick to the reason for being there. "It must have been a terrible shock for you both."

Jo nodded. "It was. But we got over it, even when nobody else did."

"What about your parents?"

"Our father died of a head attack while Jack was still in hospital."

Rhianna shook her head, unable to imagine what that must have been like.

"When Jack was sent home, nobody could deal with his sudden incapacity. Our mother was a nervous wreck."

"My sister, here…" Jack said. "She took over. She decided to dedicate her life to me, even though I told her not to."

"We're twins, you see," said Jo as if that explained everything.

"We bought this place, with the misplaced notion that we would have privacy from the gawping world. We actually thought that being behind a gate would protect us. How wrong we were."

"What do you mean?" Rihanna asked.

"It was like being trapped in a goldfish bowl with seven other fish," Jo said. "At first, they stayed away, worried about disturbing us, but then they worried they weren't being neighbourly enough."

Jack turned to look at her. "We just wanted peace and quiet, and to go about our lives without having to explain anything. They made the assumption we were married, and we decided not to enlighten them. That's the other thing we've learned about human nature, they always see bad in everything. Soon rumours would have spread about the incestuous twins, living together in plain sight of their pure unsullied eyes."

Rhianna raised a brow. She wondered how true that was. Were Jo and Jack being over-sensitive, or would it really have turned out that way?

"What about relationships?" Rhianna asked, "Girlfriends, boyfriends?"

"There have been *people,* but we found it just complicated things."

"But Jo," Rhianna said, carrying on with her blunt attitude. Soon they would kick her out for over-stepping the mark. "I can understand Jack having his writing to keep him warm at night, but, you, Jo, what about you?"

She smiled. "I have my business to keep me warm," she said.

"What kind of business?"

"You wouldn't believe me if I told you."

Rhianna's eyes widened. "You'll have to spill the beans now. I won't be able to sleep tonight."

They laughed.

"I'll show you."

She got up and gave a torch to Rhianna. They went into a small room, with a single bed against one wall and a desk with a swivelling chair on the other. On the desk was a big box with a screen and a keyboard. Over the walls were charts and formulas, randomly hung, and fixed with drawing pins.

"What's this all about."

"I'm a research consultant for an American company," Jo shrugged as if it was no big deal. "Eight years ago, in '73, I worked for a guy who developed an *Ethernet,* for connecting multiple computers."

Bemused, Rhianna shook her head. "I don't even know what you just said."

Jo laughed. "One day, we believe everyone will have access to a computer and they'll be able to connect...and maybe even talk to each other."

"I think I'd prefer a telephone."

Jo stroked a chart on the wall next to the window. She shone the torchlight upon it. "This is what I'm working on now, along with many others," she said as if it were her baby.

Rhianna stepped closer unable to decipher the numbers and formulas. "What is it."

"We call it Word processing. We think it might be big one day, especially since we hope to add a print function."

"That reminds me," Rhianna said. "Do you have a typewriter I can borrow?"

At No. 7

IT WAS ALMOST SIX. Marigold realised that the cocktail party would start soon, and she was nowhere near ready. "Oh, my god," she announced as they sat huddled together.

Alarmed by her outburst, Sandra exclaimed. "What?"

"I still haven't checked on Mrs Butler next door. I should go."

Gladys stood up. "Wait." Marigold shone her torch just past her. "We need to know if you're going to keep this to yourself. We need to be prepared, you see."

"I'm not going to say anything, but honestly I'm at a loss to know what to do. You could perhaps make it look like suicide, but now that you've buried the wetsuit, it wouldn't fit into the scheme of things."

"You're being very matter-of-fact about the whole thing."

"I don't know what else to say." Marigold's anxiety levels were increased by the minute. All of this…well, the burden was too much. Goodness knows what Clive was going to say about it all. He wouldn't want her involved.

She shone the torch on Sandra's slumped shoulders, and she softened. "Look, I never liked Eddie and what he did to you, as far as I'm concerned, he deserved everything he got. But honestly, I can't afford to get involved in all of this. My husband will kill me. You understand, don't you?"

"Yes, of course," Sandra said softly. "You mustn't worry, as soon as the phone comes back on, we'll call the police. It's time to end this."

Marigold squeezed her shoulder. "I'll come back later, to see how you are."

"What will you say to Eva?" Gladys asked.

"Nothing. I'll simply say you're not well."

And then she left.

SHE WENT NEXT DOOR to No.8. It was dark as hell. Usually, the gate lights illuminated the Butler's garden, but without any light to guide her, and with the matter of Eddie still on her mind, unable to shed a feeling of foreboding, she felt like she was walking around a graveyard at night.

She couldn't see any candles burning inside. Maybe they had gone to their daughters after all.

She didn't know what made her open the garage, but she felt it was prudent to do so. Just to exhaust all possibilities. Sandra said she hadn't seen Mrs B all day, but perhaps they'd been too wrapped up in their own problems to notice.

Marigold twisted the handle and the garage door glided upwards. The car was still in there. *Odd!* She squeezed between the car and the breezeblock walls to the door at the far end. She banged loudly on it and waited to hear footsteps or for Mrs B to call out. Anything to let her know she was all right.

When no one came, she went out of the garage and around the other side. She looked up at the bedroom window at the back. It was the same place she'd stood earlier when she heard Sandra and Gladys plotting the downfall of Eddie. She saw no lights, candles or otherwise, but maybe that was because the curtains were closed.

She wondered if they had a spare key. She decided to try the greenhouse.

She opened the door inwards and shone her light.

The horror of what she saw made her gag, and scream - more like a high-tone moan- and drop her torch from her widespread fingers and go running – stumbling more like- to the house next door to bang on the windows of Sandra's house before her knees gave way.

Chapter Twenty-five

At No. 5

EVA OPENED THE DOOR TO HER FIRST GUEST. It was Kimberly from No.1. "Come in, Kim," she said, "Come in."

Kimberly looked splendid. She wore a red dress and black boots. A gold pendant hung around her neck and above it all she wore a denim jacket. With her long dark hair falling down her back and gold hoops in her ears, she looked sassy. She was only 5'5", but she was most obviously her own woman, independent and smart. Eva admired her and wished she could look that good.

"What can I get you to drink?"

They walked through to the kitchen. Jade was in there, mixing martinis in a shaker. She still wore her sparkly top, since she hadn't brought anything to change into. Compared to Kim, Jade looked like a chic-less tart.

She introduced them. "Kim works at Phillips with Roger," Eva said.

"Really?" said Jade. "Are you a secretary or something?"

Kim curled her lip in a half-snarl while she tilted her head. "What makes you ask that?"

Jade shrugged. "I just thought…"

"Yep, I know. Because I'm a female right?"

"Well, of course, I don't know anything about you…"

Eva was watching Jade's discomfort and Eva enjoyed every second of it. "She's management," Eva said touching Kim's arm. "A very clever lady."

Turning her back, Jade poured a martini from the shaker. She placed a cherry on a stick on the side.

Kim was frowning, trying to get a better look at Jade's face. "Have we met?"

Jade shook her head. "I don't think so."

The air between them was thick as mud and even though Eva had thoroughly enjoyed, immensely, the uncomfortable tete-a-tete, she didn't want the party ruined. She placed her hand on Kim's arm and guided her away. "I can't believe the power's not on yet."

"I know. I intend to put in a serious complaint on Monday," said Kim. They went into the lounge. "Pretty with just candles, though."

"Thank you."

"I thought Marigold might have been here already."

"She'll be here soon. Last time I saw her she was going around the houses with a torch checking on everyone."

Kim chuckled. "Typical Marigold."

They laughed together as they sat down.

The fire was glowing, keeping the room warm and cosy. What with the candle flames dancing in shadows over the walls, the room looked like it was moving, alive, despite anyone being there yet. "The other guests will be here soon," said Eva. "I told everyone six."

Then Kim held her finger in the air. "I've just realised where I've seen your friend before."

"Jade? Where?"

Kim hesitated as if she was reluctant to say anything. "Well…at work. She was with your husband in his office."

At No. 7

MARIGOLD STUMBLED HER WAY across the Butler's lawn to the house next door, to Sandra's house. She could hardly get her breath as if she'd been struck dumb. She literally couldn't force any sound from her mouth. She almost tripped up the step to the patio and then she caught her foot on the hose attached to the tap, abandoned on the floor like a preying snake.

For the second time that day, she banged on the glass of Sandra's patio doors. Now she was gasping for air as a stray tear fell down her left cheek. She didn't know if it had been the wind stinging her eyes that had made that happen, or that it was indeed tears of fear.

Sandra quickly slid open the window and the wind blew Marigold inside. She leaned against the door as Gladys rushed to bring her a cup of water. "Here, drink this," she said as Marigold sat down.

"What is it, Marigold?" Sandra yelled. "What's wrong?"

"The Greenhouse…" she spluttered. "I looked inside."

"What, what?"

"Mrs Butler's cat," she sobbed. "He was hanging from a chain around his neck." She took a breath. "His body had been slit from the neck down to his belly…blood everywhere…and guts…spilling out…" She couldn't finish. She put her hands over her face to block out the gruesome sight. "I've never seen anything like it."

"But who would do something like that?" Sandra said.

She shook her head. "I don't know, but now I'm worried…about where Mrs B is right now."

At No. 5

RHIANNA HADN'T CHANGED her clothes and she hoped the hostess wouldn't mind.

"Come in," Eva said when she opened the door.

Rhianna stepped around some lanterns on the front doorstep with candles burning inside. Even though they were surrounded by glass, the flames still flickered as the wind picked up.

Eva shut the door. She looked as if she had something on her mind. Rhianna was often good at picking up on things like that. Her mother often called her psychic, but that wasn't true.

"The wind is strong," Eva said. "It may prevent the power coming back on if this keeps up."

"They might be fixing it as we speak," Rhianna said, optimistically.

"I hope you're right. We really could do with a break, don't you think?"

They went into the lounge. Two women were sitting on the sofa. One was Jade, whom she'd met earlier that afternoon, but she didn't know the other one.

"This is Kim from No.1," Eva said.

"Hi."

She looked at Rhianna as she introduced her. "This is Rolf's at No.6's niece," she said.

"Rhianna." She offered a little wave.

"What would you like to drink?"

"Do you have wine?"

"Blue Nun?"

"Lovely."

"Sit down," Jade said. Rhianna noticed Eva give Jade a look of distaste. Rhianna wondered why Jade was there if Eva didn't like her. She may never find out.

She directed her attention to Kim. "Lived here long?"

"Almost two years. I rent."

Rhianna nodded. The small talk would be difficult to get through while her mind was still on Jack.

After Jo had shown her the work she was doing, they'd returned to the sitting room.

Jack was back in his wheelchair.

"I should go," said Rhianna. "Eva's party starts around about now."

Jack propelled toward her. *Wow*, she was enamoured by him, his strength, his dignity, his intelligence. "I wish I had more time to talk about writing," she offered. "I'd love to know about your preferred genre."

"There's always tomorrow," he said.

WHEN EVA GUIDED RHIANNA into the sitting room, Kim was sitting with her legs elegantly crossed, and her smart black leather boots up to her knees. Eva made introductions and offered Rhianna a drink, Jade invited her to sit down. The nerve of her, thought Eva. Whose house was it? Certainly not Jades.

Eva had a shock earlier. Kim said that she'd seen Jade in Roger's office at work. It didn't quite make sense and she planned to quiz Roger about it when he got back from his golf trip. Why would Jade be there, at Philips Electronics? Then she stopped as realisation hit her like a bowling ball smashing into a cluster of ninepins. The two of them! No, it couldn't be. She thought back to the times she'd heard Jade's name associated with her husbands. That night of the dinner party when Harry accused them of having an affair! Was it true? Would Roger betray her with an ageing tart like Jade? She didn't know what to think. But she was going to think about it. She was going to think about it really hard.

Chapter Twenty-six

At No. 7

SANDRA WAS TRYING TO PLACATE MARIGOLD. She had been shaken by the vision of the cat in the greenhouse, shaken to the core. "Listen to me," Sandra said.

Marigold blew her nose in a handkerchief tucked up her sleeve.

"Your eyes were probably deceiving you. You saw something else, maybe a stuffed cat...or something...It wouldn't surprise me that you were spooked after hearing what had happened to Eddie, but I honestly think you're off the mark here." Sandra looked at Gladys who had her arm around Marigold's shoulder. "I just think you were seeing things...that you'd had a shock. After all, you only had the torchlight. The beam from a torch can distort things, make things look worse than they are."

Marigold took a long sniff through her nose. "You really think so?"

"I do."

Gladys squeezed Marigold's arm. "We can go together and prove it, okay?"

Marigold nodded. "I dropped my torch."

"That's okay, we have a torch."

"Mum," Sandra said. "Stay here. I don't want you tripping up."

Sandra surprised herself. She was in charge for what seemed like the first time in years. And she wasn't afraid. She felt invigorated and she welcomed the distraction from the issue that hung over her head, the issue of Eddie. When the lights came back on, she would ring the police and confess to killing her husband. She couldn't let Gladys take the blame for what she'd done. Maybe the courts would be lenient. She had enough witnesses to attest to Eddie's behaviour toward her. He was gone now. She wouldn't have to fear him anymore. She could start again.

Marigold seemed happier now that she'd been talked around. Maybe she had seen something that resembled a dead cat. A plant or something. "I'd still like to check on Mrs B," Marigold said. "Just to see if she has indeed gone to her daughters."

"To her daughters? No, that can't be right. Mr Butler has been in bed with the flu. She wouldn't have gone anywhere."

"If that's true, then why haven't we seen them all day?"

Then Sandra had a notion. "Oh, my goodness," she said. "Maybe Mrs B went down with the flu too. They could both be laid up."

"The poor things!" Gladys said. "And with no power on."

"I'll take the key," said Sandra.

Marigold looked relieved. "You have a spare key!"

"Yes, and she has mine."

MARIGOLD COULD HARDLY BELIEVE she was going back to the greenhouse. Sandra had tried to convince her she'd been seeing things, but the more Marigold thought about it, she was convinced she saw a hanging, slaughtered cat.

Leaving Gladys in the house with the candles, Sandra led with a torch shining down into their path. "Don't trip," Sandra said stepping over the discarded hosepipe.

Marigold followed close behind.

Up in the heavens, dark clouds blocked the light from the moon while the wind stirred them up like a whisk in a pot of beef consommé. The sky moved far quicker than life in Seaview. In Seaview, everything was moving slowly, as if the day had been stretched into the night and now the night stretched before them, first light so far away.

They arrived at the greenhouse door and Sandra bent down and picked up Marigold's torch. It still worked even though it had shut down on impact when she dropped it on the floor. The door had closed on its own, so now, Sandra offered a reassuring smile before she pushed it inward. The torchlight shone inside to potted seeds and tomato plants, but there was no cat, dead or otherwise.

Marigold moved past Sandra standing in the doorway. Now she *was* spooked because she was utterly convinced that only ten minutes before she had definitely seen that hanging slaughtered cat. "I don't understand it," she murmured.

"I told you," Sandra said. "You were spooked, and you saw something that *looked like* a dead cat. It's the only explanation."

"I suppose so." But deep down, Marigold wasn't entirely convinced.

"Come on, let's go check on Mrs B."

They went around the front and put the key in the latch. The door opened, then shuddered as it hit the security chain. "Damn," Sandra said. She pushed it open again until it stopped six inches in. "Hello," she called. "Mrs Butler are you there? Are you all right?"

The two women stopped and listened, but they got no response.

"I've got the strangest feeling," said Marigold.

Sandra remained upbeat, but Marigold was sure she was trying to be brave for her benefit. It was a side of Sandra she'd never seen before and Marigold liked it. *Good on her!*

"Let's try the back door."

As they closed the front door and removed the latch key, they both turned to look towards the top of *the eight*, to see Kim knocking on No.5's door. They watched as Eva opened it and welcomed her inside.

"The party has started," Marigold said from behind her.

SANDRA COULD FEEL HER HANDS SHAKING. She was trying to keep a brave face on things, for Marigold's sake, *and* for her own, but the day had truly taken its toll on her. After everything that had happened with Eddie, now there she was creeping around in the dark looking for Mrs Butler.

They went around the side of the house. On impulse, Sandra tested the handle and pressed it down.

The door opened.

"I can't believe it," said Marigold.

"Didn't you try the door before?"

"Well, no. I just assumed it would be locked."

They spoke no more as they stepped inside the kitchen of No.8.

Chapter Twenty-seven

At No. 5

"I THINK JO MIGHT COME," Rhianna said.

Eva looked surprised. "I don't think she will. We've invited her to many things in the past, but she never accepted."

"Did you invite Jack too?"

Eva guffawed. "No of course not. He's in a wheelchair." Eva sipped her drink. Rhianna noticed she was staring at Jade a lot, making evil eyes at her.

"Well, maybe if you'd invited him too, he could have decided himself if he wanted to come or not." Rhianna felt like kicking herself. The last thing she wanted to do was cause trouble for Jo and Jack, but honestly, were people *that* single-minded?

"Did they say as much?" Eva asked.

Now she'd torn it. If Jo did turn up to Eva's party, would Eva confront her on the issue? It wouldn't surprise Rhianna if she did. "She didn't say anything, in case you're wondering. It was just my own observation.

Eva pouted as if she was wondering if Rhianna was sincere. Yes, Rhianna had torn it, all right.

KIM WAS TRYING HER BEST not to think about Tyrone, but it was hard not to become distracted when there was little or no decent conversation. How she hated small talk.

In her mind, she'd exhausted all explanations as to his whereabouts. His car had been outside the gates since twelve last night. If it had broken down and he'd grabbed a lift, as Marigold had suggested, wouldn't he by now have collected his car?

She'd tried phoning him up until the very last moment the power had gone off. If he'd gotten a lift home, wouldn't he have answered when she rang?

Nothing made sense and the small talk that was going on was giving her a serious bloody headache. She decided to give it ten minutes and then she'd make her excuses and leave.

EVA GLANCED AT THE CLOCK on the mantelpiece where a pair of silver candlestick held white candles, making it look like an altar. "I wonder what's keeping the others," she said.

Jade was standing next to the radio. Fortunately, it had batteries, so at least they had *some* music. She watched her twiddling the dial to get a different station. She was starting to get Eva riled. Who the hell did she think she was, coming in her house and taking over?

When Simon and Garfunkel sang *The Sound of Silence*, Eva thought how apt, considering the lack of guests.

She looked at Kim. She was absently playing with the cuff of her denim jacket. "Is something wrong, Kim?" Eva asked.

She looked up, surprised that someone had targeted her. "Erhm, no. I was just thinking about a friend of mine."

Eva refrained from rolling her eyes. The party was bombing.

Then all heads turned when they heard a knock on the door. They all looked relieved.

Maybe it was someone who would stir the place up, get a few laughs going, some decent conversation...They could only hope.

Chapter Twenty-eight

At No. 7

SANDRA AND MARIGOLD were given a glass of brandy to calm their nerves. Gladys could only sit by and watch them as they came to terms with what they'd found at No.8.

Sandra felt like she was in shock, and that the vision she'd seen was as much a figment of her imagination as Marigold's when she'd imagined seeing the slaughtered cat.

They'd walked into the kitchen of the Butler's house. It was insanely quiet apart from a battery clock ticking on the windowsill. They had two torches now and the double beams of light crossed over as both women randomly searched for life.

Sandra called out, but it came out as a whisper. "Mrs Butler?"

Marigold came out of the lounge. She shook her head. No one in there. "We should try upstairs."

Sandra had watched enough films in her time, which quite frankly reminded her of the steps they were taking right now. Friday night TV was the best. There was always a late film showing before it closed down at midnight: Dracula, The Mummy, Frankenstein…all in a backdrop of dark houses with candlelight burning in the terrible gloom. But this…this was real, and it was making her feel sick to the stomach with sheer horror.

At the top of the stairs, she stopped. "You know what, this is ridiculous. We're just freaking ourselves out with our very active imaginations."

"Hardly surprising after seeing that cat."

"But Marigold, you didn't see a cat, remember? There was *no* cat."

Marigold shrugged as they walked the short length of the landing to the back bedroom where the Butlers slept. They shone the torch and took one final glance at each other. Then, expecting to dissolve into a fit of laughter when they discovered the room was empty, they pushed open the door.

Two mounds filled the bed.

It was the most curious of scenes. They looked like two long pillows covered over with a blanket, as if a couple of escapees were pretending to be fast asleep, tucked up in bed, when really, they were out on the town, painting it red.

In the dark, Sandra approached the bed while Marigold shone the torch. She shook her head as if she wanted to dispel the thoughts going through her mind. She was overdramatising the whole thing. She was convinced of it.

She grabbed the blanket and pulled it off the two forms below it, then she took a step back as if she'd been hit by a train and knocked into the wall.

Next to her, Marigold screamed as they both looked down upon the bodies of Mr and Mrs Butler, murdered in their beds, with ties still wrapped around their throttled necks, their eyes staring nowhere and their mouths agape, their tongues hanging out, as if they had each suffered a stroke.

Pinned up against the wall, the two women couldn't breathe, but that was only seconds before they ran from the room and down the stairs, crashing through the back door and spilling out into the garden.

MARIGOLD WAS SHAKING from head to toe for the second time in an hour. She'd been sledgehammer-ed over the head three times that day, what with the news of Eddie's death and now the Butlers.

"What happened?" Gladys asked after they'd downed their brandy in one straight gulp.

Sandra stared right into her eyes. "They're dead."

"Who's dead?" It was the simplest of questions.

"Mr and Mrs Butler…killed…strangled."

"That's ridiculous. They couldn't…"

Marigold sat up in the chair making her back straight as a ramrod. If she hadn't, she felt like she would have remained a hunchback forever. "It's true. They've been murdered."

Gladys sat down. How long had the three of them sat at that table deliberating the events of the day?

A silence fell between them like an invisible brick wall. None of them knew what to say. It was hard enough trying to map it out in their minds, but to speak of it…well, it just didn't seem real. Marigold wondered if she was being a victim of some cruel prank.

Maybe Sandra and Gladys were in on it…to make her look foolish. Soon, Eddie and the Butler's would jump out from the darkness shouting 'SURPRISE!'

Then her shoulders slumped again, along with a rounded spine crushed under the weight of her troubles. No, what had happened there today was no joke. It was very, very real.

"We should call the police."

As soon as Gladys said it, Marigold could tell she hadn't first thought about the statement. There was *no* phone. Her remark hung in the air like a whirling dervish, spiralling out of control while they all considered the consequences of what they'd seen. The first question to come out of their lips was Sandra's when she asked, "Who could have done it?"

They stared at her, perhaps a little aggrieved that she should ask a question they couldn't answer.

None of it made sense. Marigold had arrived an hour ago to find out that Sandra had killed her husband and now two more murders were on her mind. How could that even be? Maybe Sandra killed them. Maybe Mrs B had witnessed her killing Eddie. Maybe Mrs B threatened to tell all, so Sandra went next door and strangled her…with a tie…and Mr Butler too…and then covered up the bodies…

Marigold slammed on the brakes of her over-active imagination. No, all of that didn't make sense. In fact, there was no explanation. She was literally stumped.

She rubbed her eyes and then felt her hair. Earlier she'd put rollers in. She'd planned on waiting until the last minute to brush out the curls after she'd got dressed for the party. Why did she come over to find out if they were all okay? Why hadn't she just stayed safely in her own house, minding her own business? And to top it all, what the hell was Clive going to say when he came home?

SANDRA WAS ON THE VERGE of another breakdown. How many breakdowns could someone have in one day?

Marigold looked like she had the troubles of the world on her shoulders and now, she too was sinking into a pit of despair. All logical thought process had exited her brain. There was no explanation for what had happened next door. Why would someone want to kill them? What harm had the old couple ever done anyone?

"I'm going to walk into town," she said suddenly as the other two women looked up sharply.

"What?"

"Someone has to notify the police. It will have to be me."

"No, wait."

"Stop," said Gladys.

Marigold reached across the table and pressed her hand down on Sandra's. "You won't get through the gates. They don't work without power."

"Okay, I'll go over it."

"That's a nine-foot high gate. And besides. You'll hurt yourself trying to get over it. It has spikes remember?

"So, I'll go over the wall then. If we can find some ladders…"

Marigold shook her head. "No, we have to think about this."

"What's there to think about? Three people are dead. I don't care about Eddie, but someone needs to inform the Butler's family."

"I don't think it's as easy as that?" said Marigold.

"Why not?"

"Because, if you go and confess to killing Eddie, they'll think you killed the Butlers too."

"What?" Sandra frowned and scoffed. "Why would I want to hurt them?"

"You wouldn't, but the police won't know that."

Sandra paused, thinking things through…no, it was impossible. No one would blame her. Would they? "If I don't go into town and report this, what would you suggest we do?"

"Wait until morning."

"What difference will it make?"

Then Marigold stopped. Her eyes fixed on a place behind Sandra's shoulder. She was deep in thought. Her eyes had glazed over. Her lips had formed a pensive pout. She was still as if to move would have distracted her.

"What is it?" asked Gladys.

She broke the spell on her own accord. "I think I have an idea."

SANDRA HAD HER OWN IDEAS. "What if the murderer is still around here somewhere?"

"No, he'll be long gone by now. I think the bodies must have been in there like that all day. If they were robbed, the perpetrator would have made a dash for it hours ago."

"Unless he's still inside Seaview," Gladys said. "And he can't get out either. Maybe he's waiting to rob us too."

"I find that hard to believe," Marigold said

"I find it *all* hard to believe."

"Look, I've been thinking about something…I'm not sure how we can spin it yet, but there's a chance we could work this to our advantage."

"Our advantage?" said Sandra frowning at Marigold's evaluation.

"What if the robber or killer…whatever he is…what if the police assume that he killed Eddie too?"

"What?"

"Think about it." Marigold stood up and paced back and forth. Her head was filled with plots and tactics. She'd never felt so fired up. "Is it so hard to imagine that the guy, whoever he is, killed Eddie too? It would get you off the hook, Sandra."

Gladys tuned in, going along with Marigolds thought process. "If the killer gets caught for the murder of the Butlers, no one's going to believe him if he denies killing Eddie."

Marigold pursed her lips tight together and nodded knowingly. "Exactly."

"No, that couldn't work," Sandra said. "Could it?"

Chapter Twenty-nine

At No. 5

EVA ANSWERED THE DOOR ONCE MORE. It was Jo from next door at No.4. "Well, hello," said Eva, without any control over the surprise she felt that Jo had turned up at all.

She hesitated on the doorstep. "I…I thought I'd been invited."

Eva was confused why she'd just said that until she realised she was blocking the entrance. She stepped aside. "Of course you are. Come in. Come in."

Jo carried a bottle of red wine and a posy of flowers. She handed them to Eva. "From our garden," she said.

"Oh, lovely, thank you. That's very considerate."

She wore jeans with a black leather jacket over a white t-shirt. Eva thought she had a wonderful figure. She had long reddish hair and her skin was sublime. Her teeth were perfectly formed, and she had the most amazing green eyes. Eva couldn't remember ever noticing how attractive she was. On the rare occasions she'd met them, Eva had perhaps focused more on the husband, Jack. He was a physically frail man, and she'd dished out enough pity to satisfy any guilt she may have felt for not spending more time with them. The truth was, Eva never knew what to say to them. She was always afraid of putting her foot in it.

She'd often wondered how they coped. Surely, they were bored staying in their house day after day and not mixing socially with their neighbours. She'd noticed them going out a few times when Jo had pushed his wheelchair along *the eight* to the gates, but there had been one particular time when Eva bumped into them.

That Sunday morning the sun was shining, but a cool breeze kept the temperature down. She'd had her own brisk walk when she arrived back and thought the gates had opened on their own. That was until she looked downwards and saw Jack in his wheelchair. "Oh," she said. "I didn't see you there."

He smiled politely.

Eva had raised her voice a little. "Are you on your own?"

He didn't answer and she remembered wondering why. Perhaps he was deaf too. She repeated her question, a little louder that time, but he remained staring at her with a strange frown on his face. Behind him she saw Jo walking briskly towards them, carrying a checked blanket.

"Hi," she said.

"Here, let me help." Uninvited, Eva took the blanket from Jo's hand and put it across Jack's lap. She tucked it in at the sides, making him all cosy.

"What are you doing?" he said indignantly.

"There is quite a wind-up. You don't want to get cold."

Jo stepped forward and whipped the blanket from his lap. "I fetched the blanket so that I could sit down on the grass," she said. "He doesn't need you fussing over him," she snapped.

"Oh," Eva laughed awkwardly. "Well, that will be nice...sitting on the grass, I mean."

They didn't say any more. Jo simply took hold of the wheelchair and pushed Jack out of the gates. As it closed behind them, Eva shouted, "Enjoy your stroll."

Now Jo was as friendly as could be, so maybe she wasn't as stuck up as Eva had first assumed.

RHIANNA WAS RELIEVED when she saw Jo walk into the lounge. She stood up and went towards her. "Am I glad to see you," she whispered.

Jo chuckled. "Not as glad as I am to see you."

"Jack didn't want to come?" Rhianna was disappointed. She hoped she see him again. Before she left his house earlier, he'd shown her to the door. He was about to open it, but he stopped and touched her hand. She'd wrapped her fingers around his and they looked at each other as if they both knew what the other was thinking. It made Rhianna's heart jump to realise he felt the same way. And touching him, even if they were just holding hands, was exciting.

"He thought he'd let us get on with it," she said. "Socialising with a group of women isn't really his thing. He's writing by candlelight."

Rhianna smiled endearingly as she imagined him writing a chapter in the dark with just a candle to guide him. "Jo," she started. "Can I tell you something?"

"What, that you like my brother?"

"Don't you mind?"

"He likes you too."

"He does?" That made Rhianna feel very happy.

"Jack doesn't take to people very quickly. He seems to see straight through them and most of the time he prefers to stay away. But with you, he liked what he saw. He liked *you.*"

"Do you think we could perhaps go for a walk tomorrow? Do you think he'd come?"

"Yes, I bet he would."

EVA WAS SURPRISED that Marigold hadn't shown up. It was 6.30 now, way past the planned time of arrival. And where was Sandra? Wasn't she coming either? Maybe Eddie wouldn't let her, since he hadn't gone on the golf trip. She wished she could get in touch with Roger. Her imagination had been on overtime and she needed to talk to him.

Why would Jade have been in his office? For what reason? Harry was his best mate, surely, he wouldn't betray him, let alone Eva. But *she* had betrayed *him* with Harry, hadn't she? So, who was she to talk?

Harry had promised to call her this evening. She wondered if he'd tried and what he'd thought when he couldn't get through? Oh, why couldn't the power come back on? That damn electric company!

Then, someone else knocked on the door.

MARIGOLD WENT INSIDE with her knees shaking. Adrenalin! On her arm was Eddie's mother Gladys. She seemed frail next to her, her stride laborious as she forced one foot in front of the other. The woman was exhausted. Marigold wondered how much sleep she'd had over the past twenty-four hours.

They'd met before, Marigold and Gladys. It was on a night like that one when Marigold had popped over to talk to Sandra. Eddie was nowhere in sight. 'Down the pub,' Sandra told her. When she asked where Gladys was, uninterested, Sandra had tossed her head towards the lounge. Marigold knew there was no love lost between the two of them and she assumed that Gladys was a docile and deaf old biddy who worshipped the ground her son walked on. How wrong she was.

That night, she and Sandra had chatted about the new resident, Kimberly Cutter. They'd disapproved of her single girl status, living alone and working her way up the career ladder. They thought it was shocking. That was the end of '79.

Eddie had come home early, and a little worse for wear. Marigold could see it in his bloodshot eyes. He talked in a way that was offensive to Marigold, but at the time she put it down to him being drunk as a skunk. Sandra had whispered to her, 'You'd better go.'

Marigold resisted, wanting to prove to Sandra that she wouldn't be intimidated by any man, drunk or not. Then Eddie shoved her. 'Go home,' he said.

It was the most humiliating treatment she'd ever received, and she intended to relate the whole tale to Clive when she got home. But she never did. Because the next minute, Sandra was on the floor holding her face after Eddie had slapped her. Marigold had rushed to her defence. Sandra was crying, holding her cheek. Gladys came out of the lounge and saw her on the floor. She looked at Eddie, seemingly unperturbed by the commotion he'd caused, then she walked past them and went upstairs, not saying one word in Sandra's defence. Marigold had never told Clive because she knew he would have prevented her from going over there again. He may even have hit Eddie.

Earlier, after they'd left No.7 to walk along *the eight* towards Eva's house, Marigold brought up the subject to Gladys. Their arms were hooked together, taking it slow. 'Why didn't you do anything?' Marigold said.

"You have no idea how much I was tortured by looking the other way," she answered reluctantly. "I've seen him abuse her so many times, it broke my heart watching her struggling to survive that pointless marriage. She took it like a true survivor and I had always admired her for it. She's strong, with great fortitude. People don't see her that way, but I saw it. I saw it whenever he knocked her down and she got back up again."

"And yet, you never said anything?"

"Like what? He never listened when he was a boy. He watched his father do the same thing to me. There was nothing I could have said that was going to change him. He was raised watching an abusive relationship, and he carried it on to his own home. He wasn't clever enough to make his own history. He was weak like his father."

Marigold contemplated her words as they walked silently for the rest of the way. She was amazed at how close the two women were now. They had bonded within minutes of Eddie's demise and in conspiracy, they would be forever in each other's lives. How wonderful for Sandra, to have a mother like her. They could face the whole matter side by side. Give each other comfort and strength. Marigold almost envied them.

But then she thought about the murder hanging over their heads.

Now she was resolute to remain strong and help them through the road ahead. More importantly, she would go to the ends of the earth to keep Sandra out of jail.

Chapter Thirty

DRAKE FISHER HAD WATCHED the whole thing. It was really funny. When he saw that busybody from No.2 go along *the eight* with her torch, he wanted to jump out and grab her, drag her into the bushes and pulverise her with a rock. But he wasn't ready. And it would have been too messy.

As he watched her go into No.7, he thought about his mother to while away the time. His throat constricted and he shuddered with revulsion and ecstasy all at the same time.

After father left, and now the man of the house, one of Drake's duties was to throw a canister of disinfectant bleach down the cellar steps to disguise the smell wafting up. He knew it was his father's body rotting down there, and he often took pleasure in imagining his white, wrinkled, rotting face as it floated in the stinking water flooding the cellar.

Every week, on a Friday night, he would take the key and open the cellar door. At that time of the evening, Mother would be sitting in the front room watching TV, staying out of the way while Drake shook out the contents of the bleach canister and spewed it down the steps to the bottom. It was very effective, because, instead of having a whiff of father's rotting corpse, the clean smell of disinfectant bleach would waft up, giving the air a whole new appeal, smelling like the public swimming baths.

Mother never mentioned the cellar, except for one day when she complained about the rising damp. They were in the kitchen eating porridge when she saw the blackness in the corner of the outside wall, near the back door. "We'll have to get that cellar sumped, Drake," she said at the time.

He looked up from his bowl with his spoon in mid-air. "No, I told you, I'm in charge of the cellar and I won't let anyone go down there," he said.

"We won't have any choice soon. The damp will keep on rising, I reckon."

"Let it."

"We can't do that. It'll affect the whole house."

"I don't care. No one is allowed down there. I have the key, remember."

"But Drake…"

That was when he dropped his spoon filled with lumpy porridge and slapped himself across the face, three times on the left and twice on the right. She'd seen him do it before, but only when had turned away from her, but that day was the first time he'd faced her and done it. She looked shocked and terrified at the same time, which Drake thought was the most empowering thing to happen to him. Yes, he was in control and he liked it a lot.

"Drake," she said. "I know what you did."

"What did I do?" He picked up his spoon and shovelled the porridge into his mouth.

All he heard was her silence. Interfering old cow.

Now, tonight, when he watched Marigold come out of No.7 with her stupid torch, he saw her go next door to No.8 where the Butler's lived (used to live!!). He watched her as she opened the garage door, sidling down the side of the car to the back entrance. She knocked and called out, but no one answered. Of course, they didn't! He watched her come back out and walk around the side to the greenhouse. That was when things started to get good. She opened the door and shone her torch inside and when the light hit the cat, she'd dropped her torch and ran with her tail between her legs, back to the house next door. What a laugh!

That's when he went in and removed the hanging cat. There wasn't much blood since he'd killed it before he hung it. It had allowed him a good position to cut its belly from the neck to the navel. When Marigold saw it, her face was a picture. Drake enjoyed every moment of it.

He watched from the side of the greenhouse when she came back with her friend from No.7. They didn't see his face standing there, staring through the glass in the dark. If they had shone their torch his way, they would have had the fright of their life. *That* would have been funny. Instead, they left and went to the house looking for the Butlers. He could see them through the kitchen window shining their torches inside. Then it went dark and he knew they'd gone upstairs. He watched with much anticipation.

Soon they would find their friends and then the night games would begin.

End of part three

Part Four

Chapter Thirty-one

SANDRA WAITED FOR MARIGOLD and Gladys to go into No.5. She had a job to do and she needed to do it while everyone was inside at the party.

She had her torch in hand when she began her descent down the cliff steps to the beach. It was a hazardous journey, but she needed to get down there, *now*, before the tide came back in.

They'd planned the whole thing, talking it through…about how Sandra would relate the tale to the police.

'We waited all day and night for Eddie to make contact after we'd assumed he'd run off…'

"Wait," Sandra interrupted, "What about the car? If he was going to 'run off', why wouldn't he take the car?'

The question hung in the air like a pregnant pause, until…

'It broke down the night before after he picked up his mum from the care home. The brakes or something…'

"We could cut the brake wires," said Gladys.

"Good idea," said Marigold.

'We waited to hear from him…'

Gladys stopped them again. "How could he go anywhere…if the car didn't work?"

Another pause.

In cahoots, the three women churned the details over in their calculating minds, as if they were watching a detective show on the television.

"Columbo would see right through this," Gladys said. She looked as if she was about to panic. Her face had turned white and her lips sagged as if she had no bottom teeth. She looked drained, physically exhausted.

"He could have walked."

Gladys shook her head and rubbed her eyes. Her hands were shaking, not from old age, but from nerves and extreme tension. The whole experience was taking its toll on her and Sandra wondered how much more she could take. "No, this isn't making sense. Let's go back to the beginning."

Sandra had a fresh idea: *'Eddie wasn't feeling very well. He decided not to go on the golfing trip and to stay in bed all morning -* that will tie in with the witnesses- *After lunch, when he felt better, when the tide went back out, he decided to go and have his regular daily swim. He never came back and then the power went off so we couldn't call anyone.'*

She stopped and looked at the other two women. They gawped at her as they contemplated if the story made sense.

"What about the wetsuit?"

'We found Eddie's wetsuit in the greenhouse next door. We thought that perhaps the killer had taken him there, removed the wetsuit, bashed him over the head, and then pushed him over the cliff.'

Silence.

"Wouldn't we have seen something...heard something?"

'It must have happened when it was dark because we never saw anything. We didn't hear anything, because we'd taken a nap...because of the stress of worrying about Eddie.'

That means we'll have to get the wetsuit back." Gladys said.

That's when the three women looked at each other and sighed.

Now, Sandra was making her way along *the eight*, towards the steps leading down to the beach. As soon as she planted the wetsuit in the greenhouse, she'd quickly change and then go to the party to start working on their alibi.

At No. 5

IN THE HOUSE, Marigold helped Gladys into the lounge and lowered her into a comfortable armchair. She shouldn't be there. Her feet were dragging, she should be tucked up in bed, but the alibi was important if they were going to save Sandra from spending the rest of her life in jail.

"Can you get her a glass of water, please?" she said to Eva. People were standing up, hovering over her, fussing. Gladys looked like she was ready to faint.

"What's happened?" one of them asked.

"She's had a shock."

The women in the room stood about waiting for Marigold to relate the tale. She couldn't have known that they were happy that, at last, something was happening to liven up that damn party.

KIM STOOD WATCHING AND OBSERVING. What on earth was going on? Why was that old lady there? She looked like she should be put to bed with a couple of Valium. Her speckled, wrinkled hands were trembling so hard, she couldn't possibly hold a glass of water. Her pallor was ashen like she'd just seen a ghost, and her eyes were glassy yellow as if she hadn't slept for a couple of days. Her bottom lip trembled and sagged with no substance, and her tired cheeks, lined and discoloured, hung at the sides of her face making it appear as if she was slowly melting.

Eva barged past with a glass of fresh water in her hand. Marigold took it from her and held it to the old lady's lips. She closed her eyes and sipped.

Kim watched Marigold's face. She was another one who looked exhausted. She was trembling too, but hers was adrenalin led. She eyes were bright and engaged, darting about as the women crowding around the armchair, looking as if she wanted to shout at them to stand back.

"What's been going on?" asked Jade. Marigold looked up at her and frowned. Then she looked to Eva and frowned again. Her mind was distracted for a moment, and Kim suddenly knew why. The woman called Jade was the woman Marigold had seen in the shed with Eva's husband.

My, Kim thought, *the evening was certainly heating up.*

Honestly, Kim had never seen Marigold like this. She was in the moment, in charge of someone else's wellbeing, in a kindly way, not interfering or poking her nose in where it wasn't wanted. She was caring and compassionate, her movements filled with empathy for the old lady sipping the water.

"Who is she?" Jade asked.

"This is Sandra's mother-in-law."

"So, where's Sandra?" asked Eva.

"She'll be here in a minute. She's just getting changed."

SANDRA TOOK THE STEPS SLOWLY. They were wet and the wind seemed like a ten force gale. Of course, it wasn't, but if it picked up, she'd have a hard time staying on the steps. She hung onto the ledge, like a life line, putting both feet on each step before taking the next, like a child taking the stairs for the first time.

She finally reached the bottom where she was hit by a spray of sea water that knocked her onto the beach. On her hands and knees, she picked up her torch and looked about wondering what the hell she was doing there.

What a day it had been, and it wasn't over. She still had to put some things in place, and she still had to get changed, and she still had to go to that stupid cocktail party. It was becoming too much. She was finding it hard to cope. Then she thought about Gladys and how brave she'd been, and she thought about living the rest of her life without the man who had dragged her down into the same pit he had dwelled in. Only *then* was she inspired to get up and complete the task in hand, whatever the cost.

She dragged her feet along the sand to the place where she'd buried the wetsuit. How ironic that the garden shovel she'd accidentally left behind, now acted as a marker. 'X marks the spot,' she muttered to herself.

The tide was coming back in, only half the beach was visible. She had to hurry. It would take no time at all for the cove to be flooded. She fell to her knees and grabbed the spade sticking up from the sand and started digging. Two-feet down, she touched rubber when a black sleeve poked up as if it was Eddie's arm rising from his sandy grave. It failed to move her. She was resilient of anything Eddie had to offer now. She pulled on the sleeve, and heavy with sand, the wet suit slid out of its pit. She pulled it into her arms and embraced it. She should never have buried it in the first place. What the hell had she been thinking?

Then, before she could get to her feet, a wave came out of nowhere and showered her with freezing cold seawater. She closed her eyes to the impact, waiting for it to retreat, but then she opened them when she felt something hit her.

A foot.

She cleared the water from her face and stared with her mouth agape.

At her side was the naked corpse of her dead husband, Eddie.

That's when Sandra, muffled by the din of the night-tide, screamed and screamed and screamed as if she would never stop.

Chapter Thirty-two

At No.5

"LOOK, EVERYONE," said Marigold, hoping they'd all just stop speaking and asking so many dumb questions. She was on script here and she needed to say her lines.

"Quiet," Eva yelled, but it was directed mostly at Jade. She squeezed Marigold's shoulder and sat on the arm of the chair next to Gladys. Gladys was leaning her head back, trying to regain her breath. Kim put herself on the floor next to Marigold and Rhianna kneeled down next to her. That left Jade who stood against the doorframe with her arms crossed and Jo who stood a distance from them all, next to the fire.

Marigold began.

"As you know, Eddie didn't go on the golfing trip. He was feeling poorly, so he stayed in bed all morning."

Eva nodded. She knew only too well that Eddie had made his excuses and that Roger had complained about Eddie letting them down.

"Anyway, around about lunchtime, he felt a lot better, so when the tide went out after midday, he decided to go for his usual swim." Marigold's eyes were fixed on Eva's face. She needed to fix them *somewhere* so Eva's face was as good as any. "When…"

Rhianna piped up. "Yes, I remember seeing him," she said.

Marigold shifted her gaze to the young girl with the ponytail. "What?"

"I saw him swimming. He was naked."

Marigold's face must have been a picture. She didn't know what to say. They hadn't allowed for any witnesses seeing Eddie out in the bay. Besides, she couldn't have seen him…he was dead. *Oh, god*. She must have seen his body. It must have been floating on the sea in the bay, looking like he was out there swimming. *Oh God*.

Wait, she thought. It doesn't matter. If the girl thought she saw him out there swimming, that only served to support their story. *No, this is good. It's good!*

"But it couldn't have been him," she said.

The blood on Marigold's face must surely have drained away.

"The person I saw was swimming quite early this morning. It couldn't have been the man you're talking about. You did say he went out after midday."

"Anyway," Marigold said, carrying on with her story. Everything else would have to be explained later. She just needed to say her lines. They all needed to shut the hell up. "When he didn't come back, Sandra and Gladys got worried and decided to call the police."

"The police?" said Eva. "The coast guard, surely?"

"Y...Yes," Gladys stuttered. "We were going to call the coast guard too, but then the power went off and we couldn't call anyone."

"So, he's still missing?"

"Yes, he's still missing."

SANDRA RAN UP THE STEPS with no care to any mishap. She'd done the same that morning when that girl with the ponytail had come down to the beach. She'd gone on a run and Sandra had climbed up almost two steps at a time, just as she was doing now.

Oh god. Seeing Eddie like that had shaken her to the core. His body looked disgusting. His flesh looked like tripe, white and wrinkled, and his arms were askew as if they had been broken at the joints against the force of the waves on the rocks, but it was his staring, empty eyes that had chilled her to the bone. They had looked straight into her soul, making her feel like she would be spending eternity in hell.

She'd scrambled away from him, kicking her heels into the sand, but under her arm, the wetsuit remained. She'd pulled it to her chest as if it were protection against her despicable husband, dead as he was.

Eddie's body remained lying face down on the beach as the waves washed over him, covering him over and over again in frothing white water as it ebbed and returned. The waves had covered Sandra's legs, and it was only then, she was roused from the spell she was under. She looked around her and realised the beach was almost covered. *Thank god*, she thought. Once again it would take Eddie's body into its dark depths, concealing her crime for yet one more night.

GLADYS LEANED FORWARD and touched Marigold's hand. It was a silencing hand, a motherly hand. One of love and reassurance. Marigold was glad of it. Someone had to take over the story because she couldn't go on. She just couldn't.

"Marigold came over to see how we were when the lights went off," Gladys said. "She has been very supportive." The two women smiled, knowing smiles, smiles that only they knew the cause.

"She helped us get through the day after we were terribly worried about my son. There was nothing we could do. We just had to wait until the electric came back on."

A whistle of wind blew outside the window behind Glady's armchair. The draft made the candles all flicker in unison as if the flames were performing the dance of death. "The way this wind is picking up, it may never come back on. Not tonight," said Eva.

Marigold glanced at her watch. She was to give Sandra thirty minutes to do what she needed to do.

Kim leaned in. "Well done you, for looking out for them, Marigold," she said.

"I was just being a good neighbour."

"More than that. You were a true friend."

"No problem." Marigold absentmindedly stroked her finger over the face of her watch.

AS SHE RUSHED ALONG *the eight*, Sandra glanced back towards No.5. It was hard to see inside, with just candlelight in there, but the curtains were still open and she could make out a group of women gathered around an armchair.

She was about to keep speed walking towards her house when she just happened to espy a small light inside the empty house at No.3. She stopped. *Strange,* she thought. Surely there was no one in there and yet the small light had now turned to a white glow as if there was someone in there smoking a cigarette.

With much more important things on her mind, she went straight past her house to the Butler's and went quickly around the side towards the greenhouse. She pushed open the door and stepped inside. She needed to put the wetsuit towards the back, to make it look as if the killer had tried to hide it. Just as she went three steps in, her bare feet stepped in something cold. She shone the torch to the floor and recoiled when she saw her foot covered in blackened blood. She lifted it and saw what looked like small intestines hanging from her toes. She scraped her foot on a clean slab while grimacing with horror.

"I don't know how much more I can take," she said until she realised she was talking to herself. Enough is enough. With all resolve draining from her, she threw the wetsuit into the corner of the greenhouse, leaving it draped over a large pot filled with green bean sticks.

Then Sandra backed out, pulling the door shut and running over the garden to her own house next door.

Chapter Thirty-three

At No.4

RHIANNA SLIPPED AWAY. She'd been thinking about Jack ever since she left him at the door when he'd touched her hand. Her heart pounded every time she thought about their first meeting; the way he looked; how he spoke; his whole persona; how he held himself; how assertive he was. It all added up to one hunk of a man, and she cared not for his inability to walk. Despite his incapacity, when she thought about how he'd been injured, it made her admire him more. He'd remained honourable when he'd avoided crashing his lorry into a woman driver. Even then he had been a gentleman, even then!

She wanted to be with him, spend time with him, talk to him. And even if he may never be able to make love to her, the feelings she had for him seemed to eliminate the thought of never having his children…*if* they reached that occasion in their relationship. *Relationship*! What was she thinking? Was she stepping ahead of herself? She hardly knew him. Surely it wasn't normal for a woman to think about marrying a man she'd just met. Maybe she'd romanticised the whole thing. Maybe she'd just got carried away. She was a fool…wasn't she?

Despite her hopes and doubts, she still went quietly toward his house needing to see him one more time that night.

The women in No.5 were all talking about the man who had been lost at sea, Eddie. Rhianna didn't know him, nor did she know his wife or the mother. She would help if she could if she didn't have more pressing things on her mind. As it was, the thought of seeing Jack overrode all other responsibility to neighbours and strangers.

Tonight, she was a free bird. Liberated. She had no adults watching over her. She was alone in Seaview for one night only and she meant to make the most of it.

No one saw her slip away. She'd taken her jacket and while the candles burned low, under the cover of darkness she left. The one person who could have prevented her from leaving was Jo,

Jack's protective sister. She may not have wanted Rhianna to go seeking out her brother whilst she wasn't there to defend him. And perhaps Jack needed defending because wasn't she now a stranger, seeking him out, like a lovesick predator? Wasn't it her intention to seduce the man who had seduced her in a heartbeat with a single touch…a smile…an encouraging word? She was a vamp and she'd never been a vamp in her life before. The feeling she had diminished all her control. Control was something that other people did. She didn't want that. She wanted to love with abandon, not to set parameters. Yes, she was a vamp all right.

As she went, the wind tore at her clothes and her ponytail, now loose at the back of her head, flapping in the wind like a sock on a rotary. The wind burned her face and sea spray salted her skin. She had to close her eyes to stop herself from secreting tears she never meant to shed. This wasn't a time for crying, it was a time for rejoicing, celebrating the moment she'd experienced that crazy phenomenon, *love at first sight*. She'd never be able to explain it. It was literally inexplicable. It just was. And as far as Rhianna was concerned, she didn't care about explaining it to any heathen who asked.

She reached the gate which led to the back of Jack's house.

She glanced back to the window at the front of Eva's place. No.5, where inside, shadows moved around as the women fussed over the old lady in the armchair.

Then Rhianna took a deep breath and went through the gate.

KIM SAW RHIANNA SLIP AWAY. She smiled to herself, as she thought about how much she wanted to slip away too. She could be at home, cuddled up on the sofa with the fire burning in the grate, listening to the wind whistling outside, waiting for the storm to come. Instead, she was inside Eva's house as everyone fussed over the old lady in the armchair. The women who'd lost her son.

She was surprised at the actions of Marigold. In a nice way! The woman had been a pest in her life, annoying the hell out of her every damn night, but tonight, she'd taken a family under her wing the way an honourable person cared for another human being. Her actions had cast a whole new light in Kim's eyes and that didn't happen very often.

As she sat there listening and watching, she thought about Tyrone. Where was he? What on earth had happened that would make him leave his car at the side of the road like that? How she wished the power would come back on. At least then she could call him, or he could call her.

Suddenly, she felt a surge of energy and determination. She was going to slip away, go back home, get a ladder -the Butlers had one- and climb over the wall. She would then check to see if Tyrone had left his keys in the car, and if not, she would keep on walking until she came upon a house who had a phone. Yes, that all made sense and that was what she would do.

RHIANNA KNOCKED ON THE WINDOW. She was cupping her hand over her eyes against the glass, hoping to see inside. She called his name, Jack, but the wind took it away as if she'd never uttered it at all.

She tried the back door. It was open, but that wasn't unusual. No one locked their doors in Seaview, not like in the city where relaxed security was starting to put doubt in people's minds. Never before had someone intruded upon the havens of the working classes. It just wasn't done. But now burglaries were becoming commonplace in middle-class homes, where TV's were ripe for the picking and as more electrical goods worked their way in, people were becoming cautious about keeping their possessions safe. Not in Seaview though. In Seaview, they still didn't lock their doors.

She went inside. He was probably in the sitting room, staying warm in front of the fire. She knew the way. She called his name again. "Jack." It came out a half-whisper. She didn't know why. It was as if the darkness demanded quiet.

She pushed open the door.

The room was illuminated only by the flames of the fire. No candles burned, but she guessed they weren't needed as long as the fire burned.

The sofa which had once stretched the width of the chimney-piece, facing the hearth, had been moved away. In its place was Jack's wheelchair, where Jack, his head lolling to the side was tied to it with a length of thin blue rope.

She couldn't process it. The vision wasn't something she'd expected at all. It just wouldn't fathom in her consciousness. She stepped forward, her shoes thumping on the floorboards. She reached him and saw his face. He was unconscious, as if dead, his face bloodied and bruised and his mouth gagged with a piece of duct tape.

Then the door slammed shut and when she turned sharply, she saw a man standing in the shadows.

KIM WAS OUT OF THERE. Thank the heavens! She should never have gone to the party in the first place. Let the others solve all the problems of the family from No.7. They didn't need her.

She closed the back door and went without a torch, around the back to the side of the house. She no longer needed a light to guide her. The moon was up, and it was bright, despite being lost occasionally behind black clouds whisked-up by the wind.

Her hair was blowing as she came to the front of the house. She looked back to the women inside No.5, seeing shadows dance over the walls in the candlelight. They were okay, they didn't need her. Maybe Eddie would turn up. Then they could all go back to celebrating whatever they wanted to celebrate, cocktails and all.

She was just walking along *the eight*, hoping no one would spot her, when she turned her head sideways and saw something she shouldn't have seen. It was a small flicker of light as if someone had lit a cigarette, but it was inside the empty house where no one should have been.

She stopped. How odd! The new family weren't supposed to be moving in until next week, so why would there be someone inside now? She remained staring. Then she wondered, despite her assumption being completely irrational if the person inside was Tyrone. She knew it didn't make sense, but he was missing, so anything could be possible, couldn't it?

She looked back to No.5. She had only walked a short distance. She could still see them in there, fussing over the lady in the armchair. She wondered if she should go back and alert them...Alert them to what? She'd seen a small flicker of light. If she went back and told them that, they'd say she was being paranoid. *Wouldn't they?*

The confused expression on her face lingered when she decided to go check things out. She was many things, but no one could ever call her a coward. She'd been through pain and suffering...and danger...during the early part of her life...so any challenge now was a walk in the park. Besides, there was no point trying to climb the wall if Ty was in there, despite the practicality of that not making sense at all.

She decided against ringing the doorbell since it was common knowledge the house was empty and that would be silly in the scheme of things. She went up over the sloping drive and down the side of the house. The garden was practically non-existent. The previous owners must have torn up the flowers before they'd left.

She remembered them. They'd moved in at the beginning when the houses were brand new. They'd had young children who used to ride their choppers along *the eight* or kick a ball around, in danger of smashing a window or two. The parents were middle-aged and middle class. *She* stayed at home raising the kids while *he* went off to work each day in his white company car, a four-door Zephyr. Then he lost his job. No one knew why, but it was the reason they sold up and left. They could no longer afford the mortgage. A terrible time for them, Marigold had said. Of course, it was Marigold who had told her the whole story. If she hadn't, Kim wouldn't have cared to know.

She went around the back. Of course, the doors would be locked. She tried the patio doors anyway. She was right. House secure. Maybe she hadn't seen someone light a cigarette. Maybe she'd seen something else. It could have been a reflection of something in the window. Yes, that could be it. It was probably her eyes playing tricks on her.

Just before she decided to give up and leave, to carry on with her original plan of scaling the front wall on a ladder, she placed her hand up against the kitchen window. She cupped her fingers around her eyes, but she saw nothing. Just empty cabinets with the doors slightly open.

But then she went up on her toes and in her line of sight over the stainless steel sink, she saw something on the floor. At first, she couldn't make it out. It looked like a cross, a large cross laid down on the black and white checked tiles. But then the cross moved. She couldn't understand it. What were her eyes seeing?

Then she knew when a beam of moonlight cast itself through the window into the darkened house. On the floor was a man, trussed up with a rope, in the shape of a cross as if he was Jesus on a crucifix.

Chapter Thirty-four

At No.3

DRAKE FISHER COULDN'T have been more entertained if he'd gone to see a show on Broadway. The women of Seaview were entirely incompetent, living on their emotions instead of their wits. That was dangerous! *For them.*

He'd watched the woman from No.7 stagger along *the eight* to the steps leading down to the beach. The weather was frantic and yet there she was taking an early evening stroll in the midst of it. Not long after, she reappeared, soaked to the skin, carrying something black that he couldn't quite distinguish in the dark.

He'd lit a cigarette and she stopped momentarily to look inside, wondering what she'd seen. He stubbed the end of the cigarette on the wooden parquet floor.

The woman looked bewildered as if her life was being flushed down the toilet, like his mother's had been flushed the same way.

He was twenty-five then. He'd been at Phillips for six years, working the factory floor. He worked split shifts, preferring the night to the days. They were quieter, with less fussing, less chatter from the workers who seemed to form friendships. That was something he could never understand, making friends. He'd never had a friend and he functioned just fine.

The men on transport used to rib him. He was different, he knew that, but he never quite understood their reasons for taunting him day in and day out. They used to rile him so bad that when he went home to mother, he'd give her what for. He'd shout at her for not having his meal ready, for not cleaning the house, for not buying his favourite snacks. She took it like the docile bitch she was, still calling him her little Drakey, even at that age.

One day it got so bad, he'd grabbed a hold of her arm, pulled her through the kitchen and into the lean-to, took the key out of his pocket, opened the cellar door and shoved her inside. She'd tumbled down the steps to the bottom. And after he heard her splash about in the water, she screamed, when she saw father for the first time in years. Drake had leaned against the door, laughing his head off at the thought of mother's look of surprise when she bumped into her husband. He wondered if they'd have a good bonk while she was down there, grunting and groaning, moaning and doing it all night long...

Then he heard her banging on the door. "Please son, let me out, oh god, let me out, please," she begged.

His laughter had subsided, he was no longer amused. He kept his back to the door as he shouted through it. "Who'd ya meet down there, mother?" he yelled.

"No one, son. No one," she answered sobbing behind the door.

"Why do you want out, then?"

"It's the stench. I can't stand the stench. Please, son, let me out. I'll go down the shop and get the snacks you like,"

His ears had pricked up then. "Quavers?" he said slowly. "You'll get me quavers?"

"Yes, Drakey, I'll get you Quavers and Mars bars. You love Mars bars."

That's when he let her out. She was soaked to the skin when he opened the door and she fell through onto the floor of the lean-to. He gave her a swift kick in the lower leg, and she backed off. Her face was a picture. She looked like she'd seen a ghost.

He turned the key in the lock and spat back at her. "Go and get washed," he said. "And don't forget what you promised."

She shook her head. "I won't forget. I won't."

"Quavers and Mars Bars," he reiterated.

"Yes, Quavers and Mars bars."

HE'D JUST LIT ANOTHER CIGARETTE when he saw Kimberley Cutter walk along *the eight* towards her house. She stopped suddenly and looked into the window where he sat on a lone chair in the centre of the empty room. He imagined her looking straight into his eyes and his heart soared. She was the one he wanted. And if he could have her, that prize alone would supersede all his other plans to terrorize the women of Seaview.

He held his breath as he willed her to knock on the door, to come and ask him why he was inside No.3. Honestly, he never thought she would, but knowing Kim as well as he did, knowing she had guts and gumption, he couldn't help wishing she'd come seek him out. She would be happy to see him. He was sure of it. They'd been close when they'd worked together at Phillips. She had never wanted him to leave. Her hand had been forced by that Roger Lang. *He* was the one at fault. Not Kim. She just needed a lesson in humility. That was all.

He watched her go up the path to the front door, but she didn't ring the bell. Instead, she went across the driveway to the gate at the side.

He'd felt such joy that she would want to be with him. He was flattered, beyond all conscience, as if his feelings were no longer his, and that putting up a front with people to avoid being hurt, was being stripped away, making him vulnerable in her hands. They would be so happy if they were left alone. They could live in that house, buy some furniture. He could actually move away from his mother's house for good.

He stood up and stubbed his cigarette on the floor with the others. Time for smoking later, when he and Kim were lying in each other's arms.

He went swiftly to the door leading to the terrace and quietly let himself out into the garden. There were no shrubs to hide behind, no trees, and the sound of the waves crashing against the rocks in the bay deafened him so bad he had to slap his face three times on the left and twice on the right. And then, just as he pinned himself up against the wall, next to the kitchen window, she came around the side of the house.

She was so close he could practically smell her. Her body odour was distinct. A mix of musk and something else sweet. He'd smelled her many times when she'd walked past him at work, or they'd consulted each other about an issue of some kind. She had no idea he was interested in her…that he loved her. He thought he'd dropped some good hints when he'd protected her from that shithead Tyrone, but even then, she hardly noticed him. How many more hints did the woman need?

Now, she was close. She was cupping her hand over her eyes, standing on tiptoe to see inside the kitchen. He watched as realisation hit her like a thunderclap. She'd seen the shithead on the floor. *What joy!*

THE EVENING COULDN'T HAVE WORKED OUT any better, but when he saw the girl with the ponytail snooping around No.4, Drake thought his numbers had come up.

They were all so damn stupid. He'd bated the women with the bodies of the Butlers, they had no lights and a storm was brewing, but still, they walked freely around Seaview as if they were going for a picnic in the park. Earlier, when he saw that woman Marigold with the old lady from No.7, he felt sure that when they entered the Lang's house, they would tell the rest of the women about the death of the old couple. Why then weren't they all scuttling around like rats? Instead, they were ambling about without a care in the world. Why weren't they now fearful of their lives? Who made these women, Drake wondered, Punch the Puppet?

He'd laughed at his own joke when he slipped inside No.4. He already knew the layout of the place because he'd already been in there.

Chapter Thirty-five

At No.4

RHIANNA AWOKE with a blinding headache over her temples. She couldn't focus and there was a smell she couldn't distinguish. Her eyes remained blurred no matter how many times she blinked, and they burned like a million bee stings. What scared her most, was that outside her vision, beyond the darkness of her own head, she knew the man was there.

She first saw him behind the door after she found Jack unconscious and tied to his wheelchair. The man had stepped out of the shadows and came towards her, shining a torch in her eyes, which made her bring her arm up to protect herself from the torturous light. It only took him a couple of steps to reach her and just as she tried to look up, she saw the torch over her head before it came crashing down. She remembered little else except perhaps for her body being manoeuvred as she lost all control. *What's happening?* she'd screamed…probably to herself in the dark corners of her mind.

Now as she struggled to regain her sight, she felt bile rising up from her throat as panic began to take over her body. "Jack?" she called. "Jack, I can't see. Where are you?"

Silence.

And that was the scariest thing of all.

At No.3

KIM AWOKE TO THE DARKNESS with just moonlight filtering through a window to her right. Her eyes moved upward to see the window above the kitchen sink. How odd, she thought. She was once on the other side before she felt something hit her and she passed out. She knew she was going. It was like falling into a black pit with flashes of white glistening along the way. After that…*Nothing*.

But now she was coming out of it. She had travelled up the black spiral of her unconscious mind to open her eyes. As she looked at the window up above, with the moonlight, she deduced she was lying on the kitchen floor on a lumpy cushion. It was soft and hard in different places, feeling like an old mattress that had seen better days with occasional springs poking up to snag her. She couldn't move her hands, and her legs were immobile too, but she couldn't fathom why. Below, her leg felt wet and she didn't know why. And she was finding it difficult lifting her head and she didn't know why. But most of all, she could hear someone's breath in her ear, and she didn't know why.

Then she remembered what she'd seen through the kitchen window…a crucifix…or a man…she couldn't place it in her addled brain. Her mind felt like a puzzle, needing arranging so that the picture would become clear.

A least she was able to put strength in the muscles of her neck as she lifted her head. She would have recoiled if she could have moved, but she was stuck there, stuck to a man with a bloated face, with dark patches and swollen parts. One eye was closed, and his lips half open as the breath she'd heard in her ear, whistled out of his mouth like a high pitched rattle and then a croak. She forced her head back. She could only recognise the man if she was further away, *but no*, she couldn't move any more.

How strange that her fear was held at bay. Like she was looking down at her own body, watching a film of sorts.

The fear never came until she recognised the face of the man.

Her lips trembled and her whole body shook as her face almost touched his. He was dead, or unconscious, she couldn't tell, but in any event, he was seriously hurt. "Ty," she sobbed. "Tyrone, wake up, wake up."

But he didn't awaken, and all she knew, that whatever the cause, however, she'd gotten there, her body was now mirroring his, laying atop him, shaped like a smaller version of a crucifix of the man beneath her.

At No.5

"WHERE'S KIM?" Marigold asked.

The women looked about the room. They hadn't noticed that Kim had gone. "Maybe she went home."

"And not say goodbye?" Eva said indignantly. "Why would someone do that?"

"And where's Rhianna?" Jo asked.

Nobody knew. Some didn't even care. "Maybe she went with Kim."

Marigold's heart missed a beat. She looked at Gladys who seemed to be thinking the same thing as her, that there were three women outside: Kim, Rhianna and Sandra. She hoped to god that the guy who killed the old couple had long gone.

She couldn't tell them about the Butlers yet. Not until Sandra got back. That was the plan.

Marigold stood up. "Listen, everyone," she called. Everyone turned to face her. I'm thinking someone should go and find them and bring them back."

Eva pouted. "Why?" Her party was bombing, and she was clearly miffed.

"You know...with all this uncertainty...about Eddie, I mean. I just think it might be better if we all stick together until we know what's happened to him."

They all looked blankly at her as if she was crazy.

"Okay, look. There is another problem," Marigold said.

"WHAT ARE YOU TALKING ABOUT, Marigold?" said Eva, sharply. "What do you mean there's been a murder?"

The group of women had gone silent. Their ears had heard it, but they didn't trust it. One doesn't often hear the *M* word in Seaview.

"It's the Butler's...they're dead."

Eva pushed her palms up against her mouth, the same way Marigold had done when she heard about the killing of Eddie. A natural reaction, she guessed, to muffle a reluctant scream or a reaction to someone saying something she didn't want to hear.

"That's not true," Eva said.

Marigold looked at her and frowned at her 'not true' statement. She was one of those people who thought that if she couldn't see it, it didn't exist.

"I'm afraid it is true."

Gladys entered the fray. "When Marigold went around checking on everyone after the power cut, she and Sandra went next door to see if the Butlers were all right. They found them upstairs in their bed. They'd been strangled."

"What?" Eva sang. "Both of them?" It was a strange question since they'd been referring to them as the Butlers for the past ten minutes. Marigold put Eva's reaction down to shock. "Oh my god," she yelled as realisation hit her. "We have to inform police."

"Good luck with that." Jade said dryly.

It was all that was needed to make Eva stand up and confront her. "Is that all you've got to say? You've been a bloody weight around my neck all day and you come out with a statement like that."

Jade stepped forward and faced Eva square on. "Like what?"

"Devil-may-care. As if this doesn't affect you, and that all you're good for is standing there observing...like a useless wet weekend."

Jo stepped into the fray. "Stop it," she yelled. "This isn't doing anyone any good. Marigold's right. We need to go and bring Kim and Rhianna back. Just until we know what the deal is."

"What about your husband?" said Eva.

"He's my brother."

She looked aghast. "But..."

"You assumed he was my husband and we chose not to clarify the matter. We just thought it was no one's business."

"I see." She nodded. "Let's find the girls and then I'll go get my brother."

"It'll make me feel easier having a man here," said Gladys.

Marigold shook her head, trying to communicate with Gladys. He's not the man you think he is, she thought, but of course, Gladys had no idea what she'd meant by that.

Chapter Thirty-six

At No.7

A COLLECTIVE SCREAM RANG out when Sandra bumped into two nervous women. "My God," she shouted. "What are you doing?"

Sandra had just changed. After she'd planted the wetsuit, she'd rushed from the Butler's greenhouse into her own home next door, slamming shut the patio doors and quickly locking them. She wanted to lock out the world, every invasion and intrusion that threatened to engulf her and take away her soul. All wellbeing was lost at that hour. The day had been too long, and now the night was stretching out before her like a slick of black tar. She should run away. Flee. Get in Eddie's car, crash through the gates until they were flat on the road, and then escape the confines of Seaview forever, never looking back.

If only!

She trod carefully on the kitchen floor. The blood and whatever other muck that she had stuck to her feet needed to be cleaned. She couldn't drag it upstairs to the shower. What would Eddie say? She stopped as comprehension hit her. *What would Eddie say?* She repeated in her pensive, muddled mind. Where the hell had that come from?

Still, she couldn't drag it through the house. She needed to clean it off first. She disregarded the idea of going back outside to use the same tap she'd used to clean off her feet after killing her husband. The only other solution was to do it there in the kitchen where she could clean up the remnants afterwards.

Even then…

Wait!

She stopped and looked down at the mess on her foot. Where had that blood come from? She surprised herself that she had only just pondered it, that she had accepted the blood as if it was all part of the plan. But it wasn't. There shouldn't be any blood.

The cat.

Marigold said she'd seen a slaughtered cat hanging inside the greenhouse. When they went back to investigate, they saw nothing and put it down to her troubled imagination. The Butlers had a cat. Maybe Marigold saw it after all. That posed two questions in Sandra's mind. Why would the person who killed the Butlers, kill the cat? And why, if Marigold did actually see it hanging there by a chain, slaughtered, then why wasn't it still there when they went back?

Balancing and lifting her foot into the sink, she turned on the tap. She placed the torch on the side where cups and saucers were turned upside down on the draining board. Bits of congealed blood and entrails spilt into the sink as she washed between her toes. She forced the excess bits down the drain with the power of the tap, hoping they would go and never be seen again. She couldn't *ever* see them again. Still balanced on one foot, she bent her body and reached down for a rag under the sink. There, she grabbed the bleach and poured it all over her skin. She washed it with fresh water once again as the smell wafted up her nostrils. She wondered if she would ever smell anything normal again. Would the bleach and the pungent odour of cat guts linger in her nose forever?

She wiped her foot on the rag and discarded it in the peddle bin. Then she grabbed her torch and ran out of the kitchen and up the stairs.

AFTER HER SHOWER, she quickly dried her hair. She couldn't afford the time to curl it, so it would have to do as it was. She pulled on a dress she'd had for over five years. It was her going away dress after she'd married Eddie. And it was the only decent garment she owned. How fitting, she thought, wearing her good going-away dress on the day Eddie went away for good.

When she was almost ready, she secured her watch around her wrist, quickly glancing at the time before she dashed down the stairs, grabbed her coat, and with her torch in hand, opened the front door.

That was when she bumped into the two women sneaking around with their arms linked together. They all screamed at once. If it wasn't for the terror of the night, they may even have laughed at their silliness, but it wasn't a time for laughter. It was a time of mourning.

"What are you doing?" Sandra snapped.

Eva was the one holding the torch. Her hair was blowing about in the same way the wind was hammering the loose fittings around the estate, making everything rattle and shake.

"We came to find Kim and Rhianna, but we saw no sign of them at No.1. We thought we'd check the Butler's house," Eva said.

Sandra shook her head. "Why?" She was cautious about what to say. She had no way of knowing if Marigold had told them that part of the tale yet.

"To see if they're in there."

"Why would they be?" It came out of Sandra's mouth like a hiss.

"They may have to come to check if the Butlers were okay." Jo paused. "They don't know they've been killed."

Sandra pushed her arm to get the torchlight from her eyes. "Marigold told you."

"Yes, but not right away, which was a bit lax of her if you ask me," Eva said.

"I don't think there's anyone next door."

"You can't know that for sure."

Jo had already left to follow the garden around to the side of the Butler's house. Eva followed her. The moon was up now, visibility was better, despite the speed of the wind whistling along *the eight*.

"Where are you going?" Sandra paced after them. "You can't go inside." Frankly, Sandra had had enough. This wasn't part of the plan at all. What did these women want? She had to wonder if it wasn't some sense of morbid curiosity on their part. The dark side of human nature coming to the fore.

They went inside via the back door. The place was eerily quiet. A mortuary. A house of death.

"I told you there's no one here."

"Show us the bodies."

Sandra sighed. "They're upstairs."

She followed on behind as they climbed the stairs with the torch in hand. Inside the back bedroom, she saw the blanket was once again covering the bodies. She couldn't remember covering them back up the first time when she and Marigold had seen them. All Sandra could remember was them scarpering from the room in sheer terror.

Now Jo was reaching down to pull back the cover. The corpses were revealed once more, still with ties wrapped around their necks; still with their mouths agape; still with their eyes staring nowhere.

In the dark, unable to help themselves, the women screamed. Sandra glanced at the figures on the bed. She shone her torch and gasped as bile pumped up her gullet from her empty stomach. She was retching. She was about to throw up. "We need to get out of here?" she said as her voice went flat.

"Out of the house?" one of them whispered.

She shook her head. "Out of Seaview."

Now there were three figures in the bed, where once there were two.

Between the two corpses, on bloodied sheets, was the laid-out, gutless carcass of the Butler's cat, right smack in the middle between its two dead masters.

Chapter Thirty-seven

At No.5

EVERYONE RETURNED to No.5, their faces ashen and their bodies trembling from the cold. Eva and Jo went to the fire and huddled in front of it.

Marigold greeted Sandra as she fell to her knees next to Gladys. Gladys stroked her hair as Sandra sobbed from trauma and exhaustion. Marigold pretended to embrace her, as she whispered in her ear. "Did you get the wetsuit?" Their heads were together now. Gladys, Sandra and Marigold, like the allies they had become in a matter of hours. Crucial hours.

With her eyes closed, Sandra nodded, looking as if she didn't want to talk about it any more. She'd had enough.

Sandra placed her hand on Marigold's knee. "The cat," she said out of earshot of the others. "I saw the cat."

Marigold had forgotten. She'd put that picture of the hanging slaughtered cat out of her mind, believing, *hoping,* that it had been just an apparition, a trick of the torchlight, in that most horrific night, when her imagination played tricks on her mind like she'd never known before. So, it wasn't all in her head. The cat was real. "Where?"

Sandra's throat constricted as she gulped. She struggled to utter the words. "In the bed."

"What?" Gladys stared at her, her mouth distorted, as if she'd had a stroke. "What are you talking about, love?"

Before she could explain, their heads swung about as Eva made an announcement. "Listen, everyone," she said, standing up. She was still trembling. Someone had put a sweater around her shoulders. She stabbed her arms into the sleeves and took a handkerchief from the pocket. She blew her nose, squeezing her eyes shut as she forced the memory of their ordeal into the white linen. "I think we're in a pickle here," she said.

Everyone listened, happy that someone other than themselves were in the limelight.

"Here's the deal," she said, stuffing her handkerchief up her sleeve. "We have reason to believe that there's a prowler in Seaview."

Everyone muttered something, but the statement that stood out from them all was Jo's. "We don't know that for sure."

Sandra stood up. "I know there is," she said plainly. "When we saw the Butlers the first time, they didn't have a dead cat in their bed."

Jade looked confused by the whole matter. "What does that mean?" she shouted. "A dead cat!? Who cares about a cat?"

"It wasn't just a dead cat," Sandra explained, patiently. "It was slaughtered. Its innards ripped out…"

"Don't be disgusting," Jade yelled. "I can't believe what you're saying."

"Believe it or not, that's up to you, but we know what we saw."

She stood in the centre of the room, amid her peers, and tears rolled down Jade's face. She was scared. Really scared.

"Look," Eva said. "It may not be as bad as we think it is. The killer may have gone now."

"No, I don't think so," said Sandra. All eyes turned to her. "I think he's still here."

"How can you be so sure?"

"Because the cat was put into that bed *after* the power went out. He couldn't have gotten through the gate."

"Anyone could climb over that gate," Jade said, her eyes wide, hoping that someone would agree with her.

"Actually, that's not true. Someone tried it once. It's like a damn jail cell with spikes on the top and it's about 10ft high."

"Nine," said Sandra.

Marigold got to her feet by steadying herself on the arm of Gladys' chair. "I think we have to assume that there is a killer in Seaview, and we need to stay together until it's safe, maybe until the men come back or the power comes on so that we can use the phone and call the police."

Sandra rose to her feet, looking like she'd had a revelation. "I think I know where he is," she said slowly, surprising even herself as she remembered the small glow of light when she came back from the beach. "I think he's hiding out in No.3."

Everyone stared at her, shocked that she would even suggest that an intruder would be hiding among them, watching them.

Marigold looked at the women one by one. Then, she said slowly. "We need to find Kim and Rhianna."

JO WAS ABOUT TO RUSH FROM THE ROOM when Eva stopped her. "Where are you going?"

She shrugged her off. "To get my brother."

"I'll come with you." She said it but she wasn't sure if she meant it.

"No, it's alright. He's just next door. I'll go over the gardens. Bring him back here."

"In his wheelchair?"

Jo shook her head and snarled at her. "Yes, of course," she spat.

Eva looked embarrassed. She always seemed to be putting her foot in it with those two. She wished Jo would just ease up. She was *so* sensitive.

She watched her leave and locked the door behind her. Then she went upstairs to make sure all the windows were shut. She'd already checked the garage and then bolted the inner door. No one was getting in that house, not if she could help it.

When she was upstairs, checking the windows, she had time to think about Harry, wondering what he was doing right then. They were probably at dinner now, celebrating their successes on the golf course. She wondered if he was thinking about her. Had he tried to phone? And if he had, what would he have thought when he got no reply? Would he be worried about her, or worried about Jade, his wife? She liked to think it was her. They had connected in a way that couldn't be explained. Perhaps they were meant to be together.

She went into the spare room, where he had slept the night before. She had already stripped the sheets, but she wished she hadn't. She could have smelled his aftershave on them, that musky aroma which had stirred her senses at the party last summer when he'd kissed her.

As she sat on the side of the bed, Jade came into the room carrying a candle like she was Florence Nightingale. "What do you want?" Eva spat, annoyed at Jade for disturbing her most intimate thoughts.

"I came up to use the loo. Someone else is in the downstairs one."

"The toilet isn't in here."

"I know where it is."

"Of course you do, seeing as you've been here all damn day."

"Why do you hate me so much." The candle illuminated her face, highlighting the flaws.

"You know why."

"Because of Roger and me?"

Eva's head rotated like it was on a spike. "What?" She stood up and confronted her.

Now the two women were head to head with a burning candle flickering between them.

WHEN SHE HEARD THE KERFUFFLE, Marigold grabbed the torch and ran upstairs. She could smell burning, which was the most worrisome of all. At the top, on the landing, Eva and Jade were wrestling as flames rose up from an artificial rubber plant in the corner.

She went quickly into the bathroom and grabbed a jug that held plastic flowers. She dumped them in the bath and filled up the vessel with cold water. She grabbed a towel and left the tap running over it in the sink as she darted from the bathroom and back out onto the landing. As the women screamed and pulled each other's hair, Marigold doused the flames rising from the plant, then she dashed back to the bathroom and grabbed the sodden towel. Finally, she threw it over the plant and extinguished the fire. She felt like a hero, but all that heroism was wearing her out. She'd like to lie down and take a nap, but the two women were still cursing and screaming in a mass of entwined limbs. She went between them and separated them "Stop," she screeched.

They did.

Eva pushed Jade away and offered her one last stab of the foot. Jade was crying.

"What on earth are you doing?" Marigold shouted. "As if things aren't bad enough."

"She's been sleeping with my husband," Eva yelled, still on the floor trying to regain her composure.

"Okay, but you can sort this out another time."

Eva looked up at her. "You knew."

Marigold shrugged. "My Colin walked in on them at my anniversary party."

"What?" she screamed, looking daggers at Jade.

Jade sniffed and tossed her hair behind her head. "I'm not staying here listening to this," she said as she walked down the stairs with as much dignity as she could muster.

Chapter Thirty-eight

DRAKE COULDN'T HAVE TIMED it any better. He had been in the process of creating an illusion, but now the trick he had up his sleeve was about to become a whole lot better than he'd planned.

He saw her come out of the house. She was blonde and attractive, which made the experience twice as gratifying.

He was standing on the edge of the cliff, on the left side of the headland, at the bottom of the garden at No.4. She had just come out of No.5 where all the women were hiding out.

Earlier he'd watched the whole thing, when Eva Lang and the blonde had walked out of No.5 to go along *the eight*, looking for their friends. They'd gone to No.1, calling Kim's name and then crossed the road to No.7, where they bumped into the same woman he'd seen going down to the beach just thirty minutes earlier.

Like rats in a trap they all went next door to No.8 where, five minutes later, they ran out screaming. It was the funniest thing he'd ever seen, and he had to pat himself on the back for thinking about putting the cat in the bed with two old people, nice and snug-like, three in a bed, mixed with semen and blood. It was things like that made him the man he was today.

And when he saw them scarpering back to the house at the top of the headland, he was reminded of his father, who always said of *his* father. Quote: '*He made me the man I am today*.' Drake was only ten at the time, and when he thought about it afterwards, he had the sense to deem it inappropriate when he told him the story. This is what he said:

Quote: '*You would have loved my old man. He was a coal miner and good at it too. Worked the mines till the day he died and never complained once. Highly respected in the community where I grew up. Those were the good ol' days when everyone knew their place. No one stepped out of line, thinking they were better than anyone else. Our mother was a hard worker too, but our old man used to beat her good. 'It was the only way of keeping her in line,' was what he used to say. I'll tell you this little story, Drake. When our old man came home from the mines one day, he brought one of his mates with him. He owed him, see. And father never wanted to be in debt to anyone, so he paid him in kind (wink), you know what I'm saying? (laugh). Yeah, he got our mother to pay his debt good and father, by way of keeping an eye on the situation, watched. (wink). The women never complained in those days, son. They did what they were told, no mistaking. Anyhow, after the debt was paid (wink), the three of them went at it and made me watch. I was just a young'un then, but I always remembered what happened that day. It shook me up, truth be told, but I soon got over it. Our dad said it was a good lesson learned and that's why, Drake son, I always say it was my old man who made me the man I am today (wink).*

Yes, it had been a good idea putting the cat in the bed. Now, the women would be terrified that they were going to be next, hung up and gutted alive.

When he saw the blonde walk over the gardens to No.4, he knew she was coming to find the man in the wheelchair.

That's when Drake got a little bold. "Hey," he called as she stumbled around in the dark with just the moonlight to guide her. The wind had dropped a bit, but it still whistled about and now the rain was coming, starting off light and then turning to *torrential* in the blink of an eye.

"Hey," he called again over the sound of the rain and the wind. She spun about to see where the voice had come from. She saw him next to the cliff and she was squinting, finding it hard to make out what she was seeing. Then the wet and the light from the moon reflected upon the wheels of the chair.

Her mouth fell open as she saw it totter at the side of the cliff. She was a brave one alright. Next minute she was pacing towards him before he let go of the chair.

As the contraption rolled over the side, the blonde reached the edge and he gave her a little push too. It didn't take a lot, she looked like she was crying as if she'd just lost her best friend.

Drake laughed when he glanced over the side.

There on the rocks below were the broken pieces of the wheelchair and next to it the broken body of the blonde.

Chapter Thirty-nine

At No.3

KIM WAS SOBBING. Beneath her, Ty could hardly breathe. He was dying, she could tell, and he was in such terrible pain, that his brow creased from agony even in unconsciousness. She wanted to get off, to allow his chest to breath, but she couldn't shift her weight. She was tied up like a trussed chicken and she knew who was responsible, which made the whole thing even more terrifying.

Drake Fisher! The man they had let go that week from Phillips. She could hardly believe her eyes when he'd gotten down on the floor to look her straight in the eyes. His face was as she remembered, except he had a madness about him she'd never seen before, apart from that time when Tyrone was nearly mowed down by the forklift Drake had been driving. The whole factory had come to a standstill when Tyrone got up and confronted the driver, Drake Fisher.

"You did that on purpose," he yelled.

Drake had jumped down from the cab and looked him square in the face. "Two words," he said. "Hardhat and Unions."

That was when she saw that look on his face, which had sent shivers up her spine. Drake Fisher wasn't someone you stood up to. She could see that in his eyes then and she could see it in his eyes now, and that chilled her to the bone.

"Why have you done this?" she said with a trembling voice. Her cheek was touching Ty's. Her face was cold but his was hot like he had a fever.

"Just thought I'd come visit," he said. He reached up and stroked her hair. He took his hand away and even in the darkness she saw it stained with blood. "You fired me."

"It…it wasn't my decision. It came from up above."

"Like God?" he smiled.

"No, I mean higher management."

His face was repulsive. He was pale but he had blemishes on his skin, and hairs on his chin and under his nose, undeserving of the term stubble. They were just hairs, like thin tufts of grass. But it was his eyes, like the windows to his damaged soul that defined the man he was. There was no need to look further. The eyes said it all.

"How long are you going to keep us here? Will you let us go? What are you planning?" She had so many questions rattling around her head, she didn't know which to ask first, let alone digest his answers.

"Don't know…don't know…you'll see," he said in response.

"Please, please let us go. My friend needs a doctor."

"Don't you mean he needs doctoring."

"I don't understand."

"Yes. Doctoring, like altering. He's not a good person. Not good enough for you."

"I don't…"

"You and me, Kimberly Cutter. That's what I'm saying. You and me."

RHIANNA COULD HEAR HIM, but she couldn't see him. She was blind, *oh god* she was blind.

The man had taken her from Jack's house. He'd guided her roughly. She couldn't see, and she couldn't stretch out her arms to feel her way. She had no choice but to stay as close to the man as she could, hoping he would take her somewhere safe, somewhere she could get her breath back, regroup, form ideas in her mind…just to establish what was happening to her. And what of Jack? Where was Jack?

Stumbling in the dark, each time they came to a step, he kneed her on the back of her leg. She knew he was the same height as her, just by the toxic smell of his breath against her face. And he was hard. She felt him against her, rubbing his pelvis against her. Repulsed by him, she tried to get away, but he was too strong.

He took her outside and then they walked a distance before she heard another door open and he pushed her inside a room. She didn't know where she was. She was on a hard floor, like wood, and it was cold in there. Her hands were tied in front of her, so she could only use the tips of her fingers to feel. She heard him behind her as he closed the door. His steps sounded hollow, and so did her voice when she spoke, as if they were in an empty room. "Who are you? What are you going to do? Where's Jack?"

He answered. "My Little Drake...You'll see...Gone."

Chapter Forty

At No.5

THE WOMEN OF SEAVIEW sat in darkness. It was ten o'clock at night. The power was still out, the rain was lashing down, three women were missing, and they were all terrified.

They'd arranged the furniture in a semi-circle around the fireplace, and upon the hearth all their candles burned. Around them, outside the comfort of the armchairs and sofa, was blackness, where nothing moved except for the occasional draft making a curtain blow gently as if someone had whispered their breath upon it. Beyond the bricks and mortar, the rain came down in vertical sheets, like a shop display of hanging carpets. The wind blew strong so that nothing could stand erect and even the moon had hidden its light, cowering, like they all cowered.

The silence inside was deafening. They'd already sung their songs of fear. They had already flung mud, made accusations, stamped and stomped their feet, raised their voices like shrill fishwives, poked their fingers, waved their hands in the dense, morbid air. Now they were silent, like witches watching their brew.

The party was over.

Not speaking, they stared at the flames of the low burning candles. No music played, not even *The sound of silence,* no cocktails filled glasses, no snacks enjoyed.

"Someone say something," Jade said.

No one did.

And as they stared at each other's faces, or simply nowhere, or at the flickering flames, out of the blue came a rapping on the window.

They all jumped in unison.

Marigold shot up from her chair. "It's probably one of the girls," she said hoping it was Kim.

She threw back the curtain, but there was no one there.

"Someone open the door," she called.

Sandra was about to get up when Eva placed a hand on her arm. She shook her head as her eyes widened in fear. "We don't know who it is."

Marigold stopped. She had a point, but they couldn't just leave them out there. Someone had to let them in. She closed the curtains once more and went towards the door leading out to the hall, but then she stopped and spun about when she heard the knocking on the window again. She went back and flung open the curtain, but again, there was no one there.

Now she was spooked. She imagined the ghost of Eddie, or the Butlers, their souls coming back to wreak havoc on the women's minds and senses. She pulled the curtain closed once more and took a step back. The other women had risen to their feet, except for Gladys. They all tottered on the edges of the darkness, wondering who had tapped the window.

Marigold's heart was racing. Her hands shook and her lips trembled as if she was a little girl again, being spooked by her brother. They all faced the window, just looking at the closed drapes, standing and staring, waiting for something to happen.

Then someone banged on the window at the back.

How strange that they didn't scream. It was as if acceptance had descended upon the room. They were in danger, *extreme* danger.

As they faced the back of the house, waiting to discover what would happen next, the rapping on the window resumed.

Now, they knew someone was playing games. Someone was trying to frighten them.

And it was working.

SANDRA COULD STAND IT NO MORE. She had seen the worst of the day. She had been raped by her husband, she had killed him, she had buried evidence on the beach, and then retrieved it and had seen him again. She had discovered the bodies of the Butlers and she had seen them again. She had covered up the truth and blamed a murder on someone else. She had lied and fumbled her way about and she had washed cat guts from her feet. What more could the day throw at her? Nothing to beat *that*.

"Whoever's out there is starting to piss me off," she said with a determination she didn't know she possessed. The knocking was at the back again now, so it was time to take the bull by the horns. She paced through the lounge where French doors led to a large terrace overlooking the sea. She stood firm and she threw back the curtains and there, standing looking at her was a man.

She retreated when he smiled.

She was no longer brave.

He had a smirk on his face that sent a charge of fear through her veins. She became nauseous as she stared back at him, trying to understand what on earth he was doing there getting lashed by the rain in the black of night.

"Who are you?" she screamed. "Why are you here? What do you want?"

"Little Drake…To visit…You."

EVA'S FEET TRIPPED HER UP. They weren't hers. They had a life of their own as they carried her back to the circle of armchairs placed around the fire. She had a preference to bury her face in a cushion. They were sateen, the cushions. She'd made them after a watching an old episode of *Houseparty*. She curled up, pulling those feet which weren't hers, up to her chest, lying like a foetus, protected, can't-be-harmed.

The face at the window had been too much for Eva. She couldn't comprehend it and she certainly couldn't tolerate it. The face shouldn't be there, not smiling like that, looking in, as the wind sprayed the rain over his head and against the pane of the window.

No, Eva preferred not to look. If she couldn't see it, it didn't exist and that was her ultimate preference.

Chapter Forty-one

At No.3

TYRONE WOKE UP, not wide awake, but sloth-like as if it was already Sunday and he was anticipating the morning in bed with the papers. Just one eye opened. The other was glued shut by the swelling, now just a slit in a mound like a half boiled egg, except it was black…and blue…and red.

The absence of recognition quickly flashed over his face. He was too close to distinguish Kim's face.

"Ty," she whispered. "It's me, Kim."

He groaned and closed his eyes again. He had been so badly beaten. "Move your knee," he muttered.

"I can't," she sobbed. "Wait. I'll try." The tethers around her ankles prevented any drastic reflexes, but if she concentrated on her knee…There, she'd moved it about an inch, taking the pressure from his point of pain.

"Kim, what the hell?"

"Shush, Ty. Don't speak and I'll tell you everything I know."

He blinked his only eye, after it darted to the side of her. She doubted if he could see much

"Look. We're in a spot of bother, but we're going to be okay." She was finding it hard to talk and breathe at the same time. If Tyrone felt pressure on his chest by her weight, she was equally hindered having her torso pressing down on his. "It's that Drake Fisher," she said.

His eye opened as recognition hit him. Fisher was the man who had terrorised him at work.

"He got you here, somehow. I've been trying to track you down all day…" she was speaking in short bursts, in-between breathing. "The power went out around the estate, so I couldn't phone you anymore…" She suddenly realised she'd lost track of time. "I came looking for you, but he captured me too." *Breathe.* "The next thing I knew I was here. He must have knocked me out." She allowed herself a minute to catch her breath.

Ty was listening, quietly and patiently. At random intervals, he grimaced with pain.

"I'm on top of you. We're tied up with a blue nylon rope. Our hands and feet are positioned outwards like that DaVinci sketch of the Vitruvian man. On my right, the end holding our wrists is tied to the cupboard handles. I'm not sure about the other side because I can't turn my head." A tear ran down her cheek and landed on Ty's mouth. She lifted her head and saw him open his mouth to lick it. "Ty, I think you may be in bad shape. Your face is badly beaten, but I can't see what he's done to your body."

"My legs…" he groaned.

"Listen to me. We're going to get out of this, okay? We're going to get out of this."

RHIANNA HAD BEEN LEFT ALONE. She was blinded and bound, left with only her ears to help assess her situation. She thought she could hear whispers, but she was reluctant to call out. Her survival instincts had kicked in long ago when she heard the man leave the room. He didn't speak, he just left, closing the door behind him. She knew she was near the door. She felt the draft hit her when it was opened, and a fine spray of rain put moisture on her cheek. The other side of her face was on the floor.

After he'd gone, she tried to move. With her hands bound in front of her, she was able to stretch her fingers and bend her knees. She felt her ankles bound with string, the rough kind, feeling like welts were being left on her skin every time she moved. She couldn't remember him doing that…binding her ankles. She must have passed out at some point.

She was pleased when her fingers slipped inside the string. Maybe if she worked at it, she could untie it. She began trying to find the end, a knot or something. *There it was*. It wasn't double knotted, just simply tucked into the space between her ankles. As she started to disengage herself, she wondered where her shoes were.

Then she heard a groan.

Who was that?

Was it him?

She heard it again, a sound like a wounded animal.

She whispered a name "Jack!?"

Chapter Forty-two

At No.3

EVA FELT A HAND ON HER SHOULDER. She shrugged it off. She just wanted to stay where she was hiding in the cushions. "Eva, come on. We can't deal with this without you. We need you, Eva."

She turned her tearful face upwards to see Marigold sitting next to her, stroking her hair. She offered an encouraging smile. Eva didn't reciprocate. What was there to smile about? A man…a killer was lurking around outside her house and Roger wasn't there to protect her. And she needed protecting. She couldn't do this on her own.

"Where is the man?" she garbled as her nerves took over her body in the most alarming fashion. She had been afraid before, but never like this. This was fear on a whole new level.

"Sit up." Marigold helped her to her feet. "He's gone. For now. We don't know where."

Jade joined them. "I looked but I couldn't see anything," she said. "There's nothing out there except the wind."

"Don't bank on it."

"Why do you say that?" Jade yelled as if Marigold had just destroyed all her optimism in one fell swoop.

Marigold shook her head. "Why would he leave?"

"Because he's worried about being arrested when the police come."

Marigold laughed without humour. "Don't be so naïve. The man is clearly insane. He's here to kill her us if he can. Just like he killed the Butler's."

Eva's hands rushed to the base of her neck. "Dear god!"

The others joined them. Sandra had a knife in her hand. "We've got to do something."

"Just sit it out," shouted Eva. "We can wait until morning."

"He's not going to wait that long. He'll get in somehow."

"What about the girls, poor Kim and Rhianna?" Gladys asked wide-eyed.

"And Jo," said Eva. Not wanting to exclude the girl next door.

Marigold touched Eva's arm. "I'm sure they'll be okay."

"So, what can we do? If we're not going to wait it out, there's five of us and only one of him."

"We're women," Jade said shrill-like.

"But we're not weak women," Marigold said looking at Sandra. "We're not victims."

"I am," said Eva. "Look at me. I couldn't throttle a canary."

"It's not physical strength we need. We just need to use our heads."

"What are you saying, Marigold?"

"Turn the table on the pig. Hunt him before he hunts us."

Chapter Forty-three

WHEN DRAKE LEFT HIS VICTIMS ALONE, in No.3, he knew they'd probably try to break free. That's why, after he went outside, he popped back now and then to see what they were up to.

Man, he wished he had a cellar to push them down. With water at the bottom.

Earlier, he'd managed a reconstruction of 'the cellar in the lean-to', when the blonde went over the edge of the cliff. At the time, he remembered wishing he'd had a wheelchair the day his mother died. She was one heavy bitch.

It happened when he'd turned thirty. She had turned quite insane over the years, blaming her state of mind on the notion of her husband, Manny, floating around in the cellar. The damp had crept up the walls of the house. She wasn't wrong there. She tried cleaning it the best she could, and she'd whitewashed over it a few times, but it always managed to show up again, black.

"It's making me ill, that damp," she complained to Drake.

"So, what are you saying? You want to call a plumber or the landlord?"

"Well, I…"

"No, mother," he said. "Do you want more people to end up down that cellar, then?"

"No, 'course not, Drake."

"Well, you didn't mind me going down there when I was three years old, did ya?"

"That wasn't me. It was your dad. And he was only kidding around. Manny was always kidding around."

"Is that what you call it?"

"I don't know why you get so upset over him, Drake. He was your father, he loved you."

"Loved me?" he repeated. "Are you serious? He didn't love me. He loved you…Often." He smirked at his own humour.

"Oh, you're just too sensitive."

"Really? Do you know what it was like for me when I was three, to be locked in that cellar with no light? Do you, huh?" He'd faced her square on and he saw the fear in her eyes. He loved making her scared. He felt powerful, in charge, just like he was in charge of that key to the cellar.

"I told him to get you out. I did."

"But he didn't, did he? He left me there all day, while he was upstairs bonking you."

"Now, now, None of that sort of talk."

"You really are a stupid bitch, aint ya?"

Then she slapped him. Right across the cheek. It took him by surprise. She'd never hit him before. He'd stood, like a little boy in front of his mama, with his head hanging down, his chin resting on his chest, like he was ashamed for his behaviour. He was sorry, really sorry.

Then he lifted his head, slowly, like his neck was tied with a piece of string and someone else was pulling it up. Slow…slow…Then his eyes hit her eyes and she knew she was dead.

She ran. She ran for her life. Climbing the stairs two at a time, she was heading for the bathroom. It was the only door in the house with a lock on it. She'd hide in there until he'd calmed down. She was always doing that.

She got there too. She might have been fat, but she was quick. He'd give her that.

"Drake," she called from the other side of the door, "It's your birthday today, remember, my little Drakey? We'll bake a cake, have candles. You can blow them out…You can have gifts. And balloons. Maybe invite your friends from work." Her voice sounded desperate.

He slid down the door and sat on the floor, listening to all the plans for his birthday.

But it was too little, too late.

He'd wait it out. Then the bitch was going to die.

HE WAS DISTURBED FROM HIS MEMORIES when he glanced in the window of No.3. There in the dark was the girl with the ponytail, trussed up like a dead cat.

Still there. All good, he thought as he went over the lawn to No.5 and knocked on the window.

The curtains were flung open as he stood at the side, out of sight. He couldn't help smiling, thinking about their faces when they realised no one was there. They closed the curtains once more and once again he knocked. This time he skirted around the side to the back when he knocked on that window too. He loved having a lark. The only thing spoiling his fun was the damn rain. If only it had been a clear night. The moon was his friend. He could have played more games.

He decided to give them his look of death. The look he'd used on his mother after she'd slapped him.

He stood with his face close to the window when the curtains were drawn back. The woman inside screamed and backed away. He had them in the palm of his hands. He'd let them know what fear was. Just as if they'd been locked in the cellar when they were three.

Chapter Forty-four

At No.3

"WHO'S THERE?" called Rhianna.

A moan came back.

"Jack? Jack, is that you?"

A noise she couldn't decipher.

Then a voice from somewhere else. "Help. Help us?"

"Who is it? Who's there?" she called urgently.

"It's Kim," the voice returned. "Who's that?"

"It's me, Rhianna."

"Oh, thank god," the voice said. "Please, untie us."

"I can't. I can't see. And I'm tied up too." Her imagination was spinning out of control. She didn't know where she was. She had heard a moan like an injured animal coming from the same room, and then from another room, that woman…Kimberly Cutter was calling. She'd asked Rhianna to untie her, but she was immobilised too. Maybe Kim had been trussed up in the same way. She had to get free of the ankle binding. She just needed to get free. Soon.

KIM WAS ENCOURAGED to hear someone else was inside the house. It was that girl with the ponytail, the niece of the old guy from No.6. She must have been captured too. Drake Fisher had put them in the same house, where he could keep an eye on them, probably, where he could kill them.

Ty was whispering in her ear. He was weak, really weak. She wondered how long he would last. He couldn't die. He mustn't.

"Ty," she whispered urgently. She could barely breathe herself. Her throat felt like it was on fire since she'd lain on her chest for so long. She was in dire need of cool water. Her wrists were on fire too. The skin had rubbed to sore welts from the rope that tightened on her hands every time she wriggled. "Ty, someone's coming. We're going to be okay. We're going to get out of here. Ty, stay with me, please. Oh god, please."

Chapter Forty-five

At No.5

"ARE WE JUST GOING TO SIT HERE ALL NIGHT being terrorised by that man?" Marigold challenged. She wanted to motivate the women, make them see that they didn't have to be victims, that they could survive this. And, *yes*, she'd surprised herself at the ferocity of her determination. She'd lived her whole life in the shadow of her husband and welcomed it too. She'd never had a desire to break free of that, yet, there she was that night, demanding justice and freedom for all. She felt like punching the air, standing on a box preaching her cause like those activists on Speakers Corner in Hyde Park. She'd been there once…London. But she never got to hear a speaker.

"What do you expect us to do."

"We let him in."

"Whatttt?" shouted Eva.

"Hear me out."

The women looked at Marigold as their leader. That made her feel empowered, releasing her from fear of the crazy man outside the house. "Look, we have the advantage. There are five of us, this is our territory, we can get weapons, we have the element of surprise in our favour. We could simply overcome him as soon as he enters."

"It's too dangerous," said Jade looking to the other women for their endorsement.

Sandra held up her carving knife and the women looked at it as the blade shone in the candlelight. "We could do it if we're clever. We could really do it."

"What if it goes wrong. We could be killed. Even just one of us."

"Look, just listen. We hide here in the dark like we're playing hide and seek…"

"Play…" Jade was about to interrupt before Marigold held up her hand.

"Okay, that's a bad example," Marigold said nodding her head, desperately needing to convince the women that they could do this…before she too lost her nerve. "Forget the hide and seek scenario. We hide in the house with our weapons. When he comes in, we charge him. We could set some traps too."

"What sort of traps?"

"Hell, I don't know. I can't think of everything." She was starting to sound shrill.

"String," said Gladys. She shrugged. "Saw it in a film once. We can tie string at the bottom of the doors, which will trip him up…and then we can grab him."

They nodded. Finally, they had a plan.

"Wait," said Eva. "What if it goes wrong?"

Now all the women were looking to Marigold for the answer. "Then each and every one of you get out of the house as quick as you can…and run for your lives."

HE CAME BACK TWENTY MINUTES LATER.

He knocked on the front window again as everyone remained in their allocated position.

A short squeal came from the corner where Eva and Jade hid in an alcove next to the door leading to the kitchen. Across the threshold, they'd stretched a tight length of string.

Marigold and Sandra were in the lounge down the other end, near the doors they'd left wide open. The house was completely dark and now the wind was blowing into the house, making the curtains blow inwards, creating flapping noises. The two women hid next to a dresser where they couldn't be seen.

They could see the long length of string running the width of the room, cutting it in half. The chairs had been put back against the walls, the fire had been turned off and the candles snuffed out. And in the middle, down the front end of the room was Gladys, sitting on the armchair with her feet flat on the floor, like bait, waiting for him to come in and come for her.

He knocked again on the front window, just as he'd done before.

Then they knew that within the next few seconds he'd be coming around the back.

Chapter Forty-six

At No.3

RHIANNA WAS FINALLY FREE of her lower confines. She stretched her legs and arched her back while still lying on the floor. The freedom she felt was heavenly in that hell. Her hands were still bound, but at least now she could walk…or run.

She struggled to rise to her feet. She felt giddy as if she'd topple over as soon as she got upright. But still, she did it and held herself erect against a wall. She felt so cold. Why hadn't she worn her jacket when she'd gone around to see Jack?

Jack? Where was he now? Was he even alive? And what of the other women? What was happening to them? Had the man got them too?

She stretched out her arms, while they were still tied together. She would have to use her fingers to feel for obstacles. She was blind now. Her hands were her only way of seeing. "Hello," she called softly. She was aware that the man could be back any second. For all she knew, he could be standing in front of her as she walked right into him. And then he could kill her, *just like that.*

"Hello?" she repeated as she kept walking.

When she heard someone calling her name, she found herself at a door. She reached down for the handle and pushed it open.

"HELLO?"

"Rhianna," Kim called. "Is that you?"

Rhianna's darkness prevailed but to hear Kim's voice was like an angel reaching out to guide her. "Yes, Kim it's me?"

"Thank god. Can you untie us?"

"I can't see you." Her voice cracked into a sob. Without her vision, she was simply fumbling around in the dark. She had no idea how difficult it was. If she ever got her eyesight back, she'd never complained about anything again.

"We're on the floor," Kim said.

"Who's *we*?"

"Tyrone. He's here. He's been badly hurt, but he'll be okay. We just need to get him to a hospital."

Rhianna's foot hit another foot and she nearly stumbled. Instead of straightening up, she got down on her knees. It was easier that way. She felt her way along the floor and touched legs and arms and then a face. It was Kim's. She was sobbing. "Don't cry," she said. "We're going to get out of this. I just know it."

"We have to hurry. He could be back at any moment."

Rhianna kept her thoughts to herself. But all she could think of was if the man came back, they were all going to die.

KIM FELT BLESSED. To have someone else there, appearing from the dark like an angel saviour was what she'd wished for all along. "Ty," she whispered softly in his ear. Someone has come to help us. Don't give up."

He was unconscious and she didn't know if that was a blessing or not. He couldn't feel the pain, that was true, but when they were untied, how were they going to get him out of there to a hospital? That wasn't her only fear. What if Drake Fisher came back to claim her?

She knew Fisher had a soft spot for her. She'd always known it and last year, when she noticed he'd got a job as a handyman working around Seaview, it had freaked her out a bit. She thought he'd been stalking her, but then when she saw no evidence of it, she forgot about him and went on with life as if he'd never existed. At work, last week, when she went to him to ask him to report to Roger Lang's office, was the first time she'd spoken to him in a long time.

She watched him go in. Roger's office had full-length windows, and anyone could see in if they wanted to. That's how she'd seen Jade too.

She knew Fisher was going to be let go.

She felt bad for the other two that were laid off, but not for Drake Fisher. The sooner he left the building the better, she thought at the time. It wasn't that he'd done anything bad. It was just his demeanour, the way he looked sometimes, the way his eyes seemed to penetrate like they were lasers intruding on your soul. He wasn't a good looking guy either and he wasn't married. In fact, according to his records, he still lived with his mother.

Who knew what was going on his mind when he'd captured her and tied her up to Tyrone? What the hell had he been thinking? And Ty, why had he beaten him like that? Tyrone had managed to talk earlier. He'd told her that Fisher had cut his leg from behind after he left her house early this morning. And after he'd dragged him to the empty house, he'd beaten him while he was tied up, and Ty couldn't fight back, nor resist.

"He wanted my car keys," he told Kim in gasps, "But I'd accidentally left them inside your house, and I couldn't tell him that. I didn't want him to go looking for them whilst you were alone."

She had cried then, cried for the man beneath her, for his bravery in the face of adversity.

Now, she could feel the rope around her feet loosening. Her foot was free. *Thank god.* Now her hand. *Thank god.* She could finally move the right side of her body. With her other hand still tied, despite the pain of her body distorting to a different position, she managed to work her way off Ty. Then he breathed as if he'd been underwater and he'd finally found air.

Chapter Forty-seven

At No.5

DRAKE SAW THE DOOR WAS OPEN and he wondered if the women had fled. That was until he looked inside and saw the old lady in the front room like she was bait. He almost laughed at their ridiculous plan. *Whose idea was that?* he thought. They'd have to get up earlier in the morning to catch Drake Fisher so easily.

Seeing the old lady inside the room, her yellowed eyes illuminated by the moon finding its way in through the flapping curtains, he was reminded of mother and the occasion of his thirtieth birthday.

She had remained in the bathroom for three hours, talking to him through the gap at the bottom of the door. She'd talked about his cuteness when he was a baby, how he'd made them chuckle with his antics when he was a toddler, how proud they were when he got through school with four GCE O'Levels and then when he'd gotten the job at Philips straight out of college. She talked about his birthday and how they could have balloons, jelly and blancmange, presents, and Mars Bars and he softened when she mentioned that one day she would buy him a car.

"So, what do you think, son?" she'd said.

He nodded, until out of his stupor, he realised that she couldn't see him nodding. "Yes, all right, mother." He rose to his feet. "You can come out now."

"I tell you what," she said. "You go down and put the kettle on and I'll wait here a while. Then, I'll come down and make a cuppa and we'll put a list together for your party. How's that sound?"

"That sounds good. Okay, I'll see you when you come down." He walked down the stairs and into the kitchen to switch on the kettle. It was a warm day in June and the stink from the cellar was wafting up to the lean-to. He should throw some disinfectant down.

He grabbed a piece of string from the messy drawer and a pair of scissors. Then he went back and tied a length of that string to the bannister in the middle of the stairs and hooked the other end to a nail in the wall. He'd hammered that into the skirting board earlier when he'd planned what he was going to do.

He kept silent, waiting for her to emerge from the bathroom.

When she still hadn't appeared, he called up. "I've got the tea brewing, mother," he said.

Then he waited around the corner with the scissors in his hand, pointing downwards as if it were a dagger.

Now, he imagined the women of Seaview had done the same. *Great minds think alike*, he chuckled.

MOTHER HAD EVENTUALLY come out of the bathroom, but only when she was sure he had gone, or he'd calmed down. What she didn't know about her son, was that he could wait for as long as it took, that he had the patience of a saint.

He heard the door open and he heard her at the top trying to look over the banister to see if he was there. Untrusting woman that she was.

She made her descent one step at a time.

He held his breath with a smile on his face as she came halfway down. He heard her reach the middle as she misplaced her step and her ankle snapped before she tumbled down sounding like a giant boulder rolling down a mountainside.

At the bottom, she writhed in pain. Her ankle fell at a curious angle and she had a cut on her head where it had banged against the umbrella stand.

In a daze, she looked at his feet standing right next to her. She knew she was dead when she looked up and saw his eyes. When the scissors came plunging down into her neck, she had been right about *that*.

Yes, now he wished he'd had a wheelchair when he had to drag her body down the hall to the lean-to. It took him a long time to get her there and he was only mildly irritated by the mess her blood made on the linoleum floor, like red tracks left behind a barrow.

When she rolled down those cellar steps and before he closed and locked the door, he thought about his parents, together at last after all those years.

Chapter Forty-eight

At No.5

FROM WHERE SHE WAS STANDING, Marigold couldn't see him waiting outside the open doors, but she knew he was there. The wind still flapped the curtains so hard she feared they'd be ripped from their hooks and then they would really be open to the elements.

What was he waiting for? She held her scissors pointing outwards like a silver dagger.

Next to her, Sandra was silently crying and shaking from head to toe. Marigold wondered how much more she could stand. The suspense was clearly playing on her mind as much as it was on Marigolds. And god knows how the others were faring.

She could see Eva and Jade in the shadows across the other side of the room, hiding in an alcove next to the kitchen door. She wished they'd hold their knives closer to their chests, worried he might see the tips of them poking out and they would be rumbled. *What was he waiting for?*

Gladys was a star. She never complained, even after the day she'd had. She was an amazing woman, a survivor, a credit to them all. There she was, her face stony as she sat in wait, like bait. Marigold was confident he wouldn't reach her. He'd trip over the string before he got that close. Then they would overpower him, tie him up and let the police deal with him in the morning.

All good in theory.

What the hell was he waiting for?

EVA HELD HER BREATH without realising she was doing it. At her side, Jade was panting and now she was worried she'd alert the intruder to their presence and all would be lost. She reached up and placed her hand over her mouth. Jade's eyes widened in the dark. Then she blinked to let Eva know she understood. She pulled up the neck of her sweater and covered her mouth.

Eva had dished out sweaters and coats to everyone before they'd turned off the fire. Eva also wore a woolly hat and gloves since she always felt the cold.

She wanted to peep around the corner of the alcove to see what was happening. Where was the man? *What was he waiting for?*

FROM WHERE SHE STOOD at the side of the dresser, next to Marigold, Sandra had a clear view of Gladys.

She'd died only five minutes ago.

Sandra had seen the look on her face when the heart attack came. Her mouth had gaped open, but, like a trooper, she hadn't moved from her spot.

Sandra's tears flowed freely when she knew Gladys had gone. She had seen her die, even if the others hadn't, but only *she* mattered. Gladys had been her mother for one night only and it broke her heart to realise that their relationship wouldn't continue after that night. Her heart ached when she saw her just sitting there, unmoving, with her feet flat on the floor. The moon from the back of the house shone inside and illuminated her eyes, making her appear alive and well, like bait.

Now, while she watched the corpse of Gladys, she waited and wondered what the man was waiting for.

Suddenly, as all the women in the room screamed with fright, the man burst in through the front when he should have come through the back.

And as he stood there like a clown ready to do tricks, he had a smile on his face, as if he was about to play a cruel game.

Chapter Forty-nine

At No.3

THE PEOPLE OF SEAVIEW SCATTERED. It would be their one last stand before Drake Fisher got the better of them and killed them one by one.

EVA FLED WITH JADE. They'd tripped over their own trap of string across the doorway to the kitchen. They scrambled around on the floor, kicking the door closed before they helped each other rise to their feet. Then they scarpered through the garage to outside where the wind blew, and the rain came down, and the skies looked like hell above their heads. On *the eight,* outside Eva's house where inside a killer rampaged, they looked from side to side, wondering where they should go.

Their eyes fell on the house next door. No.6. They would go there. And they would hide if it took forever.

MARIGOLD HELD OUT the silver scissors as the darkness of the house engulfed her. Her eyes had adjusted to the non-light, but now pixels appeared in them like a kaleidoscope cylinder. She knew what it was. She'd had it before. It was a sugar rush mixed with adrenalin mixed with a lack of food. She slammed her back against the wall after Sandra dashed from the side of the dresser.

Marigold held out the scissors in front of her like a sword, waiting for him to pounce.

SANDRA DASHED PAST THE MAN wondering why he didn't seem to care if she escaped. It was as if he was just in it for the thrills and when the women panicked, he was immediately pleasured. It spurred him on to go further with his tirade of fear.

After bursting through the front door, as if he'd used a sledgehammer, he'd stepped forward, past Gladys sitting dead in the chair. Then he'd paced to the back of the house and calmly closed the doors. When the curtains no longer flapped, and he turned about, it was then that Sandra fled from the house, regretfully leaving behind Gladys and her friend Marigold.

She escaped through the front door from where the killer had entered. The whole door had been kicked in and splinters hung from the frame where once the lock had been. Once outside, she didn't know where to go. She couldn't go home. He might see her running along *the eight* and then, by the time she reached it, he would know exactly where she was.

To her left was the small path leading to the big rock, *Descend at your peril...* The steps would take her down to the beach where she could hide in the cave. The tide was out now. She would be safe. But the wind was still blowing like a gale. Should she even attempt the steps she had already climbed down twice that day?

She'd have to try. She had no choice.

KIM WAS RELEASED FROM HER SHACKLES. *Finally.* Her saviour, Rhianna had loosened the binds that tethered her to Tyrone and now she was frantically grabbing and grasping and pulling at the rope on Tyrone's limbs.

As she fumbled, she looked up to see the girl with the ponytail. Her eyes were badly bruised and red raw, as if she'd had something sprayed on them. No wonder she couldn't see. Now Kim would have to be her eyes and get them all out of there.

But what of Ty?

She guided Rhianna's hands to his ankles, putting her fingers between the ropes. "Do the best you can," she rushed. She went to the sink and tried the tap, but the water was off. *Damn.*

Wait.

She buried her head in the cupboard under the sink, praying the plumbing was the same as hers. From memory, in the dark, she found the stopcock. She turned the water back on. Underneath were some old rags, which she soaked with water from the tap and went back to Ty, pressing the cloths against his face and squeezing water into his open mouth. He moaned as he was refreshed.

"He's free," Rhianna said.

"Thank you." Kim bent down and spoke softly in his ear. "Ty, wake up. Can you get up? Can you walk?"

But he remained unconscious.

"I can't leave him. I can't," Kim cried as she felt Rhianna next to her on the floor.

"I'll stay," Rhianna said. "He'll be okay. You go and get help."

"I couldn't…"

"Look, you're the only one who can get out of here. You have to leave if you want to save us."

Kim looked at the girl who was now the guardian of her man on the floor. She kissed her forehead and then stood up, charging out of the house as if their lives depended on it.

It did.

RHIANNA HEARD HER LEAVE. Now she was alone with Tyrone. She tried to rouse him, but he was too far gone. She dabbed more water on his face.

Then, slowly, her eyes began to see. *Oh god.* Her eyes were beginning to focus. They still stung like bees, but she wasn't blind. *Thank god, she wasn't blind.* Her vision was dim, clouded, but it was enough to see Ty's face so that she could dab him with the wet cloth.

Then she stopped as everything around her became suspended in time.

She turned her head as her senses alerted her to danger like she could smell it.

Behind her, inside the door frame, was the man.

"WHERE'S KIMBERLY?" he asked.

Rhianna shook her head. As her eyes focused, she could see the outline of him, but now she couldn't speak. Never before had she appreciated her senses. Now she relied on them in order to survive, but as her voice failed her, her essential body parts were letting her down.

He came closer. "Where's Kim?" he said again.

The moonlight hit his face and she recoiled. He was a bizarre looking person. He had caused all that turmoil in Seaview but now he was standing there as if he were paying a visit.

Her voice croaked out of her. "She's gone,"

"Will she come back?"

"I don't know."

Suddenly his eyes came alive like he'd just woken up from a stupor. "I warned her. Now I'll have to kill *him*..." He pointed to Ty. "I have no choice now."

He stepped closer.

Rhianna screamed. "Get away, you crazy bastard," she yelled.

He stopped and looked at her. Her outburst was the game changer.

He took one step.

Then he toppled forward as a figure tackled him to the ground.

Jack.

He was on the floor using the strength in his arms as the lower part of his body dragged along behind him. Where was his wheelchair? Would it have helped? She didn't know.

The man lashed out, but Jack pulled him to the ground. Now they were on a level footing. Jack would knock the man out. Kill him even.

They would be saved.

Rhianna lay close to Tyrone, protecting his body with her own. Her whole being trembled as she watched the two men wrestle on the ground. Jack's arms flailed and his face was strained as he struggled to take the advantage. He took the crazy man in a stranglehold around his neck. Then, just as he had him, the man struck out his elbow and knocked the wind out of Jack.

He fell backwards and the man got free.

He rose up and offered one last kick into Jack's stomach before he fled from the room.

.

KIM HAD FLED FROM THE HOUSE at No.3, searching for a way to escape. *Somewhere* on the left side of the headland, there might be a place she could climb down. She searched and searched in the dark but there was nothing that resembled the steps on the other side. She was trapped. They were all trapped. A crazy man was on the loose and she didn't know what to do, where to go.

She looked out over the bay to the horizon where through the storm, the moon still shone, reflecting on the water like a runway to heaven.

Then, as she turned back towards the house where Rhianna and Ty were hiding out, her knees gave way when she saw Drake Fisher come out. He had blood on him, and he was staggering as if he'd just been in a fight.

A howl of despair escaped her lips, and as the wind carried her voice to him, he stopped and turned.

"What have you done?" she screamed using the last ounce of strength she had left, and he paced towards her like a raging devil. He was. He was the devil.

"Kim," he growled as he lowered his hands and placed them around her neck. The touch of him repulsed her. He was bent over her as she struggled pointlessly on the grass. The rain pelted them, but she was half sheltered by his body. The rain fell over his head like a halo as the moon shone behind him, and as he squeezed the breath out of her, she thought she saw angels before her eyes where the devil had once been.

Chapter Fifty

At No.5

THE PARTY WAS WELL AND TRULY OVER.

The women were gone.

Marigold was the only one left in No.5. She hugged the wall while her eyesight cleared of the pixels that had momentarily blinded her. She'd experienced it before, the day she'd met her husband Clive, fifteen years ago.

She had been standing at the bus stop waiting for the twenty-nine, after going for an interview for a bookkeeping job, before she met someone and got married. That's how it was in those days. The women weren't as independent as they were in that modern world, in 1981. In the old days, the women had just a basic education and were simply raised to care for the menfolk, while the husbands went out to earn the bacon. That day, she'd eaten nothing, out of nerves more than anything. She'd had a successful interview with an up and coming firm from Taunton. It was a company that was going places, the man behind the desk said. And as she stood waiting for the twenty-nine to go back home, pixels had formed in her eyes, like they had that night in Seaview. She'd fainted outright and when she came to, she was in the arms of the man behind the desk, the man who had interviewed her. Clive. They were married one year later, and he had protected her ever since.

Now, with her eyesight impaired, she was alone in a room with a killer and just a pair of scissors as protection.

He was standing right in front of her, just looking at her, as if he was waiting to see what she'd do. He was insane, but how could she know what was going on in his head as he watched her? And what would he do if she ran? Would she even see her way in the dark? Would he catch her as she stumbled? Would he kill her from behind? Strangle her maybe, or even use her own weapon against her. She would die. She'd never see her husband or her children again.

But she didn't want to die. *Not here like this.*

"What do you want from us?" she said.

"I want Mrs Lang."

"Eva?" she gulped. For a moment she was relieved he wasn't after her.

"Yes, Eva," he said plainly. "I want Eva. I want to kill her."

A sob caught in her throat as she imagined the man killing Eva, maybe doing to her what he'd done to the Butlers. He had no boundaries. After what he'd already done, it didn't it matter to him how much more pain he inflicted now. He would go to prison. It wouldn't matter how many he killed. It wouldn't matter. He would have no remorse. He would kill them all and that would be that.

Marigold hugged the wall as it became her only support. It was her strength as she stood there facing the killer.

He took one step towards her.

This is it.

She saw his eyes glaze over as if he was experiencing his own blurred vision and his shoulders were slumped as if he was thinking about something else. His hair clung to his head in a greasy wet mess and his speckled, spotted skin shone as the raindrops on his face picked up the reflection of the moon outside the windows.

Without further consideration, Marigold knew it was time to put an end to this man's nonsense. With one deep breath, she raised the scissors and plunged them into his right breast.

At No.6

EVA DIDN'T KNOW THE HOUSE. She couldn't remember a time she'd ever set foot in it. and now, there she was alongside her husband's mistress, going through the backdoor like a thief in the night.

Jade was muttering her fear incoherently. Eva was forced to tell her to shut up, but deep down, she was glad to have someone, *anyone* with her while she went through the motions of hiding from a killer on the loose.

It was dark in there and it was cold. Outside, the storm raged, making the terror of their plight more terrifying. But it was also a blessing. It gave her something to hang onto, a cover, a sound in the quiet of the night to fill her ears beyond the beating of her own heart.

She took Jade's hand and guided her through the kitchen to the sitting room, towards the front of the house. There, at the window, they kept low as Eva reached up and peered through the curtains.

She could see her own house. No.5. The door was open and through it came the killer, staggering, with a large patch of blood on to his right shoulder. He seemed unperturbed by his wound, carrying on as if it were nothing. He turned his head and almost as if he was looking straight at her, Eva watched the shadow of his body become a giant on the front façade of the house when a vehicle's headlights illuminated Seaview.

He threw his arm up to cover his eyes from the glaring light. Then he went to the side towards the steps to the beach.

Descend at your peril.

Chapter Fifty-one

KIM AWOKE ON THE GRASS. She had survived the strangulation. She wasn't dead. *Oh, god* she was alive. Her throat was burning like hell itself, but her limbs moved, and she could stand, and she could walk, and she could run.

As she came around the side of the garden to the front, she was forced to turn away when she was blinded by headlights from a vehicle behind the gates.

She stood on the lawn like a vulnerable deer caught in a beam of light. She looked, covering her eyes with her hands. Then the light dimmed.

The rain came down over the minibus where, returning from their trip, the men attempted to work the keypad to open the gates. They must have looked at the estate. They must have seen the lack of light. They must now realise the power was out.

Then, out of the house at No.6 two women ran, like crazy, howling, charging demons waving down the bus as it waited at the gate. A man got out. It was too dark to see who.

Unable to get inside, he was rattling the gates as the two women, Eva and Jade charged towards him, their tears mixing with the rain.

Now, Kim was running too, running towards the gates.

SANDRA WAS ALONE IN THE CAVE. She was cold. Really cold. It was pitch black in there and through the opening looking outward, the rain spilt down like a tropical waterfall.

She was safe.

The sea was pounding against the rocks and only half of the beach was visible while the water swelled and the waves crashed over and over, washing the sand.

She wondered when it would be safe to leave the cave and go back to Seaview. Were the others okay? She didn't know. She had abandoned them. She had abandoned her friend Marigold, the woman who had gallantly supported her when she had no one else…except for Gladys. Poor Gladys. She didn't deserve to die that way.

She pinned her back against the rock wall, waiting, and then, as if all her nightmares had come at once, the man...the crazy man slipped inside the cave and hid as if he too had seen his own nightmares.

Her breath was all but lost. It failed her. The air from her lungs had strangled her. Soon she would turn blue and slip away, just like Gladys.

Then she began to laugh.

Hysteria.

She couldn't stop. She almost choked with it...the laughing. Her eyes bulged as her mouth turned upwards, smiling and laughing and chuckling and croaking. She couldn't help herself. She felt as crazy as he was.

Then he turned around, and his eyes widened when he saw her hidden in the shadows, laughing.

DRAKE FISHER WAS NO ONE'S FOOL.

The woman, Marigold, had stabbed him with the scissors, just as he had stabbed his mother. Scissors were so handy. They did everything. He wholly approved of the woman's tactics. She was a worthy opponent, not like the other women who'd escaped like scurrying rats. No, this one was a survivor, and she'd do anything to stay living. Not like his mother when she walked around on eggshells all the damn time. No, this one was brave, like him, *Drake*. She was a leader. Someone to admire. *Yes*, he liked her.

Shame she had to die.

Before he could unscramble his thoughts, she'd pushed him and rushed away, going through the back door.

Damn, he thought as he looked at the blood on his chest. He reached upwards and pulled out the scissors. It didn't hurt.

He was injured, but he wasn't dead. Not yet. Anytime now, he hoped.

He went out the front. He thought he might even bump into Marigold as she ran away. That would be fun. They could die together.

Then the headlights from a vehicle almost blinded him.

What the hell?

Was it the police? Maybe they'd broken into his house and discovered mother and father in the cellar bonking and banging all day long. He didn't envy them getting the bodies out. What a stink that would be, Drake. Quack, quack.

Yes, maybe it *was* the police. They'd found his parents and now they'd come to take him off in handcuffs. He wouldn't like it in jail. No Mars Bars there. Better to get away, to die in peace and quiet without every damn person judging him and torturing him and banging all night long.

He looked to the side and saw the path leading down to the beach. *Descend at your peril.*

He fled. He took the steps one at a time, but what he really wanted to do was sail down them. That would be a lark.

Then he stopped.

He saw father.

Oh god, father was in the cellar, there to get revenge.

His white wrinkled naked body was floating on the surf, back and forth, in and out, bang, bang, banging all night long. Drake felt his heart lurch at the thought of father locking him in the cellar again. He wouldn't like that at all. "Get away from me," he screamed, but his voice was carried away by the wind and the rain.

He slipped the rest of the way down the steps. It hurt his back a lot, just like when he was three and he slipped down the cellar steps. It was dry in those days. No water. But what he saw down there made him the man he was today. The walls were painted red and from them, red curtains hung like they'd been fashioned to cover a window where there was no window. Instead, there was an old couch. It was dirty and worn and attached to it were small lengths of rope as if the person sitting on the sofa would be tied up. Then from above, father had turned the lights off and laughed. Drake scrambled to the top of the cellar stairs and banged on the door, but father didn't let him out all day.

Now the cellar was flooded, and the water was splashing, like the sound of father's body hitting the bottom of the steps when the mirror went down with him. Drake wished the splashing would stop. He didn't like the splashing.

It was black everywhere. Dark. And cold. 'Get away from me,' he called as father's corpse washed upon the sand with the white raging waves and the splashing....

He almost collided with the body as the water went past the steps, but to his left was a cave. He would hide in there until father had gone.

He went inside and hid, pressing his sore back against the rocks of the cellar.

He waited.

And then from behind him, he heard his mother laughing.

Chapter Fifty-two

"ROGER," EVA CALLED as she ran along *the eight*.

She could see him through the bars, rocking the gates. Someone was trying to climb up. It was Harry, but the wet on the metal allowed him no grip and he slid back down. He went around the side of the minibus and climbed to the top. He stood there with the rain lashing down, not close enough to scale the gates.

The men were shouting. She couldn't hear what they were saying. They could only see her and Jade, and now Kim too, running towards them, running for their lives.

"Stand back," one of them yelled.

The women stopped, drenched, huddling each other in the cold of the night.

The minibus reversed into the road and then it came toward the gates at speed.

Marigold's husband, Clive, was at the wheel. The bus knocked out the hinges on the top left side, but it wasn't enough. He reversed again, the gears scraping, and the tyres spinning and the engine roaring.

The minibus came right through and the men entered Seaview like they were the cavalry.

No.3

THE RESIDENTS OF SEAVIEW gathered inside the empty house, taking immediate shelter from the ghastly weather. The bus had been parked facing them so that the light shone in through the windows and illuminated their troubled, disturbed faces.

They exchanged stories, quickly, the women firing details at the men as they explained their plight against the crazy man who had killed the Butlers.

"Where's Marigold?" Clive shouted to anyone who would listen. "Where's my wife?"

"I'm here," the voice said behind him as she entered through the back. The couple rushed into each other's arms.

Marigold was relieved to see him. She had experienced independence and she'd enjoyed that, but now her husband was back and she felt safe and loved.

ROGER FACED EVA square on. Over his shoulder, Harry was holding Jade as she trembled and cried in his arms.

"The house is ruined," Eva sobbed as if it mattered.

He hugged her closer as his eyes moved around the room, taking it all in, scouring the place. He was pensive and alert, but Eva didn't once wonder why.

"What made you come back?" she asked trying to drag her eyes away from Harry.

"We felt it was best after none of you answered the phone," he said. "We knew there was a severe weather warning and guessed you'd had a power cut, but we couldn't be sure."

"So, you decided to come back?" Eva had hope in her eyes, hope that her husband still loved her…and not Jade.

"Well, no, it was Harry, but I agreed straight away."

KIM WAS IN THE KITCHEN, attempting to revive Tyrone, while Rhianna's Uncle Rolf, tended his wounds the best he could. Kim was beside herself. Drake Fisher had been after her, but poor Ty had taken the brunt of the killer's wrath. She wondered how he would mend, as she knew he surely would.

"I think he's going to be all right," Rolf said as he bound one of his legs. "One leg is broken but the other is cut quite badly at the back of the knee. He'll be fine, as long as we can get an ambulance out here. I think I'll go now, drive to Taunton or the nearest phone box. They could be here within the hour."

"Okay, thank you," Kim said.

"Keep him warm and hydrated."

"I will."

JACK SAT EXHAUSTED against the wall, his head thrown back and his legs splayed on the floor in front of him. Rhianna held his hand. "Where's Jo?" he panted. "Where's my sister?"

"I don't know, Jack, but we'll find her. Don't worry."

"Worried is my middle name."

"I'd help you up, but we can't find your wheelchair."

"The guy tipped me out of it when he brought me in here," Jack said. "Not before beating me up while my hands were tied. The bloody coward. At least when we fought in the kitchen, I was able to hold my own."

"You were so brave."

"Hey," he said "When he kicked me in the legs, I didn't feel a thing. I call that, one up on me."

She laughed as she straightened his shirt. "I'm sorry if you think I'm fussing over you."

"Don't be. I like it. As long as it's you."

SOMEONE ELSE CRASHED INTO THE ROOM. It was Sandra.

She was out of breath and exhausted as she fell to her knees in the unfurnished sitting room. She thought about Glady, alone in No.5, but there was nothing she could do for her now. She just wished she'd had longer with her, that brave wonderful woman.

Roger bent down and kneeled on the floor next to her. "Where's your husband?" Roger yelled. "Where's Eddie?"

Sandra's eyes closed. After she confessed, she would be called a murderer for all time.

His question hung in the air.

She didn't know how to say it. But then Marigold stepped forward. "The man killed him," she said simply.

Roger gasped. Sandra wondered why. He'd never liked Eddie, why now did he look so upset?

"Oh, god," Roger said with an expression of disbelief on his face. "This is all my fault. I caused all of this by firing Fisher." His head dropped in shame. Then he looked up again with sheer anger. His fingers were curled together in fists. He was ready for a fight. "I'm going to fix this. I'll find that Drake Fisher and I'll send his arse back to hell where it belongs."

Sandra wondered if she should own up to killing her husband. She looked to where Marigold was standing and saw her shake her head as if she knew what she was thinking.

"Where is he?"

"On the beach."

Eva tried to stop him, but he was crazed. He tore himself from her grip and with his shoulders erect, with sheer determination, he rushed out of the house and headed towards the place that said *Descend at your peril.*

DRAKE WATCHED HIM COME DOWN THE STEPS.

Roger Lang, like a gift from the devil.

What luck.

He watched him practically run half of the way down, charging towards Drake as if he was a bull seeing red. Drake had only just emerged from the cellar...the cave...after being unable to find mother, to stop her laughing. When she did stop, he was relieved, but it still took him ten minutes to go back out into the open. By then, the tide had washed up to the entrance. It had taken out the bottom of the cliff staircase as the sea came in thick and strong.

Drake still had the scissors he'd removed from his chest after Marigold had stabbed him like the trooper she was. He admired her, but the guy coming at him now, not so much. Before he killed him, he'd give him a piece of his mind.

"You idiot," Roger screamed from the second step as he held onto the wall of the cliff, steadying himself.

Drake shook his head. He remembered his father yelling at him. It made him feel inferior, but his father was always doing that, putting him down all the time.

"I give you a simple set of instructions and you blow it," Roger Lang screamed at the top of his lungs.

Drake could hardly hear him over the noise of the crashing waves.

When he'd gone to Lang's office that week to get his notice of redundancy, it wasn't the first time he'd been there. The whole debacle had been on the cards for a while. Roger Lang had even set him up with the job last summer doing chores for the residents. It was an opportunity to stake out the place, he'd said. He'd paid him top dollar. *Eight grand.* Enough for Drake to clear out of mother's house and go abroad. If the police went looking for him, he'd be long gone, living the life of Riley in some foreign land with Kimberley at his side. Lang thought it was the money that had motivated him, but Lang didn't know about the feelings he had for Kim. He'd have given back every penny just to be with her.

But now Drake knew she didn't want him. She'd proved that tonight. He just wished he'd had the opportunity to finish it. To let Tyrone have her in death only.

Roger had paid him to get rid of his wife, Eva. It had all been planned. Lang would go off on a golfing trip and take the other men with him. That would have been his alibi. While they were gone, Drake was to find a way to dispose of Eva, so that Roger could be with that other woman, Jade. She'd been to his office a few times too, but according to Roger she didn't know a thing. He wasn't so stupid to trust a woman with a plan to murder his wife. But he had been stupid enough to trust Drake Fisher.

The way his plan had gone terribly wrong made Drake laugh his head off at the thought of Lang not getting his money's worth. It was the funniest thing, especially as he watched him now, yelling from the slippery steps while the waves crashed over the rocks.

It wasn't Drake's fault he had become distracted with Kim…and Tyrone…and the Butlers and anyone else he'd managed to injure that night. Lang should have known better, but Drake had to admit he'd had a grand ol' time.

Drake held up the scissors in front of him like a silver dagger. The tips were closed to a point facing Lang. Then, as luck would have it, a wave greater than the two of them, came out of nowhere and knocked Lang off his pedestal, making his body fall head first in front of Drake while the scissors took the brunt of his fall in his stomach, puncturing him and making a hole big enough for his blood to flow freely over the waves.

That was the end of Roger Lang. And as Drake looked down and saw the red amid the white of the wash, he was reminded of the walls in the cellar painted exactly that colour, bleeding sin all over his three-year-old mind, taking away his childhood, his life, his innocence.

Before the final wave took him, taking him out to sea, he thought about his father, around there somewhere, and he hoped more than anything he wouldn't meet him along the way.

Final

THE FUNERAL WENT ON ALL DAY. The wake went on all night.

It was held at No.5. Eva's house, appropriately, since it was her husband they'd buried.

They'd tried to piece together the events that happened down on the beach that night when Roger went after Drake Fisher. And when Eva told the tale to the press and it showed on *Panorama* two nights later, this is what she'd said:

'My husband wanted to avenge the death of his good friend, Eddie, and our dear friends, the Butler's. None of them deserved to die, so you can imagine how he felt when he went down those steps that night. Drake Fisher had been hiding out in the cave on the beach. We knew that because Eddie's wife, Sandra, had left him there. Fisher had curled into a ball on the sand, like he was a little boy again, and he watched her as she went slowly past him to escape. He looked as if he feared her, but no one could possibly fear Sandra. Anyway, when my Roger went down to the cove, he must have found him, but the tide had almost covered the beach by then. Roger drowned, along with a stab wound to the stomach, but he died a hero's death.

The news covering the story told the tale of Jo from No.4.

'She was a wonderful sister and full-time carer to her disabled brother Jack. She was brutally murdered by Drake Fisher when she was pushed over the cliff on the left side of the headland. Next to her body on the rocks below were the broken remains of her brother's wheelchair. No one knows why she had met her end, but her brother Jack told Panorama that he had been taken out of his chair by Fisher to prevent him from getting away. It was just one callous act of the perpetrator to undermine and disable his victims.'

Panorama covered the story of Eddie, the loving husband of Sandra and his mother Gladys.

'He was brutally murdered when he came upon Fisher in the Butler's greenhouse. He was undoubtedly stripped of his wetsuit and tossed over the cliff like he was garbage. His wife Sandra spoke of her remorse at the death of her husband. 'There will never be anyone like him,' *she told this reporter.* 'Not in my lifetime.'

Towards the end of the programme, the news reporter summed up:

The body of Drake Fisher has yet to be found. A representative from the Devonshire Coast Guards commented, "We're keeping our eyes open for his body. We're optimistic it will emerge over the next couple of days.'

Epilogue

One Year Later

KIMBERLY CUTTER drove home on Friday night, the same route she took every Friday. She didn't go to the wine bar after work. It wasn't expected of her anymore.

Kim and Tyrone had been married soon after the terrible episode that had occurred in Seaview. Tyrone who now walked with a limp, took his old job back at Phillips as Kimberley was promoted to Roger Lang's job, an unexpected vacancy in higher management.

The in-house newsletter reported Kimberly as being the first female to take a senior management position with Phillips Electronics in Taunton and they wished her luck for the future.

RHIANNA AND JACK were married soon after the debacle of that night in Seaview. He mourned the loss of his sister and considered her death a waste of a life.

Her work was dispatched to another electronics expert oversees in America. For now, Word Processing would have to wait, but they hoped sometime in future, someone else would take on that particular project and that the computer industry would make some small advances to benefit the world.

Jack had his first novel published. It was a thriller about a murderer on the loose in a gated community in Devon. He hoped to make it rich one day.

Rhianna was now a respected journalist. She had discovered some meaty cases after all and reported them back to London for the Evening Standard. She lived over the road from her uncle Rolf who still made her a regular fry-up of bacon and eggs on a Saturday morning.

MARIGOLD AND CLIVE had one of their children move back home. Their daughter said she was worried about leaving them alone in such a dangerous place as Seaview. Now Clive spent more time in his shed down the bottom of the garden, supping on party fours when he had a quiet moment and going down the pub to play darts with his good friend Rolf.

Marigold was happy to have her daughter back, but she wished she'd clean up after herself now and then.

She had remained great friends with Kim and Sandra, keeping an eye out for them. She and Kim still enjoyed an evening together after Kim got back from work. Marigold still couldn't understand why Kim had kept her job after getting married, but she guessed that was her decision.

Now, Marigold wondered if she too should think about a career. A few women were making it in the workplace, and she did have a degree in bookkeeping. She wondered if Philipp's had an opening for a female accountant. She might ask Kim and call in a favour.

SANDRA AND GLADYS lived together now.

After Gladys had suffered a stroke that terrible night, Sandra thought she'd died of a heart attack. It turned out Gladys' body had been paralysed down one side. Later, Gladys told of how she was unable to move when she watched Drake Fisher enter No.5 and confront Marigold. She was relieved, she said when she saw Marigold plunge the scissors into the killer's chest, but as Marigold scarpered out the back, it freaked Gladys out when she realised she was alone in the house with a murderer.

Glady had made a wonderful recovery. She still had no feeling in her left arm, but she enjoyed the relationship she had with her daughter-in-law. Her son had been killed by Drake Fisher. That's the story she told, and she wouldn't be enlightening anyone to the truth anytime soon.

The police believed everything they were told about Eddie's demise. Why wouldn't they?

Sandra took up acting again when she joined an amateur dramatics company. There she met a man, but when he asked her out on a date, she saw Eddie's face and she turned him down. She hoped one day she'd get over the abuse of her husband, but perhaps she'd been permanently scarred. Time will tell on that one.

EVA MARRIED HARRY after he divorced Jade. It turned out Jade had been seeing Roger after all. Everyone knew it when she threw herself over Roger's coffin at the funeral. She'd sobbed and sobbed, and as Harry watched, he knew that divorcing her was a no-brainer.

Eva and Harry were happy. Eva received a substantial pension and a useful insurance pay-out after the death of her previous husband, Roger.

She knew he'd loved her, despite his little sordid affair, but wherever he was now, up there in heaven, she hoped he'd think about everything he'd lost for the sake of one night only.

TWO NEW RESIDENTS moved into Seaview. A young, up-and-coming working couple took the old Butler's house at No.8. They had heard about the tragic events of the year before, but the Butler's daughter had convinced them that her parents had been very happy there. She had to reduce the asking price by a couple of thousand.

Despite the sordid history of the home, the young couple bought it for £30,000 in 1981, with the promise that house prices would take an upturn in the future and that they would surely gain some healthy equity. They didn't know if that was true, but they decided to take it anyway.

Now, in the dark of night, they would sometimes hear the screaming of an animal coming from the greenhouse. They didn't believe in ghosts, but they never found the cat no matter how hard they looked.

THE NEW FAMILY who had bought No.3 put the house back on the market. They had been horrified to learn about the events of that night and wouldn't risk their children growing up in such a dangerous place as Seaview.

They sold the property to an anonymous buyer.

No one knew much about him, but some said he was a bit strange, especially when they looked through the window and saw he'd painted the walls in the house bright red.

The End

A note from the author

Thank you for reading. I sincerely hope you enjoyed 'For One Night Only' as much as I enjoyed writing it.

Please help authors by leaving a review on Amazon. Most self-published authors make little financial returns, especially when they have to give away their books to gain readership. And even if you haven't purchased the book, because your next-door neighbour lent it to you, you can still leave a review.

And please remember spoilers. Don't give away the ending.

All reviews matter. Especially the good ones!

Check out my Facebook page:
https://www.facebook.com/wendyreakes1books/

If you enjoyed For One Night Only, look out for my other books on Amazon. I particularly recommend:

'The Song of the Underground' and 'The Birds…they're back.'

Until the next time,